The Best Horror Short Stories
1800-1849

Φ

A Classic Horror Anthology

Edited and Introduced
by
Andrew Barger

For Maeve, who enjoys jumping out from behind furniture and scaring her father while he is writing.

The Best Horror Short Stories 1800-1849
Φ
A Classic Horror Anthology

EDITED AND INTRODUCED BY
ANDREW BARGER

First Edition
Manufactured in the United States or the United Kingdom
ISBN: 978-1-933747-22-4

Printed on 100% recycled paper in both
the United States and United Kingdom
(20% Post Consumer Waste)

Fonts: Bookman Old Style – CloisterBlack BT – Times New
Roman – Copperplate Gothic Light

Acknowledgements: Special thanks to Chas Miller III, Executive Director of the Sir John Soane's Museum Foundation and Susan Palmer, Archivist of the Sir John Soane's Museum for their assistance in obtaining the rare image of George Soane found within this book.

CONTENTS

A Long List of Shorts

The number of horror short stories written for the first half of the nineteenth century is fixed in time just as they are for any period in the past. No more will be written. In light of this, the best horror short stories for this period can be quantified and are open to scholarly debate. Come one, come all. I have witnessed, however, little of either from the anthologists. This is my attempt to define the best horror stories with an initial overview of how I went about it.

To find the best horror short stories of 1800-1849 is an aggressive undertaking. Yet it did not start out as all-encompassing as it first appears. The genesis of this anthology began as a simple idea. After editing and introducing "Edgar Allan Poe's Annotated and Illustrated Entire Short Stories and Poems," my interest was piqued as to just how good Edgar Allan Poe (1809-1849) really was within the horror genre. I wondered how much he had leapfrogged those who came before him and whether Poe had any equals while alive. Sure Poe's horror stories are great and there is little disagreement in this regard, but how do they compare to the stories of his contemporaries? Poe lampooned many of his contemporaries in this genre, and for good measure. Yet Poe, one of America's harshest literary critics in this time period, was quick to give credit where credit was due. A primary example is Nathaniel Hawthorne (1804-1864), Poe's main American contemporary for horror short stories.

Though Poe was laudatory of Hawthorne's short stories as being "wild, plaintive, thoughtful, and in full accordance with his themes," in *Graham's Magazine* of April 1842, Hawthorne did not agree with all his criticisms of other writers. Four years later, on June 17, 1846, Hawthorne wrote Poe and confessed: "I admire you rather as a writer of tales than as a critic upon them, I might often – and often do – dissent from your opinions in the later capacity, but could never fail to recognize your force and originality in the former."

Partly as a result of Edgar Allan Poe and Nathaniel Hawthorne in America, the horror genre made great strides in short story form. Washington Irving (1783-1859) is another potential American contender, but he excelled in writing ghost stories, which are not included in this anthology. Poe recognized Irving's talents in the same issue of *Graham's Magazine*: "With rare exception — in the case of Mr. Irving's 'Tales of a Traveler' and a few other works of a like cast — we have had no American tales of high merit. We have had no skilful compositions — nothing which could bear examination as works of art."

In America Poe and Hawthorne caused readers to be chilled with tales of premature burials, borderlands of the mind, a deranged botanist, fate at the hands of the Spanish inquisitors, a plague of red death, the fountain of youth gone bad, a mad scientist, funerals at weddings and a minister who wears a black veil.

In Europe more horror writers—a number who were precursors to Poe and Hawthorne—excelled in penning fine short stories in this genre. From Germany, Ernst T. A. Hoffmann (1776-1822) was the acknowledged forefather to Poe and Hawthorne and many others in Europe. Hoffmann wrote about mad alchemists, an insane duchess, and took doppelganger stories to new heights. Like Washington Irving, he is best remembered today as a ghost story author. Hoffmann did, however, write one short horror tale called "The Deserted House" that rises to the high demands of this collection. Wilhelm Hauff (1802-1827), another German writer, was certainly influenced by the horror of Hoffmann. He penned a number of fantastic stories in his brief but stellar career as a man of letters. He would have been one of the all time greats in this space if he had lived even into his thirties. Hauff's tale "The Severed Hand" is one of the best horror stories of 1800-1849 and is included here.

In France, Honoré de Balzac (1799-1850) explored tales of family beheadings, the blending of religious themes with the supernatural, and insane artists. Aren't we all? Oscar Wilde stated in his "Decay of Dying: A Dialogue" of 1889: "Literature always anticipates life. It does not copy it, but moulds it to its purpose. The nineteenth century as we know it is largely an invention of Balzac." His terrifying story "The Mysterious Mansion" tops all other tales of a trapped wrongdoer in this period, including Poe's "The Cask of Amontillado" that was published years later. "The Mysterious Mansion" is planted firmly in this collection along with "El Verdugo." France also gave the genre Pierre Jules Théophile Gautier (1811-1872), who bore a striking resemblance to Honoré de Balzac in both appearance and beach ball body. Gautier wrote a number of good horror novellas, yet his short horror stories fall . . . well . . . *short* of greatness. "The Mummy's Foot" of 1840 is his best short horror tale. Frenchman Prosper Mérimée (1802-1870) penned a number of good horror short stories with none rising to the level of greatness required in this anthology. His short war tale 1829, "The Taking of Redoubt," is one of his best. Eight years later he would pen "*La Vénus d'Ille*," which became one of his most popular short stories.

In Scotland, James Hogg (1770-1835) wrote many fine short stories in the horror genre. One of his best is "The Fords of Callum" that was first published in 1837. Even more famous today than Hogg, is the Scottish author Sir Walter Scott (1771-1832). Still, neither of these superior writers penned a horror tale that rose to the level of this collection.

Ireland gave us Thomas Crofton Croker (1798-1854) who focused on the retelling of Irish legends, which are not complete without the adventures of banshees and fairies. These are cherished for their historical value in the horror genre, but mostly lack in originality and fullness of story. The fairies Croker gives us in "The Legend of Knockgrafton" are deliciously devilish in their reactions.

While English author Mary Shelley (1797-1851) gave us Frankenstein's monster in novel form, her short stories in this genre are largely a disappointment. Shelley's countryman, Dr. Nathan Drake (1766-1836), penned a few gothic horror stories, which ultimately fail for being overwritten and do not rise to the level of this anthology. Similar to Mary Shelley, at a relatively young age Mathew Gregory Lewis gave us a classic gothic novel titled "The Monk." The short horror stories of Lewis, however, tend to be drawn out and contain only flashes of terror. "The Anaconda" of 1808 is one of his best. Captain Frederick Marryat (1792-1848) is another UK author who wrote in this period and was very popular. While he did not give us many short tales of horror, "The Legend of the Bell Rock" is a solid tale as is "The Story of the Greek Slave." Marryat's "The White Wolf of the Hartz Mountains" is perhaps the greatest werewolf tale for this half century and is included in "The Best Werewolf Short Stories 1800-1849." Charles Dickens, though not considered a horror author, wrote an excellent story of revenge that made this collection. It is "The Old Man's Tale About the Queer

Client" and was collected in "The Posthumous Papers of the Pickwick Club."

I would be remiss by not paying homage in this anthology to a highly overlooked English author of the time—George Soane (1789-1860). He is primarily known as a playwright and scholarly translator of foreign poems and operas into English. Soane's strained relationship with his famous architect father, John Soane, deflected much needed attention away from his fiction. It also didn't help his literary reputation when he started publishing many of his short stories anonymously. They were also spread out over a period of decades. They were first collected in three volumes titled, "The Last Ball, and Other Stories" of 1841. They are all produced at a high level. There is hardly a bad story in the lot. This is the finest, overlooked collection of horror, ghost and fantasy short stories by one author during the period in question. "The Lighthouse" is Soane's best horror tale and is included here. Another is the excellent "Recollections of a Night Fever" that is worth a read on a dark night, as well as "The Singular Trial of Francis Ormiston."

Who was the best of them all? Can a king or queen be crowned among the foundation builders of the short horror story? Yes. As you read the stories contained in this anthology you will quickly recognize just how high Edgar Allan Poe towered above all others writing in this space. The difficulty with Poe is not figuring out which of his stories rise to the level required of this collection, but rather which of his stories to exclude from it. In my opinion Poe has amazingly penned nearly thirty percent of the best horror short stories in this time period and this is without the inclusion of his classic stories: "A Descent into the Maelström," "The Black Cat," "The Masque of the Red Death," and "The Cask of Amontillado," which all could have made the list.

I waste no time in crowning Edgar Allan Poe the undisputed king of this genre for this time period. This is done without hesitation and certainly without remorse. Though Poe towered above his competitors, any "best" anthology must consider one hit wonders; those who may have written a great short horror story and slunk into obscurity in the first half of the nineteenth century.

In this quest I gladly and dutifully turned to the best magazines and journals of the day. Two of the most popular British texts, and those with reputations for publishing tales of terror, were *Blackwood's Edinburgh Magazine* (originally called the *Edinburgh Monthly Magazine* when it began in 1817) and the *Edinburgh Review*. *Blackwood's* became known for publishing sensational tales of horror. At times they were overwritten bunk. Poe went so far as to lampoon the magazine in his "How to Write a Blackwood's Article," which he published in 1842. Both of these leading British magazines provide a wide list of stories for the time period under consideration. *The Antheneum, or the Spirit of the English Magazines* was another British publication of wide circulation that contained tales of terror.

In the United States, *Atkinson's Casket* published the best stories from other magazines and journals. It also published a number of original tales. Given the lack of international copyright protection during this period, *Atkinson's Casket* also freely published horror stories from Europe, including some of the best from *Blackwood's*. In line with its macabre title, a number of these stories were tales of horror and the supernatural.

Over three hundred short horror stories have been reviewed for this anthology. They are listed along with their respective author and earliest publication date, if available. So what are the criteria used in deciding whether a short story would be considered for this anthology?

Fear is first. It has been our oldest and most dramatic of human emotions since Adam and Eve fell trembling at the presence of God in the Garden of Eden. It is the emotion that is intertwined in all horror stories. A grand horror story therefore must evoke a sudden sense of fear at some point. This often takes the form of a shocking ending, or a pervasive sense of fear or dread throughout the story. Next, there can be no fear unless one feels for the protagonist of the story. The deeper connection the reader has to the protagonist, the greater the ability of the writer to invoke fear in the reader. This is largely why Charles Dickens's "The Old Man's Tale About the Queer Client" made this collection. Who better to make readers care about the characters in a few pages than Dickens? Last, the writing of the story, the actual text on the page, must be at a high level. The stories picked for this anthology meet all three criteria.

That being said, a great horror story does not require blood and gore, or even the supernatural. "The Pit and the

Pendulum" is a fine example of a horror story lacking both. It does, however, contain "heaps" of rats, which is always welcomed in a horror tale. "The Minister's Black Veil" is a shining example from Nathaniel Hawthorne of a story devoid of murder or the supernatural that still leaves a sticky residue of dread long after the story is put down.

I also placed tight parameters on what stories would even be considered in this anthology. It does not contain any story over fifty pages. Short stories only. Poe was quick to laud short fiction in his April 1842 review of "Twice Told Tales" in *Graham's Magazine*: "We have always regarded the *Tale* (using this word in its popular acceptation) as affording the best prose opportunity for display of the highest talent." This anthology does not contain stories of ghosts, werewolves, the devil, witches, vampires, fantasy, murder mysteries or science fiction. The later explains why William Mumford's "The Iron Shroud" is not included. Its futuristic mechanisms necessitate that the story be placed in the sci-fi genre despite its horrific elements. No excerpts from novels, which are typically called "fragments," are included here. For my purposes it is acceptable, however, to take a story from a long narrative that combines or links multiple short stories such as Dickens's "Pickwick Papers" or "Arabian Nights" by William Hauff. Finally, only fiction stories are included that have been translated into the English language at some point.

Believing that the dozen stories collected here truly are the finest horror stories for this half-century, they have been annotated for better understanding of antiquated terms. These gems deserve as much. If a particular story was annotated as published, such as Samuel Warren's "The Thunder-Struck and the Boxer," those annotations are provided.

As you begin reading the list of stories considered for this anthology, you will notice that there are some horror gems that failed to make the cut for this anthology, but are excellent stories nonetheless. They are not to be forgotten.

Please read them for yourself and make your own decision as to whether the horror short stories contained in this anthology are the greatest from 1800-1849. No anthology, no matter how scholarly and open in regards to the stories considered, will be without controversy.

Hopefully you will agree that this collection hits closer to the mark than the others.

Andrew Barger
June 22, 2010

Edgar Allan Poe
(1809-1849)

Φ

The Facts in the Case of M. Valdemar

The first story in this collection is about flirting with death. Who better to pen it than Poe? At the time it was written the medical community was experimenting with putting patients under "magnetic sleep" so they would not feel pain during surgery. Purported cases of mesmeric treatment were spreading across New England. Poe, a literary practical joker, was quick to play on the misguided beliefs of the medical community and society at large.

When the story was published in the *American Review* of 1845, it garnered much attention from practicing mesmerists, who so badly wanted the story to be true. One of the most prominent, Robert Collyer, queried Poe from Boston on December 16, 1845: "Your account of M. Valdemar's case has been universally copied in this city, and has created a very great sensation." He then asked Poe to confirm that the story was true "to put at rest the growing impression that your account is merely a splendid creation of your own brain, not having any truth in fact."

Poe placed Collyer's letter in the *Broadway Journal* of December 27, 1845, and responded to it there. "We have no doubt that Mr. Collyer is perfectly correct in all that he says – and all that he desires us to say – but the truth is, there was a very small modicum of truth in the case of M. Valdemar – which, in consequence, may be called a hard case – very hard for M. Valdemar, for Mr. Collyer, and ourselves."

"The Facts in the Case of M. Valdemar," which followed on the heels of Poe's "Mesmeric Revelation," was reprinted seven times in December of 1845 alone.

In 1846 it was reprinted another three times. Philip Pendleton Cooke read the story while hunting and had this to add in his letter to Poe dated August 4, 1846, "The 'Valdemar Case' I read in a number of your Broadway Journal last winter – as I lay in a Turkey blind, muffled to the eyes in overcoats, &c., and pronounce it without hesitation the most damnable, vraisemblable, horrible, hair-lifting, shocking, ingenious chapter of fiction that any brain ever conceived, or hands traced. That gelatinous, viscous sound of man's voice! there never was such an idea before. That story scared me in broad day, armed with a double-barrel Tryon Turkey gun. What would it have done at midnight in some old ghostly countryhouse? I have always found some one remarkable thing in your stories to haunt me long after reading them."

Yet, as Poe admitted to Arch Ramsay on December 30th of the same year, "'Hoax' is precisely the word suited to M. Valdemar's case. The story appeared originally in 'The American Review', a Monthly Magazine, published in this city. The London papers, commencing with the 'Morning Post' and the 'Popular Record of Science', took up the theme. The article was generally copied in England and is now circulating in France. Some few persons believe it–but I do not–and don't you."

The Facts in the Case of
M. Valdemar

OF COURSE I SHALL not pretend to consider it any matter for wonder, that the extraordinary case of M. Valdemar has excited discussion. It would have been a miracle had it not-especially under the circumstances. Through the desire of all parties concerned, to keep the affair from the public, at least for the present, or until we had farther opportunities for investigation – through our endeavors to effect this – a garbled or exaggerated account made its way into society, and became the source of many unpleasant misrepresentations, and, very naturally, of a great deal of disbelief.

It is now rendered necessary that I give the *facts* – as far as I comprehend them myself. They are, succinctly, these:

My attention, for the last three years, had been repeatedly drawn to the subject of Mesmerism;[1] and, about nine months ago it occurred to me, quite suddenly, that in the series of experiments made hitherto, there had been a very remarkable and most unaccountable omission: – no person had as yet been mesmerized *in articulo mortis*.[2] It remained to be seen, first, whether, in such condition, there existed in the patient any susceptibility to the magnetic influence; secondly, whether, if any existed, it was impaired or increased by the condition; thirdly, to what extent, or for how long a period, the encroachments of Death might be arrested by the process. There were other points to be ascertained, but these most excited my curiosity – the last in especial, from the immensely important character of its consequences.

In looking around me for some subject by whose means I might test these particulars, I was brought to think of my friend, M. Ernest Valdemar, the well-known

---

[1] Hypnotic Trance Brought on by Hypnosis and Magnetism
[2] Death of Joints or Muscles

compiler of the "Bibliotheca Forensica,"[3] and author (under the *nom de plume*[4] of Issachar Marx) of the Polish versions of "Wallenstein"[5] and "Gargantua."[6] M. Valdemar, who has resided principally at Harlaem, N.Y., since the year 1839, is (or was) particularly noticeable for the extreme sparseness of his person – his lower limbs much resembling those of John Randolph;[7] and, also, for the whiteness of his whiskers, in violent contrast to the blackness of his hair – the latter, in consequence, being very generally mistaken for a wig. His temperament was markedly nervous, and rendered him a good subject for mesmeric experiment.

On two or three occasions I had put him to sleep with little difficulty, but was disappointed in other results which his peculiar constitution had naturally led me to anticipate. His will was at no period positively, or thoroughly, under my control, and in regard to *clairvoyance*, I could accomplish with him nothing to be relied upon. I always attributed my failure at these points to the disordered state of his health. For some months previous to my becoming acquainted with him, his physicians had declared him in a confirmed phthisis.[8] It was his custom, indeed, to speak calmly of his approaching dissolution, as of a matter neither to be avoided nor regretted.

When the ideas to which I have alluded first occurred to me, it was of course very natural that I should think of M. Valdemar. I knew the steady philosophy of the man too well to apprehend any scruples from *him*; and he had no relatives in America who would be likely to interfere. I spoke to him frankly upon the subject; and, to my surprise, his interest seemed vividly excited. I say to my surprise, for, although he had always yielded his person freely to my experiments, he had never before given me any tokens of sympathy with what I did. His disease was if

---

[3] Bible of forensics
[4] Penname
[5] Play written in 1800 by Johann Christoph Friedrich von Schiller (1759-1805), German poet and historian
[6] Comic Novel ("Gargantua and Pantagruel") by Francois Rabelais (1494-1553), which tells the story of the giant Gargantua and his son Pantagruel
[7] John Randolph (1773-1833), Virginia Congressman
[8] Tuberculosis of the lungs

that character which would admit of exact calculation in respect to the epoch[9] of its termination in death; and it was finally arranged between us that he would send for me about twenty-four hours before the period announced by his physicians as that of his decease.

It is now rather more than seven months since I received, from M. Valdemar himself, the subjoined note:

MY DEAR P– ,

You may as well come *now*. D– and F– are agreed that I cannot hold out beyond tomorrow midnight; and I think they have hit the time very nearly.

VALDEMAR

I received this note within half an hour after it was written, and in fifteen minutes more I was in the dying man's chamber. I had not seen him for ten days, and was appalled by the fearful alteration which the brief interval had wrought in him. His face wore a leaden hue; the eyes were utterly lusterless; and the emaciation[10] was so extreme that the skin had been broken through by the cheek-bones. His expectoration[11] was excessive. The pulse was barely perceptible. He retained, nevertheless, in a very remarkable manner, both his mental power and a certain degree of physical strength. He spoke with distinctness – took some palliative medicines without aid – and, when I entered the room, was occupied in penciling memoranda in a pocket-book. He was propped up in the bed by pillows. Doctors D– and F– were in attendance.

After pressing Valdemar's hand, I took these gentlemen aside, and obtained from them a minute account of the patient's condition. The left lung had been for eighteen months in a semi-osseous[12] or cartilaginous[13] state, and was, of course, entirely useless for all purposes of vitality. The right, in its upper portion, was also partially, if not thoroughly, ossified, while the lower region

---

[9] Point in time
[10] Becoming extremely thin by lack of food
[11] Eject from mouth by spitting
[12] Resembling Bone
[13] Skeleton consisting mainly of cartilage

was merely a mass of purulent tubercles,[14] running one into another. Several extensive perforations existed; and, at one point, permanent adhesion to the ribs had taken place. These appearances in the right lobe were of comparatively recent date. The ossification had proceeded with very unusual rapidity; no sign of it had been discovered a month before, and the adhesion had only been observed during the three previous days. Independently of the phthisis, the patient was suspected of aneurism of the aorta;[15] but on this point the osseous symptoms rendered an exact diagnosis impossible. It was the opinion of both physicians that M. Valdemar would die about midnight on the morrow (Sunday). It was then seven o'clock on Saturday evening.

On quitting the invalid's bed-side to hold conversation with myself, Doctors D– and F– had bidden him a final farewell. It had not been their intention to return; but, at my request, they agreed to look in upon the patient about ten the next night.

When they had gone, I spoke freely with M. Valdemar on the subject of his approaching dissolution, as well as, more particularly, of the experiment proposed. He still professed himself quite willing and even anxious to have it made, and urged me to commence it at once. A male and a female nurse were in attendance; but I did not feel myself altogether at liberty to engage in a task of this character with no more reliable witnesses than these people, in case of sudden accident, might prove. I therefore postponed operations until about eight the next night, when the arrival of a medical student with whom I had some acquaintance, (Mr. Theodore L–l,) relieved me from farther embarrassment. It had been my design, originally, to wait for the physicians; but I was induced to proceed, first, by the urgent entreaties of M. Valdemar, and secondly, by my conviction that I had not a moment to lose, as he was evidently sinking fast.

Mr. L–l was so kind as to accede to my desire that he would take notes of all that occurred, and it is from his memoranda that what I now have to relate is, for the most part, either condensed or copied *verbatim*.

It wanted about five minutes of eight when, taking the patient's hand, I begged him to state, as distinctly as he

---

[14] Pus from the lungs

[15] Expansion of great artery to all parts of the body except the lungs

could, to Mr. L–l, whether he (M. Valdemar) was entirely willing that I should make the experiment of mesmerizing him in his then condition.

He replied feebly, yet quite audibly, "Yes, I wish to be "I fear you have mesmerized" – adding immediately afterwards, deferred it too long."

While he spoke thus, I commenced the passes which I had already found most effectual in subduing him. He was evidently influenced with the first lateral stroke of my hand across his forehead; but although I exerted all my powers, no farther perceptible effect was induced until some minutes after ten o'clock, when Doctors D–and F–called, according to appointment. I explained to them, in a few words, what I designed, and as they opposed no objection, saying that the patient was already in the death agony, I proceeded without hesitation – exchanging, however, the lateral passes for downward ones, and directing my gaze entirely into the right eye of the sufferer.

By this time his pulse was imperceptible and his breathing was stertorous,[16] and at intervals of half a minute.

This condition was nearly unaltered for a quarter of an hour. At the expiration of this period, however, a natural although a very deep sigh escaped the bosom of the dying man, and the stertorous breathing ceased – that is to say, its stertorousness was no longer apparent; the intervals were undiminished. The patient's extremities were of an icy coldness.

At five minutes before eleven I perceived unequivocal signs of the mesmeric influence. The glassy roll of the eye was changed for that expression of uneasy *inward* examination which is never seen except in cases of sleep-waking, and which it is quite impossible to mistake. With a few rapid lateral passes I made the lids quiver, as in incipient[17] sleep, and with a few more I closed them altogether. I was not satisfied, however, with this, but continued the manipulations vigorously, and with the fullest exertion of the will, until I had completely stiffened the limbs of the slumberer, after placing them in a seemingly easy position. The legs were at full length; the arms were nearly so, and reposed on the bed at a

---

[16] Heavy breathing

[17] Beginning to appear

moderate distance from the loin. The head was very slightly elevated.

When I had accomplished this, it was fully midnight, and I requested the gentlemen present to examine M. Valdemar's condition. After a few experiments, they admitted him to be an unusually perfect state of mesmeric trance. The curiosity of both the physicians was greatly excited. Dr. D– resolved at once to remain with the patient all night, while Dr. F– took leave with a promise to return at daybreak. Mr. L–l and the nurses remained.

We left M. Valdemar entirely undisturbed until about three o'clock in the morning, when I approached him and found him in precisely the same condition as when Dr. F– went away – that is to say, he lay in the same position; the pulse was imperceptible; the breathing was gentle (scarcely noticeable, unless through the application of a mirror to the lips); the eyes were closed naturally; and the limbs were as rigid and as cold as marble. Still, the general appearance was certainly not that of death.

As I approached M. Valdemar I made a kind of half effort to influence his right arm into pursuit of my own, as I passed the latter gently to and fro above his person. In such experiments with this patient had never perfectly succeeded before, and assuredly I had little thought of succeeding now; but to my astonishment, his arm very readily, although feebly, followed every direction I assigned it with mine. I determined to hazard a few words of conversation.

"M. Valdemar," I said, "are you asleep?" He made no answer, but I perceived a tremor about the lips, and was thus induced to repeat the question, again and again. At its third repetition, his whole frame was agitated by a very slight shivering; the eyelids unclosed themselves so far as to display a white line of the ball; the lips moved sluggishly, and from between them, in a barely audible whisper, issued the words:

"Yes; – asleep now. Do not wake me! – let me die so!"

I here felt the limbs and found them as rigid as ever. The right arm, as before, obeyed the direction of my hand. I questioned the sleep-waker again:

"Do you still feel pain in the breast, M. Valdemar?"

The answer now was immediate, but even less audible than before: "No pain – I am dying."

I did not think it advisable to disturb him farther just then, and nothing more was said or done until the arrival of Dr. F – , who came a little before sunrise, and expressed unbounded astonishment at finding the patient still alive. After feeling the pulse and applying a mirror to the lips, he requested me to speak to the sleep-waker again. I did so, saying:

"M. Valdemar, do you still sleep?"

As before, some minutes elapsed ere a reply was made; and during the interval the dying man seemed to be collecting his energies to speak. At my fourth repetition of the question, he said very faintly, almost inaudibly:

"Yes; still asleep – dying."

It was now the opinion, or rather the wish, of the physicians, that M. Valdemar should be suffered to remain undisturbed in his present apparently tranquil condition, until death should supervene – and this, it was generally agreed, must now take place within a few minutes. I concluded, however, to speak to him once more, and merely repeated my previous question.

While I spoke, there came a marked change over the countenance of the sleep-waker. The eyes rolled themselves slowly open, the pupils disappearing upwardly; the skin generally assumed a cadaverous hue, resembling not so much parchment as white paper; and the circular hectic spots which, hitherto, had been strongly defined in the centre of each cheek, *went out* at once. I use this expression, because the suddenness of their departure put me in mind of nothing so much as the extinguishment of a candle by a puff of the breath. The upper lip, at the same time, writhed itself away from the teeth, which it had previously covered completely; while the lower jaw fell with an audible jerk, leaving the mouth widely extended, and disclosing in full view the swollen and blackened tongue. I presume that no member of the party then present had been unaccustomed to death-bed horrors; but so hideous beyond conception was the appearance of M. Valdemar at this moment, that there was a general shrinking back from the region of the bed.

I now feel that I have reached a point of this narrative at which every reader will be startled into positive disbelief. It is my business, however, simply to proceed.

There was no longer the faintest sign of vitality in M. Valdemar; and concluding him to be dead, we were consigning him to the charge of the nurses, when a strong vibratory motion was observable in the tongue. This continued for perhaps a minute. At the expiration of this period, there issued from the distended and motionless jaws a voice – such as it would be madness in me to attempt describing. There are, indeed, two or three epithets[18] which might be considered as applicable to it in part; I might say, for example, that the sound was harsh, and broken and hollow; but the hideous whole is indescribable, for the simple reason that no similar sounds have ever jarred upon the ear of humanity. There were two particulars, nevertheless, which I thought then, and still think, might fairly be stated as characteristic of the intonation – as well adapted to convey some idea of its unearthly peculiarity. In the first place, the voice seemed to reach our ears – at least mine – from a vast distance, or from some deep cavern within the earth. In the second place, it impressed me (I fear, indeed, that it will be impossible to make myself comprehended) as gelatinous or glutinous matters impress the sense of touch.

I have spoken both of "sound" and of "voice." I mean to say that the sound was one of distinct – of even wonderfully, thrillingly distinct – syllabification. M. Valdemar *spoke* – obviously in reply to the question I had propounded to him a few minutes before. I had asked him, it will be remembered, if he still slept. He now said:

"Yes; – no; – I *have been* sleeping – and now – now – *I am dead.*

No person present even affected to deny, or attempted to repress, the unutterable, shuddering horror which these few words, thus uttered, were so well calculated to convey. Mr. L – l (the student) swooned. The nurses immediately left the chamber, and could not be induced to return. My own impressions I would not pretend to render intelligible to the reader. For nearly an hour, we busied ourselves, silently – without the utterance of a word – in endeavors to revive Mr. L – l. When he came to himself, we addressed ourselves again to an investigation of M. Valdemar's condition.

It remained in all respects as I have last described it, with the exception that the mirror no longer afforded evidence of respiration. An attempt to draw blood from the arm failed. I should mention, too, that this limb was no farther subject to my will. I endeavored in vain to make it follow the direction of my hand. The only real indication, indeed, of the mesmeric influence, was now found in the

---

[18] Term used to characterize

vibratory movement of the tongue, whenever I addressed
M. Valdemar a question. He seemed to be making an effort
to reply, but had no longer sufficient volition. To queries
put to him by any other person than myself he seemed
utterly insensible – although I endeavored to place each
member of the company in mesmeric *rapport* with him. I
believe that I have now related all that is necessary to an
understanding of the sleep-waker's state at this epoch.
Other nurses were procured; and at ten o'clock I left the
house in company with the two physicians and Mr. L – l.

In the afternoon we all called again to see the patient.
His condition remained precisely the same. We had now
some discussion as to the propriety and feasibility of
awakening him; but we had little difficulty in agreeing that
no good purpose would be served by so doing. It was
evident that, so far, death (or what is usually termed
death) had been arrested by the mesmeric process. It
seemed clear to us all that to awaken M. Valdemar would
be merely to insure his instant, or at least his speedy
dissolution.

From this period until the close of last week – *an
interval of nearly seven months* – we continued to make
daily calls at M. Valdemar's house, accompanied, now and
then, by medical and other friends. All this time the
sleeper-waker remained *exactly* as I have last described
him. The nurses' attentions were continual.

It was on Friday last that we finally resolved to make
the experiment of awakening or attempting to awaken
him; and it is the (perhaps) unfortunate result of this
latter experiment which has given rise to so much
discussion in private circles – to so much of what I cannot
help thinking unwarranted popular feeling.

For the purpose of relieving M. Valdemar from the
mesmeric trance, I made use of the customary passes.
These, for a time, were unsuccessful. The first indication
of revival was afforded by a partial descent of the iris. It
was observed, as especially remarkable, that this lowering
of the pupil was accompanied by the profuse out-flowing
of a yellowish ichor[19] (from beneath the lids) of a pungent
and highly offensive odor.

It was now suggested that I should attempt to
influence the patient's arm, as heretofore. I made the

---

[19] Acrid discharge from a wound

attempt and failed. Dr. F– then intimated a desire to have me put a question. I did so, as follows:

"M. Valdemar, can you explain to us what are your feelings or wishes now?"

There was an instant return of the hectic circles on the cheeks; the tongue quivered, or rather rolled violently in the mouth (although the jaws and lips remained rigid as before;) and at length the same hideous voice which I have already described, broke forth:

"For God's sake! – quick! – quick! – put me to sleep – or, quick! – waken me! – quick! – *I say to you that I am dead!*"

I was thoroughly unnerved, and for an instant remained undecided what to do. At first I made an endeavor to re-compose the patient; but, failing in this through total abeyance of the will, I retraced my steps and as earnestly struggled to awaken him. In this attempt I soon saw that I should be successful – or at least I soon fancied that my success would be complete – and I am sure that all in the room were prepared to see the patient awaken.

For what really occurred, however, it is quite impossible that any human being could have been prepared.

As I rapidly made the mesmeric passes, amid ejaculations of "dead! dead!" absolutely *bursting* from the tongue and not from the lips of the sufferer, his whole frame at once – within the space of a single minute, or even less, shrunk – crumbled – absolutely *rotted* away beneath my hands. Upon the bed, before that whole company, there lay a nearly liquid mass of loathsome – of detestable putridity.

WILHELM HAUFF
(1802-1827)

Φ

The Severed Hand

This little gem of a tale was penned by Wilhelm Hauff, the German author of a number of outstanding horror and ghost stories during his brief life. It was first published in his 1826 collection of original short stories entitled *"Die Karavane"* ("The Caravan"). Later in the century the title was changed to "Arabian Days' Entertainments." This story is set is Constantinople, which is our modern Turkish city of Istanbul.

Sigmund Freud, in Part III of his cursory review of horror tales called "The Uncanny," referenced the story as having "an uncanny effect . . .." The extremely poor effort by Freud in discussing this genre in "The Uncanny" makes us all glad he focused the vast majority of his attention on psychology, which he understood much better than horror fiction.

Of Hauff's many talents developed at a young age, one is his ability to turn a story on a dime and send it careening off into another direction. "The Severed Hand" contains a sparkling and horrific example of this style that works extremely well. The story is firmly planted in this collection of the best horror short stories of 1800-1849.

The Severed Hand

I WAS BORN IN CONSTANTINOPLE; my father was a dragoman[1] at the Porte, and besides, carried on a fairly lucrative business in sweet-scented perfumes and silk goods. He gave me a good education; he partly instructed me himself, and also had me instructed by one of our priests. He at first intended me to succeed him in business one day, but as I showed greater aptitude than he had expected, he destined me, on the advice of his friends, to be a doctor; for if a doctor has learned a little more than the ordinary charlatan, he can make his fortune in Constantinople.

Many Franks[2] frequented our house, and one of them persuaded my father to allow me to travel to his native land to the city of Paris, where such things could be best acquired and free of charge. He wished, however, to take me with himself gratuitously on his journey home. My father, who had also travelled in his youth, agreed, and the Frank told me to hold myself in readiness three months hence. I was beside myself with joy at the idea of seeing foreign countries, and eagerly awaited the moment when we should embark. The Frank had at last concluded his business and prepared himself for the journey. On the evening before our departure my father led me into his little bedroom. There I saw splendid dresses and arms lying on the table. My looks were however chiefly attracted to an immense heap of gold, for I had never before seen so much collected together.

My father embraced me and said: "Behold, my son, I have procured for thee clothes for the journey. These weapons are thine; they are the same which thy grandfather hung around me when I went abroad. I know that thou canst use them aright; but only make use of them when thou art attacked; on such occasions, however, defend thyself bravely. My property is not large; behold I have divided it into three parts, one part for thee, another for my support and spare money, but the third is to me a sacred and untouched property, it is for thee in

---

[1] Travel guide who speaks Arabic, Turkish and Persian
[2] People from Germanic tribes

the hour of need." Thus spoke my old father, tears standing in his eyes, perhaps from some foreboding, for I never saw him again.

The journey passed off very well; we had soon reached the land of the Franks, and six days later we arrived in the large city of Paris. There my Frankish friend hired a room for me, and advised me to spend wisely my money, which amounted in all to two thousand dollars. I lived three years in this city, and learned what is necessary for a skilful doctor to know. I should not, however, be stating the truth if I said that I liked being there, for the customs of this nation displeased me; besides, I had only a few chosen friends there, and these were noble young men.

The longing after home at last possessed me mightily; during the whole of that time I had not heard anything from my father, and I therefore seized a favorable opportunity of reaching home. An embassy from France left for Turkey. I acted as surgeon to the suite of the Ambassador and arrived happily in Stamboul. My father's house was locked, and the neighbors, who were surprised on seeing me, told me my father had died two months ago. The priest who had instructed me in my youth brought me the key; alone and desolate I entered the empty house. All was still in the same position as my father had left it, only the gold which I was to inherit was gone. I questioned the priest about it, and he, bowing, said: "Your father died a saint, for he has bequeathed his gold to the Church."

This was and remained inexplicable to me. However, what could I do? I had no witness against the priest, and had to be glad that he had not considered the house and the goods of my father as a bequest. This was the first misfortune that I encountered. Henceforth nothing but ill-luck attended me. My reputation as doctor would not spread at all, because I was ashamed to act the charlatan; and I felt everywhere the want of the recommendation of my father, who would have introduced me to the richest and most distinguished, but who now no longer thought of the poor Zaleukos! The goods of my father also had no sale, for his customers had deserted him after his death, and new ones are only to be got slowly.

Thus when I was one day meditating sadly over my position, it occurred to me that I had often seen in France men of my nation travelling through the country exhibiting their goods in the markets of the towns. I remembered that the people liked to buy of them, because they came from abroad, and that such a business would be most lucrative. Immediately I resolved what to do. I disposed of my father's house, gave part of the money to a trusty friend to keep for me, and with the rest I bought what are very rare in France, shawls, silk goods, ointments, and oils, took a berth on board a ship, and thus entered upon my second journey to the land of the Franks. It seemed as if fortune had favored me again as soon as I had turned my back upon the Castles of the Dardanelles.[3]

Our journey was short and successful. I travelled through the large and small towns of the Franks, and found everywhere willing buyers of my goods. My friend in Stamboul always sent me fresh stores, and my wealth increased day by day. When I had saved at last so much that I thought I might venture on a greater undertaking, I travelled with my goods to Italy. I must however confess to something, which brought me not a little money: I also employed my knowledge of physic. On reaching a town, I had it published that a Greek physician had arrived, who had already healed many; and in fact my balsam and medicine gained me many a sequin.[4] Thus I had at length reached the city of Florence in Italy.

I resolved upon remaining in this town for some time, partly because I liked it so well, partly also because I wished to recruit myself from the exertions of my travels. I hired a vaulted shop, in that part of the town called Sta. Croce, and not far from this a couple of nice rooms at an inn, leading out upon a balcony. I immediately had my bills circulated, which announced me to be both physician and merchant. Scarcely had I opened my shop when I was besieged by buyers, and in spite of my high prices I sold more than any one else, because I was obliging and friendly towards my customers. Thus I had already lived four days happily in Florence, when one evening, as I was about to close my vaulted room, and on examining once more the contents of my ointment boxes, as I was in the habit of doing, I found in one of the small boxes a piece of paper, which I did not remember to have put into it.

I unfolded the paper, and found in it an invitation to be on the bridge which is called Ponto Vecchio[5] that night

---

[3] Castles of the Turkish Straits

[4] In this context, gold coins

[5] Commonly "Ponte Vecchio"

exactly at midnight. I was thinking for a long time as to who it might be who had invited me there; and not knowing a single soul in Florence, I thought perhaps I should be secretly conducted to a patient, a thing which had already often occurred. I therefore determined to proceed thither, but took care to gird on the sword which my father had once presented to me. When it was close upon midnight I set out on my journey, and soon reached the Ponte Vecchio. I found the bridge deserted, and determined to await the appearance of him who called me. It was a cold night; the moon shone brightly, and I looked down upon the waves of the Arno, which sparkled far away in the moonlight. It was now striking twelve o'clock from all the churches of the city, when I looked up and saw a tall man standing before me completely covered in a scarlet cloak, one end of which hid his face.

At first I was somewhat frightened, because he had made his appearance so suddenly; but was however myself again shortly afterwards, and said: "If it is you who have ordered me here, say what you want?" The man dressed in scarlet turned round and said in an undertone:

"Follow!"

At this, however, I felt a little timid to go alone with this stranger. I stood still and said: "Not so, sir, kindly first tell me where; you might also let me see your countenance a little, in order to convince me that you wish me no harm."

The red one, however, did not seem to pay any attention to this. "If thou art unwilling, Zaleukos, remain," he replied, and continued his way.

I grew angry. "Do you think," I exclaimed, "a man like myself allows himself to be made a fool of, and to have waited on this cold night for nothing?"

In three bounds I had reached him, seized him by his cloak, and cried still louder, whilst laying hold of my sabre with my other hand. His cloak, however, remained in my hand, and the stranger had disappeared round the nearest corner. I became calmer by degrees. I had the cloak at any rate, and it was this which would give me the key to this remarkable adventure. I put it on and continued my way home. When I was at a distance of about a hundred paces from it, some one brushed very closely by me and whispered in the language of the Franks: "Take care, Count, nothing can be done tonight."

Before I had time, however, to turn round, this

somebody had passed, and I merely saw a shadow hovering along the houses. I perceived that these words did not concern me, but rather the cloak, yet it gave me no explanation concerning the affair. On the following morning I considered what was to be done. At first I had intended to have the cloak cried in the streets, as if I had found it. But then the stranger might send for it by a third person, and thus no light would be thrown upon the matter. Whilst I was thus thinking, I examined the cloak more closely. It was made of thick Genoese velvet, scarlet in color, edged with Astrachan fur[6] and richly embroidered with gold. The magnificent appearance of the cloak put a thought into my mind which I resolved to carry out.

I carried it into my shop and exposed it for sale, but placed such a high price upon it that I was sure nobody would buy it. My object in this was to scrutinize everybody sharply who might ask for the fur cloak; for the figure of the stranger, which I had seen but superficially, though with some certainty, after the loss of the cloak, I should recognize amongst a thousand. There were many would-be purchasers for the cloak, the extraordinary beauty of which attracted everybody; but none resembled the stranger in the slightest degree, and nobody was willing to pay such a high price as two hundred sequins for it. What astonished me was that on asking somebody or other if there was not such a cloak in Florence, they all answered "No," and assured me they never had seen so precious and tasteful a piece of work.

Evening was drawing near, when at last a young man appeared, who had already been to my place, and who had also offered me a great deal for the cloak. He threw a purse with sequins upon the table, and exclaimed: "Of a truth, Zaleukos, I must have thy cloak, should I turn into a beggar over it!" He immediately began to count his pieces of gold. I was in a dangerous position: I had only exposed the cloak, in order merely to attract the attention of my stranger, and now a young fool came to pay an immense price for it. However, what could I do? I yielded; for on the other hand I was delighted at the idea of being so handsomely recompensed for my nocturnal adventure.

The young man put the cloak around him and went away, but on reaching the threshold he returned; whilst unfastening a piece of paper which had been tied to the

---

[6] Luxurious fur from this Russian city

cloak, and throwing it towards me, he exclaimed: "Here, Zaleukos, hangs something which I dare say does not belong to the cloak."

I picked up the piece of paper carelessly, but behold, on it these words were written: "Bring the cloak at the appointed hour to-night to the Ponte Vecchio, four hundred sequins are thine." I stood thunderstruck. Thus I had lost my fortune and completely missed my aim! Yet I did not think long. I picked up the two hundred sequins, jumped after the one who had bought the cloak, and said: "Dear friend, take back your sequins, and give me the cloak; I cannot possibly part with it." He first regarded the matter as a joke; but when he saw that I was in earnest, he became angry at my demand, called me a fool, and finally it came to blows.

However, I was fortunate enough to wrench the cloak from him in the scuffle, and was about to run away with it, when the young man called the police to his assistance, and we both appeared before the judge. The latter was much surprised at the accusation, and adjudicated the cloak in favor of my adversary. I offered the young man twenty, fifty, eighty, even a hundred sequins in addition to his two hundred, if he would part with the cloak. What my entreaties could not do, my gold did. He accepted it. I, however, went away with the cloak triumphantly, and had to appear to the whole town of Florence as a madman. I did not care, however, about the opinion of the people; I knew better than they that I profited after all by the bargain.

Impatiently I awaited the night. At the same hour as before I went with the cloak under my arm towards the Ponte Vecchio. With the last stroke of twelve the figure appeared out of the darkness, and came towards me. It was unmistakably the man whom I had seen yesterday. "Hast thou the cloak?" he asked me.

"Yes, sir," I replied; "but it cost me a hundred sequins ready money."

"I know it," replied the other. "Look here, here are four hundred." He went with me towards the wide balustrade of the bridge, and counted out the money. There were four hundred; they sparkled magnificently in the moonlight; their glitter rejoiced my heart. Alas, I did not anticipate that this would be its last joy. I put the money into my pocket, and was desirous of thoroughly looking at my kind and unknown stranger; but he wore a mask, through which dark eyes stared at me frightfully.

"I thank you, sir, for your kindness," I said to him; "what else do you require of me? I tell you beforehand it must be an honorable transaction."

"There is no occasion for alarm," he replied, whilst winding the cloak around his shoulders; "I require your assistance as surgeon, not for one alive, but dead."

"What do you mean?" I exclaimed, full of surprise.

"I arrived with my sister from abroad," he said, and beckoned me at the same time to follow him. "I lived here with her at the house of a friend. My sister died yesterday suddenly of a disease, and my relatives wish to bury her tomorrow. According to an old custom of our family all are to be buried in the tomb of our ancestors; many, notwithstanding, who died in foreign countries are buried there and embalmed. I do not grudge my relatives her body, but for my father I want at least the head of his daughter, in order that he may see her once more." This custom of severing the heads of beloved relatives appeared to me somewhat awful, yet I did not dare to object to it lest I should offend the stranger. I told him that I was acquainted with the embalming of the dead, and begged him to conduct me to the deceased. Yet I could not help asking him why all this must be done so mysteriously and at night? He answered me that his relatives, who considered his intention horrible, objected to it by daylight; if only the head were severed, then they could say no more about it; although he might have brought me the head, yet a natural feeling had prevented him from severing it himself.

In the meantime we had reached a large, splendid house. My companion pointed it out to me as the end of our nocturnal walk. We passed the principal entrance of the house, entered a little door, which the stranger carefully locked behind him, and now ascended in the dark a narrow spiral staircase. It led towards a dimly lighted passage, out of which we entered a room lighted by a lamp fastened to the ceiling.

In this room was a bed, on which the corpse lay. The stranger turned aside his face, evidently endeavoring to hide his tears. He pointed towards the bed, telling me to do my business well and quickly, and left the room.

I took my instruments, which I as surgeon always carried about with me, and approached the bed. Only the head of the corpse was visible, and it was so beautiful that

I experienced involuntarily the deepest sympathy. Dark hair hung down in long plaits, the features were pale, the eyes closed. At first I made an incision into the skin, after the manner of surgeons when amputating a limb. I then took my sharpest knife, and with one stroke cut the throat. But oh, horror! The dead opened her eyes, but immediately closed them again, and with a deep sigh she now seemed to breathe her last. At the same moment a stream of hot blood shot towards me from the wound. I was convinced that the poor creature had been killed by me. That she was dead there was no doubt, for there was no recovery from this wound. I stood for some minutes in painful anguish at what had happened. Had the "red-cloak" deceived me, or had his sister perhaps merely been apparently dead? The latter seemed to me more likely. But I dare not tell the brother of the deceased that perhaps a little less deliberate cut might have awakened her without killing her; therefore I wished to sever the head completely; but once more the dying woman groaned, stretched herself out in painful movements, and died.

Fright overpowered me, and, shuddering, I hastened out of the room. But outside in the passage it was dark; for the light was out, no trace of my companion was to be seen, and I was obliged, haphazard, to feel my way in the dark along the wall, in order to reach the staircase. I discovered it at last and descended, partly falling and partly gliding. But there was not a soul downstairs. I merely found the door ajar, and breathed freer on reaching the street, for I had felt very strange inside the house. Urged on by terror, I rushed towards my dwelling-place, and buried myself in the cushions of my bed, in order to forget the terrible thing that I had done.

But sleep deserted me, and only the morning admonished me again to take courage. It seemed to me probable that the man who had induced me to commit this nefarious deed, as it now appeared to me, might not denounce me. I immediately resolved to set to work in my vaulted room, and if possible to assume an indifferent look. But alas! an additional circumstance, which I only now noticed, increased my anxiety still more. My cap and my girdle, as well as my instruments, were wanting, and I was uncertain as to whether I had left them in the room of the murdered girl, or whether I had lost them in my flight. The former seemed indeed the more likely, and thus I could easily be discovered as the murderer.

At the accustomed hour I opened my vaulted room. My neighbor came in, as was his wont every morning, for he was a talkative man.

"Well," he said, "what do you say about the terrible affair which has occurred during the night?" I pretended not to know anything. "What, do you not know what is known all over the town? Are you not aware that the loveliest flower in Florence, Bianca, the Governor's daughter, was murdered last night? I saw her only yesterday driving through the streets in so cheerful a manner with her intended one, for today the marriage was to have taken place." I felt deeply wounded at each word of my neighbor. Many a time my torment was renewed, for every one of my customers told me of the affair, each one more ghastly than the other, and yet nobody could relate anything more terrible than that which I had seen myself.

About mid-day a police-officer entered my shop and requested me to send the people away. "Signor Zaleukos," he said, producing the things which I had missed, "do these things belong to you?" I was thinking as to whether I should not entirely repudiate them, but on seeing through the door, which stood ajar, my landlord and several acquaintances, I determined not to aggravate the affair by telling a lie, and acknowledged myself as the owner of the things. The police-officer asked me to follow him, and led me towards a large building which I soon recognized as the prison. There he showed me into a room.

My situation was terrible, as I thought of it in my solitude. The idea of having committed a murder, unintentionally, constantly presented itself to my mind. I also could not conceal from myself that the glitter of the gold had captivated my feelings, otherwise I should not have fallen blindly into the trap. Two hours after my arrest I was led out of my cell. I descended several steps until at last I reached a great hall. Around a long table draped in black were seated twelve men, mostly old men. There were benches along the sides of the hall, filled with the most distinguished of Florence. The galleries, which were above, were thickly crowded with spectators. When I had stepped towards the table covered with black cloth, a man with a gloomy and sad countenance rose; it was the Governor. He said to the assembly that he as the father in this affair could not sentence, and that he resigned his place on this occasion to the eldest of the Senators. The eldest of the Senators was an old man at least ninety years of age. He stood in a bent attitude, and his temples were covered with thin white hair, but his eyes were as yet very fiery, and his voice powerful and weighty. He commenced by asking me whether I confessed to the murder. I requested him to allow me to speak, and related undauntedly and with a clear voice what I had done, and what I knew.

I noticed that the Governor, during my recital, at one time turned pale, and at another time red. When I had finished, he rose angrily: "What, wretch!" he exclaimed, "dost thou even dare to impute a crime which thou hast committed from greediness to another?"

The Senator reprimanded him for his interruption, since he had voluntarily renounced his right; besides it was not clear that I did the deed from greediness, for, according to his own statement, nothing had been stolen from the victim. He even went further. He told the Governor that he must give an account of the early life of his daughter, for then only it would be possible to decide whether I had spoken the truth or not. At the same time he adjourned the court for the day, in order, as he said, to consult the papers of the deceased, which the Governor would give him. I was again taken back to my prison, where I spent a wretched day, always fervently wishing that a link between the deceased and the "red-cloak" might be discovered. Full of hope, I entered the Court of Justice the next day. Several letters were lying upon the table. The old Senator asked me whether they were in my handwriting. I looked at them and noticed that they must have been written by the same hand as the other two papers which I had received. I communicated this to the Senators, but no attention was paid to it, and they told me that I might have written both, for the signature of the letters was undoubtedly a Z., the first letter of my name. The letters, however, contained threats against the deceased, and warnings against the marriage which she was about to contract.

The Governor seemed to have given extraordinary information concerning me, for I was treated with more suspicion and rigor on this day. I referred, to justify myself, to my papers which must be in my room, but was told they had been looked for without success. Thus at the conclusion of this sitting all hope vanished, and on being brought into the Court the third day, judgment was pronounced on me. I was convicted of willful murder and condemned to death. Things had come to such a pass!

Deserted by all that was precious to me upon earth, far away from home, I was to die innocently in the bloom of my life.

On the evening of this terrible day which had decided my fate, I was sitting in my lonely cell, my hopes were gone, my thoughts steadfastly fixed upon death, when the door of my prison opened, and in came a man, who for a long time looked at me silently. "Is it thus I find you again, Zaleukos?" he said. I had not recognized him by the dim light of my lamp, but the sound of his voice roused in me old remembrances. It was Valetti, one of those few friends whose acquaintance I made in the city of Paris when I was studying there. He said that he had come to Florence accidentally, where his father, who was a distinguished man, lived. He had heard about my affair, and had come to see me once more, and to hear from my own lips how I could have committed such a crime. I related to him the whole affair. He seemed much surprised at it, and adjured me, as my only friend, to tell him all, in order not to leave the world with a lie behind me. I confirmed my assertions with an oath that I had spoken the truth, and that I was not guilty of anything, except that the glitter of the gold had dazzled me, and that I had not perceived the improbability of the story of the stranger. "Did you not know Bianca?" he asked me. I assured him that I had never seen her. Valetti now related to me that a profound mystery rested on the affair, that the Governor had very much accelerated my condemnation, and now a report was spread that I had known Bianca for a long time, and had murdered her out of revenge for her marriage with some one else. I told him that all this coincided exactly with the "red-cloak," but that I was unable to prove his participation in the affair. Valetti embraced me weeping, and promised me to do all, at least to save my life.

I had little hope, though I knew that Valetti was a clever man, well versed in the law, and that he would do all in his power to save my life. For two long days I was in uncertainty; at last Valetti appeared. "I bring consolation, though painful. You will live and be free with the loss of one hand."

Affected, I thanked my friend for saving my life. He told me that the Governor had been inexorable in having the affair investigated a second time, but that he at last, in order not to appear unjust, had agreed, that if a similar case could be found in the law books of the history of

Florence, my punishment should be the same as the one recorded in these books. He and his father had searched in the old books day and night, and at last found a case quite similar to mine. The sentence was: That his left hand be cut off, his property confiscated, and he himself banished for ever. This was my punishment also, and he asked me to prepare for the painful hour which awaited me. I will not describe to you that terrible hour, when I laid my hand upon the block in the public market-place and my own blood shot over me in broad streams.

Valetti took me to his house until I had recovered; he then most generously supplied me with money for travelling, for all I had acquired with so much difficulty had fallen a prey to the law. I left Florence for Sicily and embarked on the first ship that I found for Constantinople.

My hope was fixed upon the sum which I had entrusted to my friend. I also requested to be allowed to live with him. But how great was my astonishment on being asked why I did not wish to live in my own house. He told me that some unknown man had bought a house in the Greek Quarter in my name, and this very man had also told the neighbors of my early arrival. I immediately proceeded thither accompanied by my friend, and was received by all my old acquaintances joyfully. An old merchant gave me a letter, which the man who had bought the house for me had left behind. I read as follows:

"Zaleukos! Two hands are prepared to work incessantly, in order that you may not feel the loss of one of yours. The house which you see and all its contents are yours, and every year you will receive enough to be counted amongst the rich of your people. Forgive him who is unhappier than yourself!"

I could guess who had written it, and in answer to my question, the merchant told me it had been a man, whom he took for a Frank, and who had worn a scarlet cloak. I knew enough to understand that the stranger was, after all, not entirely devoid of noble intentions. In my new house I found everything arranged in the best style, also a vaulted room stored with goods, more splendid than I had ever had. Ten years have passed since. I still continue my commercial travels, more from old custom than necessity, yet I have never again seen that country where I became so unfortunate. Every year since, I have received a thousand gold-pieces; and although I rejoice to know that unfortunate man to be noble, yet he cannot relieve me of the sorrow of my soul, for the terrible picture of the murdered Bianca is continually on my mind.

SAMUEL WARREN
(1807-1877)

Φ

The Thunder-Struck and the Boxer

This story is one of a series of stories anonymously published in *Blackwood's Magazine* from August 1830 to August 1837. They were all by Samuel Warren. The articles were collected in "Passages from the Diary of a Late Physician" with "Dr. Harrison" placed on the title page of the three foreign editions. Much to Warren's surprise, a number of authors stepped forward in England and claimed to be the author of the collection while others asserted they penned certain of the tales contained within. Warren was forced to divulge his identity only when William Blackwood brought a legal action, in the Chancery Court of England, against copyright infringers of his magazine. Warren never, however, revealed why he published the stories anonymously in the first place.

Warren was not a doctor, but "for six years actively engaged in the practical study of physic," which he quit in 1827. In his Preface to the Fifth Edition of "Passages from the Diary of a Late Physician," Warren made clear that he eschewed the complexity of plots, which are found in many of Charles Dickens's works, and tales of sensation that had become literary fashion in *Blackwood's Magazine*. In reference to the overall nature of his stories,

Warren "selected the most ordinary incidents, the simplest [sic] combinations of circumstances; never attempting to disturb or complicate the development of character and of feeling with intricacy of plot, or novelty of incident."

Given the excellent writing, a pervasive sense of dread, and original supernatural events that happen to ordinary characters, "The Thunder-Struck and the Boxer" is one of the best short horror stories of 1800-1849. It is also the most apocalyptic.

The Thunder-Struck and the Boxer[1]

IN THE SUMMER OF 18—, London was visited by one of the most tremendous thunder-storms that have been known in this climate. Its character and effects—some of which latter form the subject of this chapter—will make me remember it to the latest hour of my life.

There was something portentous—a still, surcharged air—about the whole of Tuesday, the 10th of July 18—, as though nature were trembling and cowering beneath a common shock. In the exquisite language of one of our old dramatists,[2] there seemed

--------A calm
Before a tempest, when the gentle air
Lays her soft ear close to the earth, to listen
For that she fears steals on to ravish her.

From about eleven o'clock at noon, the sky wore a lurid threatening aspect, that shot awe into the beholder; suggesting to startled fancy the notion, that within the dim confines of the "labouring air," mischief was working to the world.

The heat was intolerable, keeping almost everybody within doors. The dogs, and other cattle in the streets, stood everywhere panting and loath to move. There was no small excitement, or rather agitation, diffused throughout the country, especially London; for, strange to say (and many must recollect the circumstance), it had been for some time confidently foretold by certain enthusiasts, religious as well as philosophic, that the

---

[1] This is a narrative—for obvious reasons somewhat varied in circumstances—of a lamentable occurrence in the author's family. About fourteen years ago, a very beautiful girl, eighteen years old, terrified at a violent thunderstorm, rushed into a cellar to escape, as she thought, from the danger, and was found there in the state described in the text. She died four days afterwards.

[2] Text from English poet and playwright George Chapman (1560-1634)

earth was to be destroyed that very day; in short, that the tremendous JUDGMENT was at hand! Though not myself over credulous, or given to superstitious fears, I own that on coupling these fearful predictions with the unusual, and almost preternatural aspect of the day, I more than once experienced sudden qualms of apprehension as I rode along on my daily rounds. I did not so much communicate alarm to the various circles I entered, as catch it from them. Then, again, I would occasionally pass a silent group of passengers clustering round a street-preacher, who, true to his vocation, "redeeming the time," seemed by his gestures, and the disturbed countenances around him, to be foretelling all that was frightful. The tone of excitement which pervaded my feelings, was further heightened by a conversation on the prevailing topic which I had in the course of the morning with the distinguished poet and scholar, Mr —. With what fearful force did he suggest possibilities; what vivid, startling colouring did he throw over them! It was, indeed, a topic congenial to his gloomy imagination. He talked to me, in short, till my disturbed fancy began to realize the wildest chimeras.

"Great God, Dr —!" said he, laying his hand suddenly on my arm, his great black eyes gleaming with mysterious awe—"Think, only think! What if, at the moment we are talking together, a comet, whose track the peering eye of science has never traced—whose very existence is known to none but God—is winging its fiery way towards our earth, swift as the lightning, and with force inevitable! Is it at this instant dashing to fragments some mighty orb that obstructed its progress, and then passing on towards us, disturbing system after system in its way?—How—when will the frightful crash be felt? Is its heat now blighting our atmosphere?—Will combustion first commence, or shall we be at once split asunder into innumerable fragments, and sent drifting through infinite space?—Whither—whither shall we fly? what must become of our species?—Is the Scriptural JUDGMENT then coming?—Oh, doctor, what if all these things *are really at hand?*"

Was this imaginative raving calculated to calm one's feelings?—By the time I reached home, late in the afternoon, I felt in a fever of excitement. I found an air of apprehension throughout the whole house. My wife, children, and a young lady, a visitor, were all together in the parlour, looking out for me, through the window, anxiously—and with paler faces than they perhaps were aware of. The visitor just alluded to, by the way, was a Miss Agnes P—, a girl of about twenty-one, the daughter of an old friend and patient of mine. Her mother, a widow (with no other child than this), resided in a village about fifty miles from town—from which she was expected, in a few days' time, to take her daughter back again into the country. Miss P— was a very charming young woman. There was a softness of expression about her delicate features, that in my opinion constitutes the highest style of feminine loveliness.

Her dark, pensive, searching eyes, spoke a soul full of feeling. The tones of her voice, mellow and various, and her whole carriage and demeanour, were in accordance with the expression of her features. In person she was about the average height, and perfectly well moulded and proportioned; and there was a Hebe-like ease and grace about all her gestures. She excelled in most feminine accomplishments; but her favourite objects were music and romance. A more imaginative creature was surely never known. It required all the fond and anxious surveillance of her friends to prevent her carrying her tastes to excess, and becoming, in a manner, unfitted for the "dull commerce of a duller earth!"

No sooner had this young lady made her appearance in my house, and given token of something like a prolonged stay, than I became the most popular man in the circle of my acquaintance. Such assiduous calls to inquire after *my* health, and that of my family!— Such a multitude of men—young ones, to boot—and so embarrassed with a consciousness of the poorness of the pretence that drew them to my house! Such matronly inquiries from mothers and elderly female relatives, into the nature and extent of "sweet Miss P—'s expectations!" During a former stay at my house, about six months before the period of which I am writing, Miss P— surrendered her affections—(to the delighted surprise of all her friends and relatives)—to the quietest, and perhaps worthiest of her claimants—a young man, then, preparing for orders at Oxford. Never, sure, was there a greater contrast between the tastes of a pledged couple; she all feeling, romance, enthusiasm; he serene, thoughtful, and matter-of-fact. It was most amusing to witness their occasional collisions on subjects which developed their respective tastes and qualities; and interesting to note that the effect was invariably to raise the one in the other's estimation—as if each prized most the qualities of the other. Young N— had spent two days in London—the greater portion of them, I need hardly say, at my house—about a week before the period of which I am writing; and he and his fair mistress had disputed rather keenly on the topic of general discussion—the predicted event of the 10th of July.

If she did not repose implicit faith in the prophecy, her belief had, somehow or another, acquired a most disturbing strength. He laboured hard to disabuse her of her awful apprehensions—and she as hard to overcome his obstinate incredulity. Each was a little too eager about the matter; and, for the first time since they had known each other, they parted with a *little* coldness—yes, although he was to set off the next morning for Oxford! In short, scarcely anything was talked about by Agnes but the coming 10th of July; and if she did not anticipate the actual destruction of the globe, and the final judgment of mankind, she at least looked forward to some event, mysterious and tremendous. The eloquent enthusiastic creature almost brought over my placid, little, matter-of-fact wife to her way of thinking!

To return from this long digression—which, however, will be presently found to have been not unnecessary. After staying a few minutes in the parlour, I retired to my library, for the purpose, among other things, of making those entries in my diary, from which these "Passages" are taken—but the pen lay useless in my hand. With my chin resting on the palm of my left hand, I sat at my desk lost in a reverie; my eyes fixed on the tree which grew in the yard and overshadowed my windows. How still—how motionless was every leaf! What sultry — oppressive — *unusual* repose! How it would have cheered me to hear the faintest "sough" of wind—to see the breeze sweep freshening through the leaves, rustling and stirring them into life! I opened my window, untied my neckerchief, and loosened my shirt-collar — for I felt suffocated with the heat. I heard at length a faint pattering sound among the leaves of the tree—and presently there fell on the window frame three or four large ominous drops of rain. After gazing upwards for a moment or two on the gloomy aspect of the sky—I once more settled down to writing; and was dipping my pen into the inkstand, when there blazed about me a flash of lightning, with such a ghastly, blinding splendour, as defies all description. It was like what one might conceive to be a glimpse of hell—and yet not a *glimpse* merely—for it continued, I think, six or seven seconds. It was followed, at scarce an instant's interval, with a crash of thunder as if the world had been smitten out of its sphere, and was rending asunder!—I hope these expressions will not be considered hyperbolical. No one, I am sure, who recollects the occurrence I am describing, will require the appeal!—May *I* never see or hear the like again! I leaped from my chair with consternation; and could think of nothing at the moment, but closing my eyes, and shutting out from my ears the stunning sound of the thunder.[3] For a moment I stood literally stupefied.

On recovering myself, my first impulse was to spring to the door, and rush down stairs in search of my wife and children. (I heard, on my way, the sound of shrieking proceed from the parlour in which I had left them. In a moment I had my wife folded in my arms, and my children clinging with screams round my knees. My wife had fainted. While I was endeavouring to restore her, there came a second flash of lightning, equally terrible

---

[3] The following fine description of a storm at sea, is to be found in Mr James Montgomery's *"Pelican Island."* I shall, I hope, be excused for transcribing it, as I believe it is not very generally known:—

"Dreary and hollow moans foretold a gale;
Nor long the issue tarried;
Then the wind, unprison'd, blew its trumpet loud and shrill;
Out flash'd the lightnings gloriously;
The rain Came down like music, and the full-toned thunder Roll'd in grand harmony throughout high heaven:
Till ocean, breaking from his black supineness, drown'd in his own stupendous uproar all the voices of the storm beside;
Meanwhile a war of mountains raged upon his surface;
Mountains each other swallowing, and again New Alps and Andes, from unfathom'd valleys upstarting, join'd the battle;
Like those sous Of earth—giants, rebounding as new-born from every fall on their unwearied mother.
I glow'd with all the rapture of the strife:
Beneath was one wild whirl of foaming surges;
Above the array of lightnings, like the swords of cherubim, wide brandish'd to repel aggression from heaven's gates;
Their naming strokes quench'd momentarily in the vast abyss."

with the first—and a second explosion of thunder, loud as one could imagine the discharge of a thousand parks of artillery, directly overhead. The windows—in fact, the whole house quivered with the shock. The noise helped to recover my wife from her swoon.

"Kneel down! Love! Husband!"—she gasped, endeavouring to drop upon her knees—"Kneel down! Pray —pray for us! *It is at hand!*" After shouting several times pretty loudly, and pulling the bell repeatedly and violently, one of the servants made her appearance—but evidently terrified and bewildered. She and her mistress, however, recovered themselves in a few minutes, roused by the cries of the children. "Wait a moment, love," said I, "and I will bring you a little sal-volatile!"[4] I stepped into the back room, where I generally kept a few phials of drugs—and poured out what I wanted. The thought then for the first time struck me, that I had not seen Miss P in the parlour I had just quitted. *Where* was she? What would *she* say to all this?—God bless me, where is she?—I thought, with increasing trepidation.

"Edward—Edward," I exclaimed, to a servant who happened to pass the door of the room where I was standing; "where's Miss P—?"

"Miss P—, sir!—Why—I don't—oh, yes!" he replied, suddenly recollecting himself, "about five minutes ago I saw her run very quickly upstairs, and haven't seen her since, sir."

"What!" I exclaimed with increasing trepidation, "was it about the time that the first flash of lightning came?" "Yes, it was, sir!"—"Take this in to your mistress, and say I'll be with her immediately," said I, giving him what I had mixed. I rushed upstairs, calling out as I went, "Agnes! Agnes! where are you?" I received no answer. At length I reached the floor where her bedroom lay. The door was closed, but not shut.

"Agnes! Where are you?" I inquired, very agitatedly, at the same time knocking at her door. I received no answer. "Agnes! Agnes! For God's sake speak!—Speak, or I shall come into your room!" No reply was made; and I thrust open the door. Heavens! Can I describe what I saw?

Within less than a yard of me stood the most fearful figure my eyes have ever beheld. It was Agnes!—She was in the attitude of stepping to the door, with both arms

[4] Ammonium carbonate liquid used in smelling salts

extended. Her hair was partially disheveled. Her face seemed whiter than the white dress she wore. Her lips were of a livid hue. Her eyes, full of awful expression, were fixed with a petrifying stare on me. Oh, language fails me—utterly!—Those eyes have seldom since been absent from me when alone! I strove to speak—but could not utter a sound. My lips seemed rigid as those I looked at. The horrors of nightmare seemed upon me. My eyes at length closed; my head seemed turning round—and for a moment or two I lost all consciousness. I revived. *There* was the frightful thing still before me—nay, close to me! Though I looked at her, I never once thought of Agnes P—. It was the tremendous appearance—the ineffable terror gleaming from her eyes, that thus overcame me. I protest I cannot conceive anything more dreadful! Miss P— continued standing perfectly motionless: and while I was gazing at her in the manner I have been describing, a peal of thunder roused me to my self-possession.

I stepped towards her, took hold of her hand, exclaiming, "Agnes—Agnes!" and carried her to the bed, where I laid her down. It required some little force to press down her arms; and I drew the eyelids over her staring eyes mechanically. While in the act of doing so, a flash of lightning flickered luridly over her—but her eye neither quivered nor blinked. She seemed to have been suddenly deprived of all sense and motion: in fact, nothing but her pulse—if pulse it should be called—and faint breathing, showed that she lived. My eye wandered over her whole figure, dreading to meet some scorching trace of lightning—but there was nothing of the kind. What had happened to her? Was she frightened — to death? I spoke to her; I called her by her name, loudly; I shook her, rather violently: I might have acted it all to a statue! — I rang the chamber bell with almost frantic violence: and presently my wife and a female servant made their appearance in the room; but I was far more embarrassed than assisted by their presence. "Is she killed?" murmured the former, as she staggered towards the bed, and then clung convulsively to me—"Has the lightning struck her?"

I was compelled to disengage myself from her grasp, and hurry her into the adjoining room—whither I called a servant to attend her; and then returned to my hapless patient. But what was I to do? Medical man as I was, I never had seen a patient in such circumstances, and felt as ignorant on the subject as agitated. It was not epilepsy—it was not apoplexy — a swoon — nor any known species of hysteria. The most remarkable feature of her case, and what enabled me to ascertain the nature of her disease, was this; that if I happened accidentally to alter the position of her limbs, they retained, for a short time, their new position. If, for instance, I moved her arm—it remained for a while in the situation in which I had last placed it, and gradually resumed its former one.

If I raised her into an upright posture, she continued sitting so without the support of pillows, or other assistance, as exactly as if she had heard me express a wish to that effect, and assented to it; but—the horrid vacancy of her aspect! If I elevated one eyelid for a moment, to examine the state of the eye, it was some time in closing, unless I drew it over myself.

All these circumstances — which terrified the servant who stood shaking at my elbow, and muttering, "She's possessed! she's possessed!—Satan has her!"—convinced me at length that the unfortunate girl was seized with CATALEPSY; that rare mysterious affection, so fearfully blending the conditions of life and death—presenting— so to speak—life in the aspect of death, and death in that of life!

I felt no doubt that extreme terror, operating suddenly on a nervous system most highly excited, and a vivid, active fancy, had produced the effects I saw. Doubtless the first terrible outbreak of the thunderstorm—especially the fierce splendour of that first flash of lightning which so alarmed myself—apparently corroborating and realising all her awful apprehensions of the predicted event, overpowered her at once, and flung her into the fearful situation in which I found her—that of one ARRESTED in her terror-struck flight towards the door of her chamber. But again—the thought struck me—had she received any direct injury from the lightning? Had it blinded her? It might be so—for I could make no impression on the pupils of the eyes. Nothing could startle them into action. They seemed a little more dilated than usual, and fixed.

I confess that, besides the other agitating circumstances of the moment, this extraordinary, this unprecedented case, too much distracted my self-possession to enable me promptly to deal with it. I had heard and read of, but never before seen such a case. No time, however, was to be lost. I determined to resort at once to strong anti-spasmodic treatment. I bled her from the arm freely, applied blisters behind the ears, immersed her feet, which, together with her hands, were cold as those of a statue, in hot water, and endeavoured to force into her mouth a little opium[5] and ether.[6] Whilst the servants were busied about her, undressing her, and carrying my directions into effect, I stepped for a moment into the adjoining room, where I found my wife just recovering from a violent fit of hysterics. Her loud laughter, though so near me, I had not once heard, so absorbed was I with the mournful case of Miss P—. After continuing with her till she recovered sufficiently to accompany me down stairs, I returned to Miss P—'s bedroom. She continued exactly in the condition in which I had left her.

Though the water was hot enough almost to parboil her tender feet, it produced no sensible effect on the circulation, or the state of the skin; and finding a strong determination of blood towards the regions of the head and neck, I determined to have her cupped between the shoulders.[7] I went down stairs to drop a line to the apothecary,[8] requesting him to come immediately with his cupping instruments. As I was delivering the note into the hands of a servant, a man rushed up to the open door where I was standing, and, breathless with haste, begged

---

[5] Narcotic drug made from the opium poppy

[6] Sweet solution used for an anesthetic

[7] "The mode of performing the operation is as follows :—A vase-shaped glass vessel called a cupping-glass is placed close to the skin. The flame of a spirit-lamp is then introduced for a moment in the glass so as to expel the air, and the glass is rapidly placed with its mouth downwards on the skin. If this be done with sufficient rapidity, the partial vacuum in the cupping-glass causes it to adhere to the skin, which is forced into it by atmospheric pressure, as shown in the illustration. The blood is, of course, drawn towards the surface by the same means.

The glass is then quickly removed, and a little brass instrument applied, which, at the touching of a spring, sends out a number of small lancet-blades so formed as to make very slight cuts. The glass is again applied, and rapidly becomes filled with blood from the cuts, the air having forced it in." *Nature's Teachings*, Rev. J. G. Wood, 1885, pg. 330.

[8] A pharmacist

my instant attendance on a patient close by, who had just met with a severe accident. Relying on the immediate arrival of Mr —, the apothecary, I put on my hat and great-coat, took my umbrella, and followed the man who had summoned me out. It rained in torrents; for the storm, after about twenty minutes' intermission, burst forth again with unabated violence. The thunder and lightning—peal upon peal—blaze upon blaze, were really terrific!

THE BOXER.

THE PATIENT WHO THUS abruptly, and, under circumstances, inopportunely, required my services, proved to be one Bill —, a notorious boxer, who, in returning that evening from a great prize-fight, had been thrown out of his gig, the horse having been frightened by the lightning, and the rider, who was much the worse for liquor, had his ankle dreadfully dislocated. He had been taken up by some passengers, and conveyed with great difficulty to his own residence, a public-house, not three minutes' walk from where I lived. The moment I entered the tap-room, which I had to pass on my way to the staircase, I heard his groans, or rather howls, overhead.

The excitement of intoxication, added to the agonies occasioned by his accident, had driven him, I was told, nearly mad. He was uttering the most revolting execrations as I entered his room. He damned himself, his ill luck (for it seemed he had lost considerable sums on the fight), the combatants, the horse that threw him, the thunder and lightning—everything, in short, and everybody about him. The sound of the thunder was sublime melody to me, and the more welcome, because it drowned the blasphemous bellowing of the monster I was visiting. Yes; there lay the burly boxer, stretched upon the bed, with none of his dress removed except the boot, which had been cut from the limb that was injured—his new blue coat, with glaring yellow buttons, and drab knee-breeches, soiled with the street mud into which he had been precipitated—his huge limbs, writhing in restless agony over the bed—his fists clenched, and his flat, iron-featured face swollen and distorted with pain and fury.

"But, my good woman," said I, pausing at the door, addressing myself to the boxer's wife, who, wringing her hands, had conducted me upstairs, "I assure you I am not the person you should have sent to. It's a surgeon's, not a physician's case; I fear I can't do much for him—quite out of my way"—

"Oh, for God's sake—for the love of God, don't say so!" gasped the poor creature with affrighted emphasis —"Oh, do *something* for him, or he'll drive us all out of our senses—he'll be killing us!"

"Do something!" roared my patient, who had overheard the last words of his wife, turning his bloated face towards me—"*do* something, indeed? ay, and be to you! Here, here look ye, doctor—look ye *here!*" he continued, pointing to the wounded foot, which, all crushed and displaced, and the stocking soaked with blood, presented a shocking appearance—"look here, indeed!—ah! That horse! that horse!" his teeth gnashed, and his right hand was lifted up, clenched, with fury—"If I don't break every bone in his body, as soon as ever I can stir this cursed leg again!"

I felt for a moment as though I had entered the very pit and presence of Satan, for the lightning was gleaming over his ruffianly figure incessantly, and the thunder rolling close overhead while he was speaking.

"Hush! hush! you'll drive the doctor away! For pity's sake hold your tongue, or Doctor won't come into the room to you!" gasped his wife, dropping on her knees beside him.

"Ha, ha! Let him go! Only let him stir a step, and lame as I am, me if I don't jump out of bed, and teach him civility! *Here,* you doctor, as you call yourself! What's to be done?" Really I was too much shocked, at the moment, to know. I was half inclined to leave the room immediately, and had a fair plea for doing so in the *surgical* nature of the case; but the agony of the fellow's wife induced me to check my outraged feelings, and stay. After directing a person to be sent off, in my name, for the nearest surgeon, I addressed myself to my task, and proceeded to remove the stocking. His whole body quivered with the anguish it occasioned; and I saw such fury gathering in his features, that I began to dread lest he might rise up in a sudden frenzy, and strike me.

"Oh! oh! oh! Curse your clumsy hands! You don't know no more nor a child," he groaned, "what you're about. Leave it—leave it alone! Give over with ye! Doctor —, I say, be off!"

"Mercy, mercy, doctor!" sobbed his wife in a whisper, fearing from my momentary pause that I was going to take her husband at his word—"Don't go away!—Oh, go on—go on! It *must* be done, you know! Never mind what he says! He's only a little the worse for liquor now—and—and then the *pain!* Go on, doctor! He'll thank you the more for it tomorrow!"

"Wife! here!" shouted her husband. The woman instantly stepped up to him. He stretched out his Herculean arm, and grasped her by the shoulder.

"So, you—! I'm drunk, am I? I'm *drunk,* eh—you lying!" he exclaimed, and jerked her violently away, right across the room, to the door, where the poor creature fell down, but presently rose, crying bitterly.

"Get away! Get off—get down stairs—if you don't want me to serve you the same again! Say I'm drunk, you beast?" With frantic gestures she obeyed, rushed down stairs, and I was left alone with her husband. I was disposed to follow her abruptly; but the positive dread of my life (for he might leap out of the bed and kill me with a blow) kept me to my task. My flesh crept with disgust at touching his! I examined the wound, which undoubtedly must have given him torture enough to drive him mad, and bathed it in warm water; resolved to pay no attention to his abuse, and quit the instant that the surgeon, who had been sent for, made his appearance. At length he came. I breathed more freely, resigned the case into his hands, and was going to take up my hat, when he begged me to continue in the room, with such an earnest apprehensive look, that I reluctantly remained. I saw he dreaded as much being left alone with his patient as I! It need hardly be said that every step that was taken in dressing the wound, was attended with the vilest execrations of the patient. Such a foul-mouthed ruffian I never encountered anywhere. It seemed as though he was possessed of a devil. What a contrast to the sweet speechless sufferer whom I had left at home, and to whom my heart yearned to return!

The storm still continued raging. The rain had comparatively ceased, but the thunder and lightning made their appearance with fearful frequency and fierceness. I drew down the blind of the window, observing to the surgeon that the lightning seemed to startle our patient.

"Put it up again! Put up that blind again, I say!" he cried impatiently. "D'ye think *I'm* afeard of the lightning, like my horse today? Put it up again—or I'll get out and do it myself!" I did as he wished. Reproof or expostulation was useless. "Ha!" he exclaimed, in a low tone of fury, rubbing his hands together—in a manner bathing them in the fiery stream, as a flash of lightning gleamed ruddily over him. "*There* it is! Curse it—just the sort of flash that frightened my horse—, d—it!" —and the impious wretch shook his fist, and grinned horribly a ghastly smile.

"Be silent, sir! Be silent! or we will both leave you instantly. Your behaviour is impious! it is frightful to witness! Forbear—lest the vengeance of God descend upon you!"

"Come, come—none o' your methodism *here!* Go on with your business! Stick to your trade," interrupted the Boxer.

"Does not *that* rebuke your blasphemies?" I inquired, suddenly shading my eyes from the vivid stream of lightning that burst into the room, while the thunder rattled overhead—evidently in most dreadful proximity. When I removed my hands from my eyes, and opened them, the first object that they fell upon was the figure of the Boxer, sitting upright in bed, with both hands stretched out, just as those of Elymas the sorcerer in the picture of Raphael—his face the colour of a corpse—and his eyes, almost starting out of their sockets, directed with a horrid stare towards the window. His lips moved not—nor did he utter a sound. It was clear what had occurred. The wrathful fire of heaven, that had glanced harmlessly around us, had blinded the blasphemer. Yes —the sight of his eyes had perished.

While we were gazing at him in silent awe, he fell back in bed speechless, and clasped his hands over his breast, seemingly in an attitude of despair. But for that motion, we should have thought him dead. Shocked beyond expression, Mr — paused in his operations. I examined the eyes of the patient. The pupils were both dilated to their utmost extent, and immovable. I asked him many questions, but he answered not a word. Occasionally, however, a groan of horror, remorse, agony (or all combined), would burst from his pent bosom; and this was the only evidence he gave of consciousness. He moved over on his right side—his "pale face turned to the wall"— and, unclasping his hands, pressed the forefinger of each with convulsive force upon the eyes. Mr — proceeded with his task. What a contrast between the present and past behaviour of our patient! Do what we would—put him to never such great pain—be neither uttered a syllable, nor expressed any symptoms of passion, as before. There was, however, no necessity for my continuing any longer; so I left the case in the hands of Mr —, who undertook to acquaint Mrs — with the frightful accident that bad happened to her husband. What two scenes had I witnessed that evening!

—

I hurried home full of agitation at the spectacle I had just quitted, and melancholy apprehensions concerning the one to which I was returning. On reaching my lovely patient's room, I found, alas! no sensible effects produced by the very active means which had been adopted. She lay in bed, the aspect of her features apparently the same as when I last saw her. Her eyes were closed—her cheeks very pale, and mouth rather open, as if she were on the point of speaking. The hair hung in a little disorder on each side of her face, having escaped from beneath her cap. My wife sat beside her, grasping her right hand— weeping and almost stupefied; and the servant that was in the room when I entered, seemed so bewildered as to be worse than useless. As it was now getting dark, I ordered candles. I took one of them in my hand, opened her eyelids, and passed and repassed the candle several times before her eyes, but it produced no apparent effect. Neither the eyelids blinked, nor the pupils contracted. I then took out my penknife, and made a thrust with the open blade, as though I intended to plunge it into her right eye; it seemed as if I might have buried the blade in the socket, for the shock or resistance called forth by the attempt. I took her hand in mine—having for a moment displaced my wife—and found it damp and cold; but when I suddenly left it suspended, it continued so for a few moments, and only gradually resumed its former situation. I pressed the back of the blade of my penknife upon the flesh at the root of the nail (as every one knows, a very tender part), but she evinced not the slightest sensation of pain. I shouted suddenly and loudly in her ears, but with similar ill success. I felt at an extremity. Completely baffled at all points—discouraged and agitated beyond expression—I left Miss P— in the care of a nurse, whom I had sent for to attend upon her, at the instance of my wife, and hastened to my study to see if my books could throw any light upon the nature of this, to me, new and inscrutable disorder. After hunting about for some time, and finding but little to the purpose, I prepared for bed, determining in the morning to send off for Miss P—'s mother, and Mr N— from Oxford, and also to call upon my eminent friend Dr D—, and hear what his superior skill and experience might be able to suggest. In passing Miss P—'s room, I stepped in to take my farewell for the evening.

"Beautiful, unfortunate creature!" thought I, as I stood gazing mournfully on her, with my candle in my hand, leaning against the bedpost. "What mystery is upon thee? What awful change has come over thee?—the gloom of the grave and the light of life—both lying upon thee at once! Is thy mind palsied as thy body? How long is this strange state to last? How long art thou doomed to linger thus on the confines of both worlds, so that those in either, who love thee, may not claim thee? Heaven guide our thoughts to discover a remedy for thy fearful disorder!" I could not bear to look upon her any longer; and after kissing her lips, hurried up to bed, charging the nurse to summon me the moment that any change whatever was perceptible in Miss P—. I dare say, I shall be easily believed when I apprise the reader of the troubled night that followed such a troubled day. The thunderstorm itself, coupled with the predictions of the day, and apart from its attendant incidents that have been mentioned, was calculated to leave an awful and permanent impression on one's mind.

"If I were to live a century, I could not forget it," said a distinguished writer, in a letter to me. "The thunder and lightning were more appalling than I ever recollect witnessing, even in the West Indies—that region of storms and hurricanes. The air had been long surcharged with electricity; and I predicted several days beforehand that we should have a storm of very unusual violence. But when with this we couple the strange prophecy that gained credit with a prodigious number of those one would have expected to be above such things—neither more nor less than that the world was to come to an end on that very day, and the judgment of mankind to follow; I say, the coincidence of the events was not a little singular, and calculated to inspire common folk with wonder and fear. I dare say, if one could but find them out, that there were instances of people frightened out of their wits on the occasion. I own to you candidly that I, for one, felt a little squeamish, and had not a little difficulty in bolstering up my courage with Virgil's *Felix qui potuit rerum cognoscere causas,"* &c.[9]

I did not so much sleep as doze interruptedly for the first three or four hours after getting into bed. I, as well as my alarmed Emily, would start up occasionally, and sit listening, under the apprehension that we heard a shriek, or some other such sound, proceed from Miss P—'s room. The image of the blinded Boxer flitted in fearful forms about me, and my ears seemed to ring with his curses.—It must have been, I should think, between two and three o'clock, when I dreamed that I leaped out of bed, under an impulse sudden as irresistible—slipped on my dressing-gown, and hurried down stairs to the back drawing room. On opening the door, I found the room lit up with funeral tapers, and the apparel of a dead-room spread about. At the further end lay a coffin on trestles, covered with a long sheet, with the figure of an old woman sitting beside it, with long streaming white hair, and her eyes, bright as the lightning, directed towards me with a fiendish stare of exultation. Suddenly she rose up—pulled off the sheet that had covered the coffin—pushed aside the lid— plucked out the body of Miss P—, dashed it on the floor, and trampled upon it with apparent triumph! This horrid dream awoke me, and haunted my waking thoughts. May I never pass such a dismal night again!

I rose from my bed in the morning feverish and unrefreshed; and in a few minutes' time hurried to Miss P—'s room. The mustard applications to the soles of the feet, together with the blisters behind the ears, had produced the usual local effects, without affecting the complaint. Both her pulse and breathing continued calm. The only change perceptible in the colour of her countenance was a slight pallor about the upper part of the cheeks, and I fancied there was an expression about her mouth approaching to a smile. She had, I found, continued, throughout the night, motionless and silent as a corpse. With a profound sigh I took my seat beside her, and examined the eyes narrowly, but perceived no change in them. What was to be done? How was she to be roused from this fearful—if not fatal lethargy?

---

[9] Fortunate is he who was able to learn the causes of things

While I was gazing intently on her features, I fancied that I perceived a slight muscular twitching about the nostrils. I stepped hastily down stairs (just as a drowning man, they say, catches at a straw) and returned with a phial of the strongest solution of ammonia,[10] which I applied freely with a feather to the interior of the nostrils. This attempt, also, was unsuccessful as the former ones. I cannot describe the feelings with which I witnessed these repeated failures to stimulate her torpid sensibilities into action; and not knowing what to say or do, I returned to dress, with feelings of unutterable despondency. While dressing, it struck me that a blister might be applied with success along the whole course of the spine. The more I thought of this expedient, the more feasible it appeared;— it would be such a direct and powerful appeal to the nervous system—in all probability the very seat and source of the disorder!

I ordered one to be sent for instantly—and myself applied it, before I went down to breakfast. As soon as I had despatched the few morning patients that called, I wrote imperatively to Mr N— at Oxford, and to Miss P—'s mother, entreating them by all the love they bore Agnes to come to her instantly. I then set out for Dr D—'s, whom I found just starting on his daily visits. I communicated the whole case to him. He listened with interest to my statement, and told me he had once a similar case in his own practice, which, alas! terminated fatally, in spite of the most anxious and combined efforts of the *elite* of the faculty in London. He approved of the course I had adopted—most especially the blister on the spine; and earnestly recommended me to resort to galvanism—if Miss P— should not be relieved from the fit before the evening—when he promised to call, and assist in carrying into effect what he recommended.

"Is it that beautiful girl I saw in your pew last Sunday, at church?" he inquired suddenly.

"The same—the same!"—I replied with a sigh.

Dr D— continued silent for a moment or two. "Poor creature!" he exclaimed with an air of deep concern," one so beautiful! Do you know I thought I now and then perceived a very remarkable expression in her eye, especially while that fine voluntary was playing. Is she an enthusiast about music?"

---

[10] Liquid smelling-salts

"Passionately—devotedly"—

"We'll try it!" he replied briskly, with a confident air—" We'll try it! First, let us disturb the nervous torpor with a slight shock of galvanism,[11] and then try the effect of your organ."[12] I listened to the suggestion with interest, but was not quite so sanguine in my expectations as my friend appeared to be.

In the whole range of disorders that affect the human frame, there is perhaps not one so mysterious, so incapable of management, as that which afflicted the truly unfortunate young lady whose case I am narrating. It has given rise to infinite speculation, and is admitted, I believe, on all hands to be—if I may so speak—a nosological[13] anomaly. Van Swieten[14] vividly and picturesquely enough compares it to that condition of the body, which, according to ancient fiction, was produced in the beholder by the appalling sight of Medusa's head—

"Saxifici Medusæ Vultus."[15]

The medical writers of antiquity have left evidence of the existence of this disease in their day—but given the most obscure and unsatisfactory descriptions of it, confounding it, in many instances, with other disorders— apoplexy,[16] epilepsy,[17] and swooning.[18] Celsus,[19] according to Van Swieten, describes such patients as these in question under the term *"attoniti,"* which is a translation of the title I have prefixed to this paper: while, in our own day, the celebrated Dr Cullen classes it as a species of apoplexy, at the same time stating that he had never seen a genuine instance of catalepsy. He had always found, he says, those cases, which were reported such, to

---

[11] Application of electrical current to parts of the body

[12] I had at home—being myself a lover, though not a scientific one, of music—a very fine organ.

[13] Medical branch that classifies diseases into various categories

[14] Gerard van Swieten (1700-1772), European physician who argued against the supernatural

[15] A petrified Face

[16] Stroke

[17] Random seizures

[18] Fainting

[19] Aulus Cornelius Celsus (25 BC – 50 AD), extensive researcher of medicine in ancient Rome

be feigned ones. More modern science, however, distinctly recognises the disease as one peculiar and independent; and is borne out by numerous unquestionable cases of catalepsy, recorded by some of the most eminent members of the profession. Dr Jebb, in particular, in the appendix to his "Select Cases of Paralysis of the Lower Extremities," relates a remarkable and affecting instance of a cataleptic patient. As it is not likely that general readers have met with this interesting case, I shall here transcribe it. The young lady who was the subject of the disorder, was seized with the fit when Dr Jebb was announced on his first visit.

She was employed in netting, and was passing the needle through the mesh; in which position she immediately became rigid, exhibiting, in a very pleasing form, a figure of deathlike sleep, beyond the power of art to imitate, or the imagination to conceive. Her forehead was serene, her features perfectly composed. The paleness of her colour—her breathing being also scarcely perceptible at a distance—operated in rendering the similitude to marble more exact and striking. The position of the fingers, hands, and arms was altered with difficulty, but preserved every form of flexure they acquired. Nor were the muscles of the neck exempted from this law; her head maintaining every situation in which the hand could place it, as firmly as her limbs.

Upon gently raising the eyelids, they immediately closed with a degree of spasm.[20] The iris contracted upon the approach of a candle, as in a state of vigilance. The eyeball itself was slightly agitated with a tremulous motion, not discernible when the eyelid had descended. About half an hour after my arrival, the rigidity of her limbs and statue-like appearance being yet unaltered, she sung three plaintive songs in a tone of voice so elegantly expressive, and with such affecting modulation, as evidently pointed out how much the most powerful passion of the mind was concerned in the production of her disorder—as, indeed, her history confirmed. In a few minutes afterwards she sighed deeply, and the spasm in her limbs was immediately relaxed. She complained that she could not open her eyes, her hands grew cold, a general tremor followed; but in a few seconds, recovering

---

[20] This was not the case with Miss P—. I repeatedly remarked the perfect mobility of her eyelids.

entirely her recollection and powers of motion, she entered into a detail of her symptoms, and the history of her complaint. After she had discoursed for some time with apparent calmness, the universal spasm suddenly returned. The features now assumed a different form, denoting a mind strongly impressed with anxiety and apprehension. At times she uttered short and vehement exclamations, in a piercing tone of voice, expressive of the passions that agitated her mind; her hands being strongly locked in each other, and all her muscles, those subservient to speech excepted, being affected with the same rigidity as before.

But the most extraordinary case on record is one[21] given by Dr Petetin, a physician of Lyons, in which *"the senses were transferred to the pit of the stomach, and the ends of the fingers and toes*—i. e. the patients, in a state of insensibility to all external impressions upon the proper organs of sense, were nevertheless capable of hearing, *seeing,* smelling, and tasting whatever was approached to the pit of the stomach, or the ends of the fingers and toes! The patients are said to have answered questions proposed to the pit of the stomach—to have told the hour by a watch placed there—to have tasted food, and smelt the fragrance of apricots, touching the part," &c. &c. It may be interesting to add, that an eminent physician, who went to see the patient, incredulous of what he had heard, returned perfectly convinced of its truth. I have also read somewhere of a Spanish monk, who was so terrified by a sudden sight which he encountered in the Asturias mountains, that, when several of his holy brethren, whom he had preceded a mile or two, came up, they found him stretched upon the ground in the fearful condition of a cataleptic patient.

They carried him back immediately to their monastery, and he was believed dead. He suddenly revived, however, in the midst of his funeral obsequies, to the consternation of all around him. When he had perfectly recovered the use of his faculties, he related some absurd matters which he pretended to have seen in a vision during his comatose state. The disorder in question, however, generally makes its appearance in the female sex, and seems to be in

---

[21] A second similar case, well authenticated, occurred not long afterwards, at the same place.—They are attributed by Dr P— to the influence of animal electricity.

many, if not in most instances, a remote member of the family of hysterical affections.—To return, however.

On returning home from my daily round, in which my dejected air was remarked by all the patients I had visited, I found no alteration whatever in Miss P—. The nurse had failed in forcing even arrowroot[22] down her mouth, and, finding it was not swallowed, was compelled to desist, for fear of choking her. We were, therefore, obliged to resort to other means of conveying support to her exhausted frame. The blister on the spine,[23] from which I had expected so much, and the renewed sinapisms[24] to the feet, had failed to make any impression! Thus was every successive attempt an utter failure! The disorder continued absolutely inaccessible to the approaches of medicine. The baffled attendants could but look at her, and lament. Good God! was Agnes to continue in this dreadful condition till her energies sunk in death? What would become of her lover?—of her mother? These considerations greatly disturbed my peace of mind. I could neither think, read, eat, nor remain anywhere but in the chamber, where, alas! my presence was so unavailing!

Dr D— made his appearance soon after dinner; and we proceeded at once to the room where our patient lay. Though a little paler than before, her features were placid as those of the chiseled marble. Notwithstanding all she had suffered, and the fearful situation in which she lay at that moment, she still looked very beautiful. Her cap was off, and her rich auburn hair lay negligently on each side of her, upon the pillow. Her forehead was white as alabaster. She lay with her head turned a little on one side, and her two small white hands were clasped together over her bosom. This was the nurse's arrangement for "poor dear young lady," she said, "I couldn't bear to see her laid straight along, with her arms close beside her like a corpse, so I tried to make her look as much asleep as possible!" The impression of beauty, however, conveyed by her symmetrical and tranquil features, was disturbed as soon as, lifting up the eyelids, we saw the fixed stare of the eyes. They were not glassy, or corpse-like, but bright

---

[22] A bland root used for those with dietary restrictions

[23] A paste applied to the skin that contains an irritant

[24] Black mustard powder applied to the skin as a counter-irritant

as those of life, with a little of the dreadful expression of epilepsy.

We raised her in bed, and she, as before, sat upright, but with a blank, absent aspect, that was lamentable and unnatural. Her arms, when lifted and left suspended, did not fall, but *sunk* down again gradually. We returned her gently to her recumbent posture, and determined at once to try the effect of galvanism upon her. My machine was soon brought into the room; and when we had duly arranged matters, we directed the nurse to quit the chamber for a short time, as the effect of galvanism is generally found too startling to be witnessed by a female spectator. I wish I had not myself seen it in the case of Miss P—! Her colour went and came—her eyelids and mouth started open—and she stared wildly about her, with the aspect of one starting out of bed in a fright. I thought at one moment that the horrid spell was broken, for she sat up suddenly, leaned forwards towards me, and her mouth opened as though she were about to speak!

"Agnes! Agnes! dear Agnes! Speak, speak! but a word! Say you live!" I exclaimed, rushing forwards. Alas! she heard me—she saw me—not, but fell back in bed in her former state! When the galvanic shock was conveyed to her limbs, it produced the usual effects—dreadful to behold in all cases—but agonising to me in the case of Miss P—. The last subject on which I had seen the effects of galvanism,[25] previous to the present instance, was the

---

[25] A word about that case, by the way, in passing. The spectacle was truly horrific. When I entered the room where the experiments were to take place, the body of a man named Carter, which had been cut down from the gallows scarce half an hour, was lying on the table; aud the cap being removed, his features, distorted with the agonies of suffocation, were visible. The crime he had been hanged for was murder; and a brawny, desperate ruffian he looked. None of his clothes were removed. He wore a fustian jacket and drab knee-breeches. The first time that the galvanic shock was conveyed to him will never, I dare say, be forgotten by any one present. We all shrunk from the table in consternation, with the momentary belief that we had positively brought the man back to life; for he suddenly sprang *up* into a sitting posture—his arms waved wildly—the colour rushed into his cheeks—his lips were drawn apart, so as to show all his teeth—and his eyes glared at us with apparent fury. One young man, a medical student, shrieked violently, and was carried out in a swoon. One gentleman present, who happened to be nearest to the upper part of the body, was

body of an executed malefactor; and the associations revived on the present occasion were almost too painful to bear. I begged my friend to desist, for I saw the attempt was hopeless, and I would not allow her tender frame to be agitated to no purpose. My mind misgave me for ever making the attempt. What, thought I, if we have fatally disturbed the nervous system, and prostrated the small remains of strength she had left? While I was torturing myself with such fears as these, Dr laid down the rod, with a melancholy air, exclaiming, "Well! what *is* to be done now? I cannot tell you how sanguine I was about the success of this experiment! Do you know whether she ever had *a* fit of epilepsy?" he inquired.

"No—not that I am aware of. I never heard of it, if she had."

"Had she generally a horror of thunder and lightning?"

"Oh—quite the contrary! she felt a sort of ecstasy on such occasions, and has written some beautiful verses during their continuance. *Such* seemed rather her hour of inspiration than otherwise!"

"Do you think the lightning itself has affected her?—Do you think her sight is destroyed?"

"I have no means of knowing whether the immobility of the pupils arises from blindness, or is only one of the temporary effects of catalepsy."

"Then she believed the prophecy, you think, of the world's destruction on Tuesday?"

"No—I don't think she exactly *believed* it; but I am sure that day brought with it awful apprehensions, or, at least, a fearful degree of uncertainty."

"Well—between ourselves—, there was something *very* strange in the coincidence, was not there? Nothing in life ever shook my firmness as it was shaken yesterday! I almost fancied the earth was quivering in its sphere!"

"It *was* a dreadful day!—One I shall never forget! *That* is the image of it," I exclaimed, pointing to the poor sufferer—"which will be engraven on my mind as long as I live! But the worst is perhaps yet to be told you: Mr N—, her lover, to whom she was very soon to have been married, HE will be here shortly to see her"—

---

almost knocked down with the violent blow he received from the left arm. It was some time before any of us could recover presence of mind sufficient to proceed with the experiments.

"My God!" exclaimed Dr D—, clasping his hands, eyeing Miss P— with intense commiseration—"What a fearful bride for him!"

"I dread his coming—I know not what we shall do! And then there's her *mother,* poor old lady!—her I have written to, and expect almost hourly!"

"Why, what an accumulation of shocks and miseries!— it will be upsetting *you!*" said my friend, seeing my distressed appearance.

"Well," he continued, "I cannot now stay here longer— your misery is catching; and, besides, I am most pressingly engaged; but you may rely on my services, if you should require them in any way."

My friend took his departure, leaving me more disconsolate than ever. Before retiring to bed, I rubbed in mustard upon the chief surfaces of the body, hoping, though faintly, that it might have some effect in rousing the system. I kneeled down, before stepping into bed, and earnestly prayed, that as all human efforts seemed baffled, the Almighty would set her free from the mortal thraldom in which she lay, and restore her to life, and those who loved her more than life! Morning came—it found me by her bedside as usual, and her in no wise altered, apparently neither better nor worse! If the unvarying monotony of my description should fatigue the reader, what must the actual monotony and hopelessness have been to me!

While I was sitting beside Miss P—, I heard my youngest boy come down stairs, and ask to be let into the room. He was a little fair-haired youngster, about three years of age, and had always been an especial favourite of Miss P—'s—her "own sweet pet"—as the poor girl herself called him. Determined to throw no chance away, I beckoned him in, and took him on my knee. He called to Miss P—, as if he thought her asleep; patted her face with his little hands, and kissed her. "Wake, wake!— Cousin Aggy, get up!" he cried—"Papa say 'tis time to get up! Do you sleep with eyes open?[26]—Eh? —Cousin Aggy?"

He looked at her intently for some moments, and seemed frightened. He turned pale, and struggled to get off my knee. I allowed him to go, and he ran to his mother, who was standing at the foot of the bed, and hid his face behind her.

---

[26] I had been examining her eyes, and had only half closed the lids.

I passed breakfast-time in great apprehension, expecting the two arrivals I have mentioned. I knew not how to prepare either the mother or the betrothed husband for the scene that awaited them, and which I had not particularly described to them. It was with no little trepidation that I heard the startling knock of the general postman; and with infinite astonishment and doubt that I took out of the servant's hands a letter from Mr N— for poor Agnes! For a while I knew not what to make of it. Had he received the alarming express I had forwarded to him; and did he write to Miss P—? Or was he unexpectedly absent from Oxford when it arrived? The latter supposition was corroborated by the post-mark, which I observed was Lincoln. I felt it my duty to open the letter. Alas! it was in a gay strain—unusually gay for N—; informing Agnes that he had been suddenly summoned into Lincolnshire, to his cousin's wedding, where he was very happy, both on account of his relative's happiness, and the anticipation of a similar scene being in store for himself! Every line was buoyant with hope and animation; but the postscript most affected me.

"P.S.—*The tenth of July,* by the way, my Agnes! *Is* it all over with us, sweet Pythonissa? Are you and I at this moment on separate fragments of the globe? I shall seal my conquest over you with a kiss when I see you! Remember, you parted from me in a pet, naughty one!—and kissed me rather coldly! But that is the way that your sex always end arguments, when you are vanquished!"

I read these lines in silence;—my wife burst into tears. I hastened to send a second summons to Mr N—, and directed it to him in Lincoln, where he had requested Miss P— to address him. Without explaining the precise nature of Miss P—'s seizure, I gave him warning that he must hurry up to town instantly; and that, even then, it was doubtful whether he would see her alive. After this little occurrence, I could hardly trust myself to go up-stairs again, and look upon the unfortunate girl. My heart fluttered at the door, and when I entered I burst into tears. I could utter no more than the words, "poor—poor Agnes!" and withdrew.

I was shocked, and indeed enraged, to find, in one of the morning papers, a paragraph stating, though inaccurately, the nature of Miss P—'s illness. Who could have been so unfeeling as to make the poor girl an object of public wonder and pity? I never ascertained, though I made every inquiry, from whom the intelligence was communicated.

One of my patients that day happened to be a niece of the venerable and honoured Dean of —, at whose house she resided. He was in the room when I called; and to explain what he called "the gloom of my manner," I gave him a full account of the melancholy event which had occurred. He listened to me till the tears ran down his face.

"But you have not yet tried the effect of *music*—of which you say she is so fond! Do not you intend to resort to it?" I told him it was our intention, and that our agitation was the only reason why we did not try the effect of it immediately after the galvanism.

"Now, doctor, excuse an old clergyman, will you?" said the venerable and pious dean, laying his hand on my arm; "and let me suggest that the experiment may not be the less successful, with the blessing of God, if it be introduced in the course of a religious service. Come, doctor, what say you?" I paused.

"Have you any objection to my calling at your house this evening, and reading the service appointed by our church for the visitation of the sick? It will not be difficult to introduce the most solemn and affecting strains of music, or to let it precede or follow."

Still I hesitated—and yet I scarce knew why.

"Come, doctor, you know I am no enthusiast—I am not generally considered a fanatic. Surely when man has done his best, and fails, he should not hesitate to turn to God!"

The good old man's words sunk into my soul, and diffused in it a cheerful and humble hope that the blessing of Providence would attend the means suggested. I acquiesced in the dean's proposal with delight, and even eagerness; and it was arranged that he should be at my house between seven and eight o'clock that evening. I think I have already observed, that I had an organ, a very fine and powerful one, in my back drawing-room; and this instrument had been the eminent delight of poor Miss P–.

She would sit down at it for hours together, and her performance would not have disgraced a professor. I hoped that on the eventful occasion that was approaching, the tones of her favourite instrument, with the blessing of Heaven, might rouse a slumbering responsive chord in her bosom, and aid in dispelling the cruel "charm that deadened her." She certainly could not last long in the condition in which she now lay. Everything that medicine could do, had been tried—in vain; and if the evening's experiment—our forlorn hope, failed —we must, though with a bleeding heart, submit to the will of Providence, and resign her to the grave. I looked forward with intense anxiety—with alternate hope and fear—to the engagement of the evening.

On returning home, late in the afternoon, I found poor Mrs P— had arrived in town, in obedience to my summons; and heart-breaking, I learnt, was her first interview, if such it may be called, with her daughter. Her groans and cries alarmed the whole house, and even arrested the attention of the neighbours. I had left instructions, that in case of her arrival during my absence, she should be shown at once, without any precautions, into the presence of Miss P—; with the hope, faint though it was, that the abruptness of her appearance, and the violence of her grief might operate as a salutary shock upon the stagnant energies of her daughter.

"My child! my child! my child!" she exclaimed, rushing up to the bed with frantic haste, and clasping the insensible form of her daughter in her arms, where she held her till she fell fainting into those of my wife. What a dread contrast was there between the frantic gestures— the passionate lamentations of the mother, and the stony silence and motionlessness of the daughter! One little but affecting incident occurred in my presence. Mrs P— (as yet unacquainted with the peculiar nature of her daughter's seizure) had snatched Miss P—'s hand to her lips, kissed it repeatedly, and suddenly let it go, to press her own hand upon her head, as if to repress a rising hysterical feeling. Miss P—'s arm, as usual, remained for a moment or two suspended, and only gradually sunk down upon the bed. It looked as if she voluntarily continued it in that position, with a cautioning air. Methinks I see at this moment the affrighted stare with which Mrs P— regarded the outstretched arm, her body recoiling from the bed, as though she expected her daughter were about to do or appear something dreadful!

I subsequently learned from Mrs P— that her mother, the grandmother of Agnes, was reported to have been twice affected in a similar manner, though apparently from a different cause; so that there seemed something like a hereditary tendency towards it, even though Mrs P— herself had never experienced anything of the kind.

As the memorable evening advanced, the agitation of all who were acquainted with, or interested in the approaching ceremony, increased. Mrs P—, I need hardly say, embraced the proposal with thankful eagerness. About half-past seven, my friend Dr D— arrived, pursuant to his promise; and he was soon afterwards followed by the organist of the neighbouring church—an old acquaintance, and who was a constant visitor at my house, for the purpose of performing and giving instructions on the organ. I requested him to commence playing Martin Luther's hymn—the favourite one of Agnes—as soon as she should be brought into the room. About eight o'clock, the dean's carriage drew up. I met him at the door.

"Peace be to this house, and to all that dwell in it!" he exclaimed as soon as he entered. I led him up-stairs; and, without uttering a word, he took the seat prepared for him, before a table on which lay a Bible and Prayer-Book. After a moment's pause, he directed the sick person to be brought into the room. I stepped up-stairs, where I found my wife, with the nurse, had finished dressing Miss P—. I thought her paler than usual, and that her cheeks seemed hollower than when I had last seen her. There was an air of melancholy sweetness and languor about her, that inspired the beholder with the keenest sympathy.

With a sigh, I gathered her slight form into my arms, a shawl was thrown over her, and, followed by my wife and the nurse, who supported Mrs P—, I carried her down stairs, and placed her in an easy recumbent posture, in a large old family chair, which stood between the organ and the dean's table. How strange and mournful was her appearance! Her luxuriant hair was gathered up beneath a cap. the whiteness of which was equaled by that of her countenance.

Her eyes were closed; and this, added to the paleness of her features, her perfect passiveness, and her being enveloped in a long white unruffled morning dress, which appeared not unlike a shroud at first sight—made her look rather a corpse than a living being! As soon as Dr D— and I had taken seats on each side of our poor patient, the solemn strains of the organ commenced. I never appreciated music, and especially the sublime hymn of Luther, so much as on that occasion. My eyes were fixed with agonizing scrutiny on Miss P—. Bar after bar of the music melted on the ear, and thrilled upon the heart; but, alas! produced no more effect upon the placid sufferer than the pealing of an abbey organ on the statues around! My heart began to misgive me: if *this* one last experiment failed! When the music ceased we all kneeled down, and the dean, in a solemn tone of voice, commenced reading appropriate passages from the service for the visitation of the sick. When he had concluded the 71st Psalm, he approached the chair of Miss P—, dropped upon one knee, held her right hand in his, and in a somewhat tremulous voice, read the following affecting verses from the 8th chapter of St Luke:—

"While he yet spake, there cometh one from the ruler of the synagogue's house, saying to him, 'Thy daughter is dead; trouble not the master.'

"But when Jesus heard it, he answered him, saying, 'Fear not; believe only, and she shall be made whole.'

"And when he came into the house he suffered no man to go in, save Peter and James, and John, and the father and the mother of the maiden. And all wept and bewailed her: but he said, 'Weep not; she is not dead, but sleepeth.' And they laughed him to scorn, knowing that she was dead.

"And he put them all out, and took her by the hand, and called, saying, '*Maid, arise. And her spirit came again, and she arose straightway.*'"

While he was reading the passage which I have marked in italics, my heated fancy almost persuaded me that I saw the eyelids of Miss P— moving. I trembled from head to foot; but, alas! it was a delusion.

The dean, much affected, was proceeding with the fifty-fifth verse, when such a tremendous and long-continued mocking was heard at the street door as seemed likely to break it open. Every one started up from their knees, as if electrified—all moved but unhappy Agnes—and stood in silent agitation and astonishment. Still the knocking was continued, almost without intermission. My heart suddenly misgave me as to the cause.

"Go—go—See if"—stammered my wife, pale as ashes—endeavouring to prop up the drooping mother of our patient. Before any one had stirred from the spot on which he was standing, the door was burst open, and in rushed Mr N—, wild in his aspect, frantic in his gesture, and his dress covered with dust from head to foot. We stood gazing at him as though his appearance had petrified us.

"Agnes!—my Agnes!" he exclaimed, as if choked for want of breath.

"AGNES!—Come!" he gasped, while a smile appeared on his face that had a gleam of madness in it.

"Mr N—! what are you about? For mercy's sake, be calm! Let me lead you, for a moment, into another room, and all shall be explained!" said I, approaching and grasping him firmly by the arm.

"AGNES!" he continued in a tone that made us tremble. He moved towards the chair in which Miss P— lay. I endeavoured to interpose, but he thrust me aside. The venerable dean attempted to dissuade him, but met with no better a reception than myself.

"Agnes!" he reiterated in a hoarse whisper, "why won't you speak to me? what are they doing to you?"

He stepped within a foot of the chair where she lay—calm and immovable as death! We stood by watching his movements, in terrified apprehension and uncertainty. He dropped his hat, which he had been grasping with convulsive force, and before any one could prevent him, or even suspect what he was about, he snatched Miss P— out of the chair, and compressed her in his arms with frantic force, while a delirious laugh burst from his lips. We rushed forward to extricate her from his grasp.

His arms gradually relaxed—he muttered, "Music! music! a dance!" and almost at the moment that we removed Miss P— from him, fell senseless into the arms of the organist. Mrs P had fainted; my wife seemed on the verge of hysterics; and the nurse was crying violently. Such a scene of trouble and terror I have seldom witnessed! I hurried with the poor unconscious girl upstairs, laid her upon the bed, shut and bolted the door after me, and hardly expected to find her alive: her pulse, however, was calm as it had been throughout the seizure. The calm of the Dead Sea seemed upon her!

*   *   *   *

I feel, however, that I should not protract these painful scenes; and shall therefore hurry to their close. The first letter which I had dispatched to Oxford after Mr N—, happened to bear on the outside the words, "*special haste!*" which procured its being forwarded by express after Mr N—. The consternation with which he received and read it may be imagined. He set off for town that instant in a post-chaise and four; but finding their speed insufficient, he took to horseback for the last fifty miles, and rode at a rate which nearly destroyed both horse and rider. Hence his sudden appearance at my house, and the frenzy of his behaviour! After Miss P— had been carried up-stairs, it was thought imprudent for Mr N— to continue at my house, as he exhibited every symptom of incipient brain fever, and might prove wild and unmanageable. He was therefore removed at once to a house within a few doors off, which was let out in furnished lodgings. Dr D— accompanied him, and bled him immediately, very copiously. I have no doubt that Mr N— owed his life to that timely measure. He was placed in bed, and put at once under the most vigorous antiphlogistic treatment.[27]

The next evening beheld Dr D—, the Dean of —, and myself around the bedside of Agnes. All of us expressed the most gloomy apprehensions. The dean had been offering up a devout and most affecting prayer.

"Well, my friend," said he to me, she is in the hands of God. All that man can do has been done; let us resign ourselves to the will of Providence!"

"Ay, nothing but a miracle can save her, I fear," replied Dr D—.

"How much longer do you think it probable, humanly speaking, that the system can continue in this state, so as to give hopes of ultimate recovery?" inquired the dean.

"I cannot say," I replied with a sigh. "She *must* sink, and speedily. She has not received, since she was first seized, as much nourishment as would serve for an infant's meal!"

"I have an impression that she will die suddenly," said Dr D—; "possibly within the next twelve hours; for I cannot understand how her energies can recover from, or bear longer, this fearful paralysis!"

"Alas, I fear so too!"   *   *   *   *

"I have heard some frightful instances of premature burial in cases like this," said the dean. "I hope you will not think of committing her remains to the earth, before you are satisfied, beyond a doubt, that life is extinct."

I made no reply—my emotions nearly choked me—I could not bear to contemplate such an event.

---

[27] Remedy to reduce fever or inflammation in the body

"Do you know," said Dr D—, with an apprehensive air, "I have been thinking latterly of the awful possibility, that, notwithstanding the stagnation of her physical powers, her MIND may be sound, and perfectly conscious of all that has transpired about her!"

"Why—why," stammered the Dean, turning pale—"what if she has—has heard all that has been said!"[28]

"Ay!" replied Dr D—, unconsciously sinking his voice to a whisper, "I know of a case—in fact, a friend of mine has just published it—in which a woman"—

There was a faint knocking at the door, and I stepped to it, for the purpose of inquiring what was wanted. While I was in the act of closing it again, I overheard Dr D—'s voice exclaim in an affrighted tone, "Great God!" and on turning round, I saw the dean moving from the bed, his face white as ashes, and he fell from his chair as if in a fit. How shall I describe what I saw on approaching the bed?

The moment before I had left Miss P— lying in her usual position, and with her eyes closed. They were now wide open, and staring upwards with an expression I have no language to describe. It reminded me of what I had seen when I first discovered her in the fit. Blood, too, was streaming from her nostrils and mouth—in short, a more frightful spectacle I never witnessed. In a moment, both Dr D— and I seemed to have lost all power of motion. Here, then, was the spell broken! The trance over!—I implored Dr D— to recollect himself, and conduct the dean from the room, while I would attend to Miss P—.

The nurse was instantly at my side, but violently agitated. She quickly procured warm water, sponges, cloths, &c., with which she at once wiped away and encouraged the bleeding. The first sound uttered by Miss P— was a long deep-drawn sigh, which seemed to relieve her bosom of an intolerable sense of oppression. Her eyes gradually closed again, and she moved her head away, at the same time raising her trembling right hand to her face. Again she sighed—again opened her eyes, and, to my delight, their expression was more natural than before. She looked languidly about her for a moment, as if examining the bed-curtains—and her eyes closed again. I sent for some weak brandy-and-water, and gave her a

---

[28] In almost every known instance of recovery from catalepsy, the patients have declared that they heard every word that had been uttered beside them!

little in a teaspoon. She swallowed it with great difficulty. I ordered some warm water to be got ready for her feet, to equalise the circulation; and while it was preparing, sat by her watching every motion of her features with the most eager anxiety.

"How are you, Agnes?" I whispered.

She turned languidly towards me, opened her eyes, and shook her head feebly—but gave me no answer.

"Do you feel pain anywhere?" I inquired. A faint smile stole about her mouth, but she did not utter a syllable. Sensible that her exhausted condition required repose, I determined not to tax her newly-recovered energies; so I ordered her a gentle composing draught and left her in the care of the nurse, promising to return by and by, to see how my sweet patient went on. I found that the dean had left. After swallowing a little wine and water, he recovered sufficiently from the shock he had received, to be able, with Dr D—'s assistance, to step into his carriage, leaving his solemn benediction for Miss P—.

As it was growing late, I sent my wife to bed, and ordered coffee in my study, whither I retired, and sat lost in conjecture and reverie till nearly one o'clock. I then repaired to my patient's room; but my entrance startled her from a sleep that had lasted almost since I had left. As soon as I sat down by her, she opened her eyes—and my heart leaped with joy to see their increasing calmness— their expression resembling what had oft delighted me while she was in health. After eyeing me steadily for a few moments, she seemed suddenly to recognise me. "Doctor!" she whispered, in the faintest possible whisper, while a smile stole over her languid features. I gently grasped her hand; and in doing so my tears fell upon her cheek.

"How strange!" she whispered again in a tone as feeble as before. She gently moved her hand into mine, and I clasped the trembling lilied fingers, with an emotion I cannot express. She noticed my agitation; and the tears came into her eyes, while her lip quivered, as though she were going to speak. I implored her, however, not to utter a word, till she was better able to do it without exhaustion; and, lest my presence should tempt her beyond her strength, I bade her good-night—her poor slender fingers once more compressed mine — and I left her to the care of the nurse, with a whispered injunction to step to me instantly if any change took place in Agnes. I could not sleep! I felt a prodigious burden removed from my mind; and woke my wife that she might share in my joy.

I received no summons during the night; and on entering her room about nine o'clock in the morning, I found that Miss P— had taken a little arrow-root in the course of the night, and slept calmly, with but few intervals. She had sighed frequently; and once or twice conversed for a short time with the nurse about *heaven*—as I understood. She was much stronger than I had expected to find her. I welcomed her affectionately, and she asked me how I was—in a tone that surprised me by its strength and firmness.

"Is the storm over?" she inquired, looking towards the window.

"Oh yes—long, long ago!" I replied, seeing at once that she seemed to have no consciousness of the interval that had elapsed.

"And are you all well?—Mrs —" (my wife), "how is she?"

"You shall see her shortly."

"Then no one was hurt?"

"Not a hair of our heads!"

"How frightened I must have been!"

"Poh, poh, Agnes! Nonsense! Forget it!"

"Then—the world is not—there has been no—is all the same as it was?" she murmured, eyeing me apprehensively.

"The world come to an end—do you mean?" She nodded, with a disturbed air—"Oh, no, no! It was merely a thunder-storm."

"And is it quite over, and gone?"

"Long ago! Do you feel hungry?" I inquired, hoping to direct her thoughts from a topic I saw agitated her.

"Did you ever see such lightning?" she asked, without regarding my question.

"Why—certainly it was very alarming"—

"Yes, it was! Do you know, doctor," she continued, with a mysterious air —"I — I — saw — yes — there were strange faces in the lightning"—

"Come, child, you rave!"

They seemed coming towards the world.

Her voice trembled, the colour of her face changed.

"Well—if you *will* talk such nonsense, Agnes, I must leave you. I will go and fetch my wife. Would you like to see her?"

"*Tell N— to come to me today*—I must see HIM. I have a message for him!" She said this with a sudden energy that surprised me, while her eye brightened as it settled on me. Her last words surprised and disturbed me. Were her intellects affected! How did she know—how could she conjecture that he was within reach? I took an opportunity of asking the nurse whether she had mentioned Mr N—'s name to her; but not a syllable had been interchanged upon the subject.

Before setting out on my daily visits, I stepped into her room, to take my leave. I was quitting the room, when, happening to look back, I saw her beckoning to me. I returned.

"I MUST see N— this evening!" said she, with a solemn emphasis that startled me; and as soon as she had uttered the words, she turned her head from me, as if she wished no more to be said.

My first visit was to Mr N—, whom I found in a very weak state, but so much recovered from his illness as to be sitting up, and partially dressed. He was perfectly calm and collected; and, in answer to his earnest inquiries, I gave him a full account of the nature of Miss P—'s illness. He received the intelligence of the favourable change that had occurred with evident though silent ecstasy. After much inward doubt and hesitation, I thought I might venture to tell him of the parting — the twice-repeated request she had made. The intelligence blanched his already pallid cheeks to a whiter hue, and he trembled violently.

"Did you tell her I was in town? Did she recollect me?"

"No one has breathed your name to her!" I replied.

*　　*　　*　　*

"Well, doctor, if, on the whole, you think so—that it would be safe," said N—, after we had talked much on the matter—"I will step over and see her; but—it looks very—very strange!"

"Whatever whim may actuate her, I think it better, on the whole, to gratify her. Your refusal *may* be attended with infinitely worse effects than an interview. However, you shall hear from me again. I will see if she continues in the same mind; and if so, I will step over and tell you."—I took my leave.

A few moments before stepping down to dinner, I sat beside Miss P—, making my usual inquiries; and was gratified to find that her progress, though slow, seemed sure. was leaving, when, with similar emphasis to that she had previously displayed, she again said—

"*Remember!* N— MUST be here tonight!"

I was confounded. What could be the meaning of this mysterious pertinacity? I felt distracted with doubt, and dissatisfied with myself for what I had told to N—. I felt answerable for whatever ill effects might ensue; and yet what could I do?

—

It was evening—a mild, though lustrous July evening. The skies were all blue and white, save where the retiring sunlight produced a mellow mixture of colours towards the west. Not a breath of air disturbed the serene complacency. My wife and I sat on each side of the bed where lay our lovely invalid, looking, despite her illness, beautiful, and in comparative health. Her hair was parted with negligent simplicity over her pale forehead. Her eyes were brilliant, and her cheeks occasionally flushed. She spoke scarce a word to us as we sat beside her. I gazed at her with doubt and apprehension. I was aware that health could not possibly produce the colour and vivacity of her complexion and eyes; and felt at a loss to what I should refer it.

"Agnes, love!—How beautiful is the setting sun!" exclaimed my wife, drawing aside the curtains.

"Raise me! Let me look at it!" replied Miss P— faintly. She gazed earnestly at the magnificent object for some minutes; and then abruptly said to me—

"He will be here soon?"

"In a few moments I expect him. But—Agnes—why do you wish to see him?"

She sighed, and shook her head.

It had been arranged that Dr D— should accompany Mr N— to my house, and conduct him upstairs, after strongly enjoining on him the necessity there was for controlling his feelings, and displaying as little emotion as possible. My heart leaped into my mouth — as the saying is— when I heard the expected knock at the door.

"N— is come at last!" said I in a gentle tone, looking earnestly at her, to see if she was agitated. It was not the case. She sighed, but evinced no trepidation.

"Shall he be shown in at once?" I inquired.

"No—wait a few moments," replied the extraordinary girl, and seemed lost in thought for about a minute. "Now!" she exclaimed; and I sent down the nurse, herself pale and trembling with apprehension, to request the attendance of Dr D— and Mr N—.

As they were heard slowly approaching the room, I looked anxiously at my patient, and kept my fingers at her pulse. There was not a symptom of flutter or agitation.

At length the door was opened, and Dr D— slowly entered, with N— upon his arm. As soon as his pale trembling figure was visible, a calm and heavenly smile beamed upon the countenance of Miss P—. It was full of ineffable loveliness! She stretched out her right arm; he pressed it to his lips, without uttering a word.

My eyes were riveted on the features of Miss P—. Either they deceived me, or I saw a strange alteration—as if a cloud were stealing over her face. I was right!—We all observed her colour fading rapidly. I rose from my chair; Dr B— also came nearer, thinking she was on the verge of fainting. Her eye was fixed upon the flushed features of her lover, and gleamed with radiance. She gently elevated both her arms towards him, and he leaned over her.

"PREPARE!" she exclaimed, in a low thrilling tone;—her features became paler and paler—her arms fell. She had spoken—she had breathed her last.

She was dead!

Within twelve months poor N— followed her; and, to the period of his death, no other word or thought seemed to occupy his mind but the momentous warning which had issued from the lips of Agnes P—, PREPARE!

I have no mystery to solve, no denouement to make. I tell the facts as they occurred; and hope they may not be told in vain!

ERNST THEODOR WILHELM HOFFMANN
(1776-1822)

Φ

The Deserted House

Sir Walter Scott, who was no stranger to tales of the fantastic and supernatural, saw fit to pen a long article on the novels of E. T. A. Hoffmann. It was later collected in "Sir Walter Scott: Periodical Criticism," Vol. VI, 1838, pg. 340. On Hoffmann's appearance, Sir Walter Scott commented, *Even his outward appearance bespoke the state of his nervous system: a very little man with a quantity of dark-brown hair, and eyes looking through his elf-flocks, that*

"E'en like grey goss-hawk'a Blared wild,"

indicated that touch of mental derangement, of which he seems to have been himself conscious, when entering the following fearful memorandum in his diary:—

"Why, in sleeping and in waking, do I, in my thoughts, dwell upon the subject of insanity? The out-pouring of the wild ideas that arise in my mind may perhaps operate like the breathing of a vein."

This is not the first time a person writing in the horror genre for this period (or any period) has been accused of being mentally instable. This is purportedly the enabler of their fantastic ideas. Edgar Allan Poe, even to this day, carries the reputation of an author who labored under mental derangement, and this derangement allowed him to somehow produce great works of terror beyond the borders of the lucid mind. In a letter to George Eveleth on January 4, 1848, Poe stated, *I became insane, with long intervals of horrible sanity.* This statement is frequently quoted out of context as applying to Poe's persistent state of mind when it was actually made in reference to the bouts of tuberculosis that plagued his young wife, Virginia, for many years, leading up to her ultimate death from the disease in 1847 at the age of twenty-five.

Sir Walter Scott was of the belief that mental derangement was the cause of Hoffmann's fantastic story ideas. I am of a different belief. If insanity fosters creative genius, we would look to our sanatoriums for our greatest literature. Insanity does not foster creative genius. It is creative genius acting at the highest of levels that cracks open the door to insanity. Some authors choose to step through it while the truly great ones only step one foot inside while leaving the other planted firmly on the solid floor of lucidity.

E. T. A. Hoffmann never entered the creaky-hinged door of "The Deserted House," he merely stepped one trembling foot inside.

The Deserted House

THEY WERE ALL AGREED in the belief that the actual facts of life are often far more wonderful than the invention of even the liveliest imagination can be.

"It seems to me," spoke Lelio, "that history gives proof sufficient of this. And that is why the so-called historical romances seem so repulsive and tasteless to us, those stories wherein the author mingles the foolish fancies of his meager brain with the deeds of the great powers of the universe."

Franz took the word. "It is the deep reality of the inscrutable secrets surrounding us that oppresses us with a might wherein we recognize the Spirit that rules, the Spirit out of which our being springs."

"Alas," said Lelio, "it is the most terrible result of the fall of man, that we have lost the power of recognizing the eternal verities."

"Many are called, but few are chosen," broke in Franz. "Do you not believe that an understanding of the wonders of our existence is given to some of us in the form of another sense? But if you would allow me to drag the conversation up from these dark regions where we are in danger of losing our path altogether up into the brightness of light-hearted merriment, I would like to make the scurrilous suggestion that those mortals to whom this gift of seeing the Unseen has been given remind me of bats. You know the learned anatomist Spallanzani has discovered a sixth sense in these little animals which can do not only the entire work of the other senses, but work of its own besides."

"Oho," laughed Edward, "according to that, the bats would be the only natural-born clairvoyants. But I know one who possesses that gift of insight, of which you were speaking, in a remarkable degree. Because of it he will often follow for days some unknown person who has happened to attract his attention by an oddity in manner, appearance, or garb; he will ponder to melancholy over some trifling incident, some lightly told story; he will combine the antipodes and raise up relationships in his imagination which are unknown to everyone else."

"Wait a bit," cried Lelio. "It is our Theodore of whom

you are speaking now. And it looks to me as if he were having some weird vision at this very moment. See how strangely he gazes out into the distance."

Theodore had been sitting in silence up to this moment. Now he spoke: "If my glances are strange it is because they reflect the strange things that were called up before my mental vision by your conversation, the memories of a most remarkable adventure—"

"Oh, tell it to us," interrupted his friends.

"Gladly," continued Theodore. "But first, let me set right a slight confusion in your ideas on the subject of the mysterious. You appear to confound what is merely odd and unusual with what is really mysterious or marvelous, that which surpasses comprehension or belief. The odd and the unusual, it is true, spring often from the truly marvelous, and the twigs and flowers hide the parent stem from our eyes. Both the odd and the unusual and the truly marvelous are mingled in the adventure which I am about to narrate to you, mingled in a manner which is striking and even awesome." With these words Theodore drew from his pocket a notebook in which, as his friends knew, he had written down the impressions of his late journeyings. Refreshing his memory by a look at its pages now and then, he narrated the following story.

You know already that I spent the greater part of last summer in —. The many old friends and acquaintances I found there, the free, jovial life, the manifold artistic and intellectual interests—all these combined to keep me in that city. I was happy as never before, and found rich nourishment for my old fondness for wandering alone through the streets, stopping to enjoy every picture in the shop windows, every placard on the walls, or watching the passers-by and choosing some one or the other of them to cast his horoscope secretly to myself.

There is one broad avenue leading to the — Gate and lined with handsome buildings of all descriptions, which is the meeting place of the rich and fashionable world. The shops which occupy the ground floor of the tall palaces are devoted to the trade in articles of luxury, and the apartments above are the dwellings of people of wealth and position. The aristocratic hotels are to be found in this avenue, the palaces of the foreign ambassadors are there and you can easily imagine that such a street would be the center of the city's life and gayety.

I had wandered through the avenue several times,

when one day my attention was caught by a house which contrasted strangely with the others surrounding it.

Picture to yourselves a low building but four windows broad, crowded in between two tall, handsome structures. Its one upper story was little higher than the tops of the ground-floor windows of its neighbors, its roof was dilapidated, its windows patched with paper, its discolored walls spoke of years of neglect. You can imagine how strange such a house must have looked in this street of wealth and fashion. Looking at it more attentively I perceived that the windows of the upper story were tightly closed and curtained, and that a wall had been built to hide the windows of the ground floor. The entrance gate, a little to one side, served also as a doorway for the building, but I could find no sign of latch, lock, or even a bell on this gate. I was convinced that the house must be unoccupied, for at whatever hour of the day I happened to be passing I had never seen the faintest signs of life about it. An unoccupied house in this avenue was indeed an odd sight. But I explained the phenomenon to myself by saying that the owner was doubtless absent upon a long journey, or living upon his country estates, and that he perhaps did not wish to sell or rent the property, preferring to keep it for his own use in the eventuality of a visit to the city.

You all, the good comrades of my youth, know that I have been prone to consider myself a sort of clairvoyant, claiming to have glimpses of a strange world of wonders, a world which you, with your hard common sense, would attempt to deny or laugh away. I confess that I have often lost myself in mysteries which after all turned out to be no mysteries at all. And it looked at first as if this was to happen to me in the matter of the deserted house, that strange house which drew my steps and my thoughts to itself with a power that surprised me. But the point of my story will prove to you that I am right in asserting that I know more than you do. Listen now to what I am about to tell you.

One day, at the hour in which the fashionable world is accustomed to promenade up and down the avenue, I stood as usual before the deserted house, lost in thought. Suddenly I felt, without looking up, that some one had stopped beside me, fixing his eyes on me. It was Count P., whom I had found much in sympathy with many of my imaginings, and I knew that he also must have been deeply interested in the mystery of this house. It surprised me not a little, therefore, that he should smile ironically when I spoke of the strange impression that this deserted dwelling, here in the gay heart of the town, had made upon me. But I soon discovered the reason for his irony. Count P. had gone much farther than myself in his imaginings concerning the house. He had constructed for himself a complete history of the old building, a story weird enough to have been born in the fancy of a true poet. It would give me great pleasure to relate this story to you, but the events which happened to me in this connection are so interesting that I feel I must proceed with the narration of them at once.

When the count had completed his story to his own satisfaction, imagine his feelings on learning one day that the old house contained nothing more mysterious than a cake bakery belonging to the pastry cook whose handsome shop adjoined the old structure. The windows of the ground floor were walled up to give protection to the ovens, and the heavy curtains of the upper story were to keep the sunlight from the wares laid out there. When the count informed me of this I felt as if a bucket of cold water had been suddenly thrown over me. The demon who is the enemy of all poets caught the dreamer by the nose and tweaked him painfully.

And yet, in spite of this prosaic explanation, I could not resist stopping before the deserted house whenever I passed it, and gentle tremors rippled through my veins as vague visions arose of what might be hidden there. I could not believe in this story of the cake and candy factory. Through some strange freak of the imagination I felt as a child feels when some fairy tale has been told it to conceal the truth it suspects. I scolded myself for a silly fool; the house remained unaltered in its appearance, and the visions faded in my brain, until one day a chance incident woke them to life again.

I was wandering through the avenue as usual, and as I passed the deserted house I could not resist a hasty glance at its close-curtained upper windows. But as I looked at it, the curtain on the last window near the pastry shop began to move. A hand, an arm, came out from between its folds. I took my opera glass from my pocket and saw a beautifully formed woman's hand, on the little finger of which a large diamond sparkled in unusual brilliancy; a rich bracelet glittered on the white, rounded arm. The hand set a tall, oddly formed crystal bottle on the window ledge and disappeared again behind the curtain.

I stopped as if frozen to stone; a weirdly pleasurable sensation, mingled with awe, streamed through my being with the warmth of an electric current. I stared up at the mysterious window and a sigh of longing arose from the very depths of my heart. When I came to myself again, I was angered to find that I was surrounded by a crowd which stood gazing up at the window with curious faces. I stole away inconspicuously, and the demon of all things prosaic whispered to me that what I had just seen was the rich pastry cook's wife, in her Sunday adornment, placing an empty bottle, used for rose-water or the like, on the window sill. Nothing very weird about this.

Suddenly a most sensible thought came to me. I turned and entered the shining, mirror-walled shop of the pastry cook. Blowing the steaming foam from my cup of chocolate, I remarked: "You have a very useful addition to your establishment next door." The man leaned over his counter and looked at me with a questioning smile, as if he did not understand me. I repeated that in my opinion he had been very clever to set up his bakery in the neighboring house, although the deserted appearance of the building was a strange sight in its contrasting surroundings. "Why, sir," began the pastry cook, "who told you that the house next door belongs to us? Unfortunately every attempt on our part to acquire it has been in vain, and I fancy it is all the better so, for there is something queer about the place."

You can imagine, dear friends, how interested I became upon hearing these words, and that I begged the man to tell me more about the house.

"I do not know anything very definite, sir," he said. "All that we know for a certainty is that the house belongs to the Countess S., who lives on her estates and has not been to the city for years. This house, so they tell me, stood in its present shape before any of the handsome buildings were raised which are now the pride of our avenue, and in all these years there has been nothing done to it except to keep it from actual decay. Two living creatures alone dwell there, an aged misanthrope of a steward and his melancholy dog, which occasionally howls at the moon from the back courtyard. According to the general story the deserted house is haunted. In very truth my brother, who is the owner of this shop, and myself have often, when our business kept us awake during the silence of the night, heard strange sounds from the other side of the wall. There was a rumbling and a scraping that frightened us both And not very long ago we heard one night a strange singing which I could not describe to you.

It was evidently the voice of an old woman, but the tones were so sharp and clear, and ran up to the top of the scale in cadences and long trills, the like of which I have never heard before, although I have heard many singers in many lands. It seemed to be a French song, but I am not quite sure of that, for I could not listen long to the mad, ghostly singing, it made the hair stand erect on my head. And at times, after the street noises are quiet, we can hear deep sighs, and sometimes a mad laugh, which seem to come out of the earth. But if you lay your ear to the wall in our back room, you can hear that the noises come from the house next door.

He led me into the back room and pointed through the window. "And do you see that iron chimney coming out of the wall there? It smokes so heavily sometimes, even in summer when there are no fires used that my brother has often quarreled with the old steward about it, fearing danger. But the old man excuses himself by saying that he was cooking his food. Heaven knows what the queer creature may eat, for often, when the pipe is smoking heavily, a strange and queer smell can be smelled all over the house."

The glass doors of the shop creaked in opening. The pastry cook hurried into the front room, and when he had nodded to the figure now entering he threw a meaning glance at me. I understood him perfectly. Who else could this strange guest be, but the steward who had charge of the mysterious house! Imagine a thin little man with a face the color of a mummy, with a sharp nose tight-set lips, green cat's eyes, and a crazy smile; his hair dressed in the old-fashioned style with a high toupet and a bag at the back, and heavily powdered. He wore a faded old brown coat which was carefully brushed, gray stockings, and broad, flat-toed shoes with buckles. And imagine further, that in spite of his meagerness this little person is robustly built, with huge fists and long, strong fingers, and that he walks to the shop counter with a strong, firm step, smiling his imbecile smile, and whining out: "A couple of candied oranges—a couple of macaroons—a couple of sugared chestnuts—" Picture all this to yourself and judge whether I had not sufficient cause to imagine a mystery here.

The pastry cook gathered up the wares the old man had demanded. "Weigh it out, weigh it out, honored neighbor," moaned the strange man, as he drew out a little leathern bag and sought in it for his money. I noticed that he paid for his purchase in worn old coins, some of which were no longer in use. He seemed very unhappy and murmured: "Sweet—sweet—it must all be sweet! Well, let it be! The devil has pure honey for his bride—pure honey!"

The pastry cook smiled at me and then spoke to the old man. "You do not seem to be quite well. Yes, yes, old age, old age! It takes the strength from our limbs."

The old man's expression did not change, but his voice went up: "Old age?—Old age?—Lose strength?—Grow weak?—Oho!" And with this he clapped his hands together until the joints cracked, and sprang high up into the air until the entire shop trembled and the glass vessels on the walls and counters rattled and shook. But in the same moment a hideous screaming was heard; the old man had stepped on his black dog, which, creeping in behind him, had laid itself at his feet on the floor. "Devilish beast—dog of hell!" groaned the old man in his former miserable tone, opening his bag and giving the dog a large macaroon.[1]

The dog, which had burst out into a cry of distress that was truly human, was quiet at once, sat down on its haunches, and gnawed at the macaroon like a squirrel. When it had finished its tidbit, the old man had also finished the packing up and putting away of his purchases.

"Good night, honored neighbor," he spoke, taking the hand of the pastry cook and pressing it until the latter cried aloud in pain. "The weak old man wishes you a good night, most honorable Sir Neighbor," he repeated, and then walked from the shop, followed closely by his black dog. The old man did not seem to have noticed me at all. I was quite dumfounded in my astonishment.

"There, you see," began the pastry cook. "This is the way he acts when he comes in here, two or three times a month, it is. But I can get nothing out of him except the fact that he was a former valet of Count S., that he is now in charge of this house here, and that every day—for many

_____

[1] Coconut cookies

years now—he expects the arrival of his master's family. My brother spoke to him one day about the strange noises at night; but he answered calmly, 'Yes, people say the ghosts walk about in the house.' But do not believe it, for it is not true."

The hour was now come when fashion demanded that the elegant world of the city should assemble in this attractive shop. The doors opened incessantly, the place was thronged, and I could ask no further questions.

This much I knew, that Count P.'s information about the ownership and the use of the house were not correct; also that the old steward, in spite of his denial, was not living alone there, and that some mystery was hidden behind its discolored walls. How could I combine the story of the strange and gruesome singing with the appearance of the beautiful arm at the window? That arm could not be part of the wrinkled body of an old woman; the singing, according to the pastry cook's story, could not come from the throat of a blooming and youthful maiden. I decided in favor of the arm, as it was easy to explain to myself that some trick of acoustics had made the voice sound sharp and old, or that it had appeared so only in the pastry cook's fear-distorted imagination.

Then I thought of the smoke, the strange odors, the oddly formed crystal bottle that I had seen, and soon the vision of a beautiful creature held enthralled by fatal magic stood as if alive before my mental vision. The old man became a wizard who perhaps quite independently of the family he served, had set up his devil's kitchen in the deserted house. My imagination had begun to work, and in my dreams that night I saw clearly the hand with the sparkling diamond on its finger, the arm with the shining bracelet. From out thin, gray mists there appeared a sweet face with sadly imploring blue eyes, then the entire exquisite figure of a beautiful girl. And I saw that what I had thought was mist was the fine steam flowing out in circles from a crystal bottle held in the hands of the vision.

"Oh, fairest creature of my dreams," I cried in rapture. "Reveal to me where thou art, what it is that enthralls thee. Ah, I know it! It is black magic that holds thee captive—thou art the unhappy slave of that malicious devil who wanders about brown-clad and bewigged in pastry shops, scattering their wares with his unholy springing, and feeding his demon dog on macaroons, after they have howled out a Satanic measure in five-eight time.

Oh, I know it all, thou fair and charming vision. The diamond is the reflection of the fire of thy heart. But that bracelet about thine arm is a link of the chain which the brown-clad one says is a magnetic chain. Do not believe it, O glorious one! See how it shines in the blue fire from the retort. One moment more and thou art free. And now, O maiden, open thy rosebud mouth and tell me—" In this moment a gnarled fist leaped over my shoulder and clutched at the crystal bottle, which sprang into a thousand pieces in the air. With a faint, sad moan, the charming vision faded into the blackness of the night.

When morning came to put an end to my dreaming I hurried to the avenue and placed myself before the deserted house. Heavy blinds were drawn before the upper windows. The street was still quite empty, and I stepped close to the windows of the ground floor and listened and listened; but I heard no sound. The house was as quiet as the grave. The business of the day began, the passers-by became more numerous, and I was obliged to go on. I will not weary you with the recital of how for many days I crept about the house at that hour, but without discovering anything of interest. None of my questionings could reveal anything to me, and the beautiful picture of my vision began finally to pale and fade away.

At last as I passed, late one evening, I saw that the door of the deserted house was half open and the brown-clad old man was peeping out. I stepped quickly to his side with a sudden idea. "Does not Councilor Binder live in this house?" Thus I asked the old man, pushing him before me as I entered the dimly lighted vestibule.

The guardian of the old house looked at me with his piercing eyes, and answered in gentle, slow tones: "No, he does not live here, he never has lived here, he never will live here, he does not live anywhere on this avenue. But people say the ghosts walk about in this house. Yet I can assure you that it is not true. It is a quiet, a pretty house, and tomorrow the gracious Countess S. will move into it. Good night, dear gentleman."

With these words the old man maneuvered me out of the house and locked the gate behind me. I heard his feet drag across the floor, I heard his coughing and the rattling of his bunch of keys, and I heard him descend some steps.

Then all was silent.

During the short time that I had been in the house I had noticed that the corridor was hung with old tapestries and furnished like a drawing-room with large, heavy chairs in red damask.

And now, as if called into life by my entrance into the mysterious house, my adventures began. The following day, as I walked through the avenue in the noon hour, and my eyes sought the deserted house as usual, I saw something glistening in the last window of the upper story. Coming nearer I noticed that the outer blind had been quite drawn up and the inner curtain slightly opened. The sparkle of a diamond met my eye. O kind Heaven! The face of my dream looked at me, gently imploring, from above the rounded arm on which her head was resting. But how was it possible to stand still in the moving crowd without attracting attention? Suddenly I caught sight of the benches placed in the gravel walk in the center of the avenue, and I saw that one of them was directly opposite the house. I sprang over to it, and leaning over its back, I could stare up at the mysterious window undisturbed. Yes, it was she, the charming maiden of my dream! But her eye did not seem to seek me as I had at first thought; her glance was cold and unfocused, and had it not been for an occasional motion of the hand and arm, I might have thought that I was looking at a cleverly painted picture.

I was so lost in my adoration of the mysterious being in the window, so aroused and excited throughout all my nerve centers, that I did not hear the shrill voice of an Italian street hawker, who had been offering me his wares for some time. Finally he touched me on the arm, I turned hastily and commanded him to let me alone. But he did not cease his entreaties, asserting that he had earned nothing today, and begging me to buy some small trifle from him. Full of impatience to get rid of him I put my hand in my pocket.

With the words: "I have more beautiful things here," he opened the under drawer of his box and held out to me a little, round pocket mirror. In it, as he held it up before my face, I could see the deserted house behind me, the window, and the sweet face of my vision there.

I bought the little mirror at once, for I saw that it would make it possible for me to sit comfortably and inconspicuously, and yet watch the window. The longer I looked at the reflection in the glass, the more I fell captive to a weird and quite indescribable sensation, which I might almost call a waking dream. It was as if a lethargy had lamed my eyes, holding them fastened on the glass beyond my power to loosen them. Through my mind there rushed the memory of an old nurse's tale of my earliest childhood. When my nurse was taking me off to bed, and I showed an inclination to stand peering into the great mirror in my father's room, she would tell me that when children looked into mirrors in the night time they would see a strange, hideous face there, and their eyes would be frozen so that they could not move them again. The thought struck awe to my soul, but I could not resist a peep at the mirror, I was so curious to see the strange face. Once I did believe that I saw two hideous glowing eyes shining out of the mirror. I screamed and fell down in a swoon.

All these foolish memories of my early childhood came trooping back to me. My blood ran cold through my veins. I would have thrown the mirror from me, but I could not. And now at last the beautiful eyes of the fair vision looked at me, her glance sought mine and shone deep down into my heart. The terror I had felt left me, giving way to the pleasurable pain of sweetest longing.

"You have a pretty little mirror there," said a voice beside me. I awoke from my dream, and was not a little confused when I saw smiling faces looking at me from either side. Several persons had sat down upon my bench, and it was quite certain that my staring into the window, and my probably strange expression, had afforded them great cause for amusement.

"You have a pretty little mirror there," repeated the man, as I did not answer him. His glance said more, and asked without words the reason of my staring so oddly into the little glass. He was an elderly man, neatly dressed, and his voice and eyes were so full of good nature that I could not refuse him my confidence. I told him that I had been looking in the mirror at the picture of a beautiful maiden who was sitting at a window of the deserted house. I went even farther; I asked the old man if he had not seen the fair face himself. "Over there? In the old house—in the last window?" He repeated my questions in a tone of surprise.

"Yes, yes," I exclaimed.

The old man smiled and answered: "Well, well, that was a strange delusion. My old eyes—thank Heaven for my old eyes! Yes, yes, sir. I saw a pretty face in the window there, with my own eyes; but it seemed to me to be an excellently well-painted oil portrait."

I turned quickly and looked toward the window; there was no one there, and the blind had been pulled down.

"Yes," continued the old man, "yes, sir. Now it is too late to make sure of the matter, for just now the servant, who, as I know, lives there alone in the house of the Countess S., took the picture away from the window after he had dusted it, and let down the blinds."

"Was it, then, surely a picture?" I asked again, in bewilderment.

"You can trust my eyes," replied the old man. "The optical delusion was strengthened by your seeing only the reflection in the mirror. And when I was in your years it was easy enough for my fancy to call up the picture of a beautiful maiden."

"But the hand and arm moved," I exclaimed. "Oh, yes, they moved, indeed they moved," said the old man smiling, as he patted me on the shoulder. Then he arose to go, and bowing politely, closed his remarks with the words, "Beware of mirrors which can lie so vividly. Your obedient servant, sir."

You can imagine how I felt when I saw that he looked upon me as a foolish fantast. I began to be convinced that the old man was right, and that it was only my absurd imagination which insisted on raising up mysteries about the deserted house.

I hurried home full of anger and disgust, and promised myself that I would not think of the mysterious house, and would not even walk through the avenue for several days. I kept my vow, spending my days working at my desk, and my evenings in the company of jovial friends, leaving myself no time to think of the mysteries which so enthralled me. And yet, it was just in these days that I would start up out of my sleep as if awakened by a touch, only to find that all that had aroused me was merely the thought of that mysterious being whom I had seen in my vision and in the window of the deserted house. Even during my work, or in the midst of a lively conversation with my friends, I felt the same thought shoot through me like an electric current. I condemned the little mirror in which I had seen the charming picture to a prosaic daily use. I placed it on my dressing-table that I might bind my cravat before it, and thus it happened one day, when I was about to utilize it for this important business, that its glass seemed dull, and that I took it up and breathed on it to rub it bright again. My heart seemed to stand still, every fiber in me trembled in delightful awe. Yes, that is all the name I can find for the feeling that came over me, when, as my breath clouded the little mirror, I saw the beautiful face of my dreams arise and smile at me through blue mists. You laugh at me? You look upon me as an incorrigible dreamer? Think what you will about it—the fair face looked at me from out of the mirror! But as soon as the clouding vanished, the face vanished in the brightened glass.

I will not weary you with a detailed recital of my sensations the next few days. I will only say that I repeated again the experiments with the mirror, sometimes with success, sometimes without. When I had not been able to call up the vision, I would run to the deserted house and stare up at the windows; but I saw no human being anywhere about the building. I lived only in thoughts of my vision; everything else seemed indifferent to me. I neglected my friends and my studies. The tortures in my soul passed over into, or rather mingled with, physical sensations which frightened me, and which at last made me fear for my reason. One day, after an unusually severe attack, I put my little mirror in my pocket and hurried to the home of Dr. K., who was noted for his treatment of those diseases of the mind out of which physical diseases so often grow. I told him my story; I did not conceal the slightest incident from him, and I implored him to save me from the terrible fate which seemed to threaten me.

He listened to me quietly, but I read astonishment in his glance. Then he said: "The danger is not as near as you believe, and I think that I may say that it can be easily prevented. You are undergoing an unusual psychical disturbance, beyond a doubt. But the fact that you understand that some evil principle seems to be trying to influence you, gives you a weapon by which you can combat it. Leave your little mirror here with me, and force yourself to take up with some work which will afford scope for all your mental energy. Do not go to the avenue; work all day, from early to late, then take a long walk, and spend your evenings in the company of your friends. Eat heartily, and drink heavy, nourishing wines. You see I am endeavoring to combat your fixed idea of the face in the window of the deserted house and in the mirror, by diverting your mind to other things, and by strengthening your body. You yourself must help me in this."

I was very reluctant to part with my mirror. The physician, who had already taken it, seemed to notice my hesitation.

He breathed upon the glass and holding it up to me, he asked: "Do you see anything?"

"Nothing at all," I answered, for so it was.

"Now breathe on the glass yourself," said the physician, laying the mirror in my hands.

I did as he requested. There was the vision even more clearly than ever before.

"There she is!" I cried aloud.

The physician looked into the glass, and then said: "I cannot see anything. But I will confess to you that when I looked into this glass, a queer shiver overcame me, passing away almost at once. Now do it once more."

I breathed upon the glass again and the physician laid his hand upon the back of my neck. The face appeared again, and the physician, looking into the mirror over my shoulder, turned pale. Then he took the little glass from my hands, looked at it attentively, and locked it into his desk, returning to me after a few moments' silent thought.

"Follow my instructions strictly," he said. "I must confess to you that I do not yet understand those moments of your vision. But I hope to be able to tell you more about it very soon."

Difficult as it was to me, I forced myself to live absolutely according to the doctor's orders. I soon felt the benefit of the steady work and the nourishing diet, and yet I was not free from those terrible attacks, which would come either at noon, or, more intensely still, at midnight. Even in the midst of a merry company, in the enjoyment of wine and song, glowing daggers seemed to pierce my heart, and all the strength of my intellect was powerless to resist their might over me. I was obliged to retire, and could not return to my friends until I had recovered from my condition of lethargy. It was in one of these attacks, an unusually strong one, that such an irresistible, mad longing for the picture of my dreams came over me, that I hurried out into the street and ran toward the mysterious house. While still at a distance from it, I seemed to see lights shining out through the fast-closed blinds, but when I came nearer I saw that all was dark. Crazy with my desire I rushed to the door; it fell back before the pressure of my hand. I stood in the dimly lighted vestibule, enveloped in a heavy, close atmosphere. My heart beat in strange fear and impatience. Then suddenly a long, sharp tone, as from a woman's throat, shrilled through the house. I know not how it happened that I found myself suddenly in a great hall brilliantly lighted and furnished in old-fashioned magnificence of golden chairs and strange Japanese ornaments. Strongly perfumed incense arose in blue clouds about me.

"Welcome—welcome, sweet bridegroom! the hour has come, our bridal hour!" I heard these words in a woman's voice, and as little as I can tell, how I came into the room, just so little do I know how it happened that suddenly a tall, youthful figure, richly dressed, seemed to arise from the blue mists. With the repeated shrill cry: "Welcome, sweet bridegroom!" she came toward me with outstretched arms—and a yellow face, distorted with age and madness, stared into mine!

I fell back in terror, but the fiery, piercing glance of her eyes, like the eyes of a snake, seemed to hold me spellbound. I did not seem able to turn my eyes from this terrible old woman, I could not move another step.

She came still nearer, and it seemed to me suddenly as if her hideous face were only a thin mask, beneath which I saw the features of the beautiful maiden of my vision.

Already I felt the touch of her hands, when suddenly she fell at my feet with a loud scream, and a voice behind me cried: "Oho, is the devil playing his tricks with your grace again? To bed, to bed, your grace. Else there will be blows, mighty blows!"

I turned quickly and saw the old steward in his night clothes, swinging a whip above his head. He was about to strike the screaming figure at my feet when I caught at his arm.

But he shook me from him, exclaiming: "The devil, sir! That old Satan would have murdered you if I had not come to your aid. Get away from here at once!"

I rushed from the hall, and sought in vain in the darkness for the door of the house. Behind me I heard the hissing blows of the whip and the old woman's screams. I drew breath to call aloud for help, when suddenly the ground gave way under my feet; I fell down a short flight of stairs, bringing up with such force against a door at the bottom that it sprang open, and I measured my length on the floor of a small room. From the hastily vacated bed, and from the familiar brown coat hanging over a chair, I saw that I was in the bedchamber of the old steward.

There was a trampling on the stair, and the old man himself entered hastily, throwing himself at my feet. "By all the saints, sir," he entreated with folded hands, "whoever you may be, and however her grace, that old Satan of a witch has managed to entice you to this house, do not speak to anyone of what has happened here. It will cost me my position. Her crazy excellency has been punished, and is bound fast in her bed. Sleep well, good sir, sleep softly and sweetly. It is a warm and beautiful July night. There is no moon, but the stars shine brightly. A quiet good night to you."

While talking, the old man had taken up a lamp, had led me out of the basement, pushed me out of the house door, and locked it behind me. I hurried home quite bewildered, and you can imagine that I was too much confused by the gruesome secret to be able to form any explanation of it in my own mind for the first few days. Only this much was certain, that I was now free from the evil spell that had held me captive so long.

All my longing for the magic vision in the mirror had disappeared, and the memory of the scene in the deserted house was like the recollection of an unexpected visit to a madhouse. It was evident beyond a doubt that the steward was the tyrannical guardian of a crazy woman of noble birth, whose condition was to be hidden from the world. But the mirror? and all the other magic? Listen, and I will tell you more about it.

Some few days later I came upon Count P. at an evening entertainment. He drew me to one side and said, with a smile, "Do you know that the secrets of our deserted house are beginning to be revealed?"

I listened with interest; but before the count could say more the doors of the dining-room were thrown open, and the company proceeded to the table. Quite lost in thought at the words I had just heard, I had given a young lady my arm, and had taken my place mechanically in the ceremonious procession. I led my companion to the seats arranged for us, and then turned to look at her for the first time. The vision of my mirror stood before me, feature for feature, there was no deception possible! I trembled to my innermost heart, as you can imagine; but I discovered that there was not the slightest echo even, in my heart, of the mad desire which had ruled me so entirely when my breath drew out the magic picture from the glass. My astonishment, or rather my terror, must have been apparent in my eyes.

The girl looked at me in such surprise that I endeavored to control myself sufficiently to remark that I must have met her somewhere before. Her short answer, to the effect that this could hardly be possible, as she had come to the city only yesterday for the first time in her life, bewildered me still more and threw me into an awkward silence. The sweet glance from her gentle eyes brought back my courage, and I began a tentative exploring of this new companion's mind. I found that I had before me a sweet and delicate being, suffering from some psychic trouble.

At a particularly merry turn of the conversation, when I would throw in a daring word like a dash of pepper, she would smile, but her smile was pained, as if a wound had been touched. "You are not very merry tonight, countess. Was it the visit this morning?" An officer sitting near us had spoken these words to my companion, but before he could finish his remark his neighbor had grasped him by the arm and whispered something in his ear, while a lady at the other side of the table, with glowing cheeks and angry eyes, began to talk loudly of the opera she had heard last evening.

Tears came to the eyes of the girl sitting beside me. "Am I not foolish?" She turned to me. A few moments before she had complained of headache.

"Merely the usual evidences of a nervous headache," I answered in an easy tone, "and there is nothing better for it than the merry spirit which bubbles in the foam of this poet's nectar." With these words I filled her champagne glass, and she sipped at it as she threw me a look of gratitude. Her mood brightened, and all would have been well had I not touched a glass before me with unexpected strength, arousing from it a shrill, high tone. My companion grew deadly pale, and I myself felt a sudden shiver, for the sound had exactly the tone of the mad woman's voice in the deserted house.

While we were drinking coffee I made an opportunity to get to the side of Count P. He understood the reason for my movement. "Do you know that your neighbor is Countess Edwina S.? And do you know also that it is her mother's sister who lives in the deserted house, incurably mad for many years? This morning both mother and daughter went to see the unfortunate woman. The old steward, the only person who is able to control the countess in her outbreaks, is seriously ill, and they say that the sister has finally revealed the secret to Dr. K. This eminent physician will endeavor to cure the patient, or if this is not possible, at least to prevent her terrible outbreaks of mania. This is all that I know yet."

Others joined us and we were obliged to change the subject. Dr. K. was the physician to whom I had turned in my own anxiety, and you can well imagine that I hurried to him as soon as I was free, and told him all that had happened to me in the last days. I asked him to tell me as much as he could about the mad woman, for my own peace of mind; and this is what I learned from him under promise of secrecy.

"Angelica, Countess Z.," thus the doctor began, "had already passed her thirtieth year, but was still in full possession of great beauty, when Count S., although much younger than she, became so fascinated by her charm that he wooed her with ardent devotion and followed her to her father's home to try his luck there. But scarcely had the count entered the house, scarcely had he caught sight of Angelica's younger sister, Gabrielle, when he awoke as from a dream. The elder sister appeared faded and colorless beside Gabrielle, whose beauty and charm so enthralled the count that he begged her hand of her father. Count Z. gave his consent easily, as there was no doubt of Gabrielle's feelings toward her suitor. Angelica did not show the slightest anger at her lover's faithlessness. 'He believes that he has forsaken me, the foolish boy! He does not perceive that he was but my toy, a toy of which I had tired.' Thus she spoke in proud scorn, and not a look or an action on her part belied her words. But after the ceremonious betrothal of Gabrielle to Count S., Angelica was seldom seen by the members of her family. She did not appear at the dinner table, and it was said that she spent most of her time walking alone in the neighboring wood.

"A strange occurrence disturbed the monotonous quiet of life in the castle. The hunters of Count Z., assisted by peasants from the village, had captured a band of gypsies who were accused of several robberies and murders which had happened recently in the neighborhood. The men were brought to the castle courtyard, fettered together on a long chain, while the women and children were packed on a cart. Noticeable among the last was a tall, haggard old woman of terrifying aspect, wrapped from head to foot in a red shawl. She stood upright in the cart, and in an imperious tone demanded that she should be allowed to descend. The guards were so awed by her manner and appearance that they obeyed her at once.

"Count Z. came down to the courtyard and commanded that the gang should be placed in the prisons under the castle. Suddenly Countess Angelica rushed out of the door, her hair all loose, fear and anxiety in her pale face. Throwing herself on her knees, she cried in a piercing voice, 'Let these people go! Let these people go! They are innocent! Father, let these people go! If you shed one drop of their blood I will pierce my heart with this knife!' The countess swung a shining knife in the air and then sank swooning to the ground. 'Yes, my beautiful darling—my golden child—I knew you would not let them hurt us,' shrilled the old woman in red. She cowered beside the countess and pressed disgusting kisses to her face and breast, murmuring crazy words. She took from out the recesses of her shawl a little vial in which a tiny goldfish seemed to swim in some silver-clear liquid. She held the vial to the countess's heart. The latter regained consciousness immediately. When her eyes fell on the gypsy woman, she sprang up, clasped the old creature ardently in her arms, and hurried with her into the castle.

"Count Z., Gabrielle, and her lover, who had come out during this scene, watched it in astonished awe. The gypsies appeared quite indifferent. They were loosed from their chains and taken separately to the prisons. Next morning Count Z. called the villagers together. The gypsies were led before them and the count announced that he had found them to be innocent of the crimes of which they were accused, and that he would grant them free passage through his domains. To the astonishment of all present, their fetters were struck off and they were set at liberty. The red-shawled woman was not among them It was whispered that the gypsy captain, recognizable from the golden chain about his neck and the red feather in his high Spanish hat, had paid a secret visit to the count's room the night before. But it was discovered, a short time after the release of the gypsies, that they were indeed guiltless of the robberies and murders that had disturbed the district.

"The date set for Gabrielle's wedding approached. One

day, to her great astonishment, she saw several large wagons in the courtyard being packed high with furniture, clothing, linen, with everything necessary for a complete household outfit. The wagons were driven away, and the following day Count Z. explained that, for many reasons, he had thought it best to grant Angelica's odd request that she be allowed to set up her own establishment in his house in X. He had given the house to her, and had promised her that no member of the family, not even he himself, should enter it without her express permission. He added also, that, at her urgent request, he had permitted his own valet to accompany her, to take charge of her household.

"When the wedding festivities were over, Count S. and his bride departed for their home, where they spent a year in cloudless happiness. Then the count's health failed mysteriously. It was as if some secret sorrow gnawed at his vitals, robbing him of joy and strength. All efforts of his young wife to discover the source of his trouble were fruitless. At last, when the constantly recurring fainting spells threatened to endanger his very life, he yielded to the entreaties of his physicians and left his home, ostensibly for Pisa. His young wife was prevented from accompanying him by the delicate condition of her own health.

"And now," said the doctor, "the information given me by Countess S. became, from this point on, so rhapsodical that a keen observer only could guess at the true coherence of the story. Her baby, a daughter, born during her husband's absence, was spirited away from the house, and all search for it was fruitless. Her grief at this loss deepened to despair, when she received a message from her father stating that her husband, whom all believed to be in Pisa, had been found dying of heart trouble in Angelica's home in X., and that Angelica herself had become a dangerous maniac. The old count added that all this horror had so shaken his own nerves that he feared he would not long survive it.

"As soon as Gabrielle was able to leave her bed, she hurried to her father's castle. One night, prevented from sleeping by visions of the loved ones she had lost, she seemed to hear a faint crying, like that of an infant, before the door of her chamber. Lighting her candle she opened the door. Great Heaven! there cowered the old gypsy woman, wrapped in her red shawl, staring up at her with eyes that seemed already glazing in death. In her arms she held a little child, whose crying had aroused the countess. Gabrielle's heart beat high with joy—it was her child—her lost daughter! She snatched the infant from the gypsy's arms, just as the woman fell at her feet lifeless. The countess's screams awoke the house, but the gypsy was quite dead and no effort to revive her met with success.

"The old count hurried to X. to endeavor to discover something that would throw light upon the mysterious disappearance and reappearance of the child. Angelica's madness had frightened away all her female servants; the valet alone remained with her. She appeared at first to have become quite calm and sensible. But when the count told her the story of Gabrielle's child she clapped her hands and laughed aloud, crying: 'Did the little darling arrive? You buried her, you say? How the feathers of the gold pheasant shine in the sun! Have you seen the green lion with the fiery blue eyes?' Horrified the count perceived that Angelica's mind was gone beyond a doubt, and he resolved to take her back with him to his estates, in spite of the warnings of his old valet. At the mere suggestion of removing her from the house Angelica's ravings increased to such an extent as to endanger her own life and that of the others.

"When a lucid interval came again Angelica entreated her father, with many tears, to let her live and die in the house she had chosen. Touched by her terrible trouble he granted her request, although he believed the confession which slipped from her lips during this scene to be a fantasy of her madness. She told him that Count S. had returned to her arms, and that the child which the gypsy had taken to her father's house was the fruit of their love. The rumor went abroad in the city that Count Z. had taken the unfortunate woman to his home; but the truth was that she remained hidden in the deserted house under the care of the valet. Count Z. died a short time ago, and Countess Gabrielle came here with her daughter Edwina to arrange some family affairs. It was not possible for her to avoid seeing her unfortunate sister. Strange things must have happened during this visit, but the countess has not confided anything to me, saying merely that she had found it necessary to take the mad woman away from the old valet. It had been discovered that he had controlled her outbreaks by means of force and physical cruelty; and that also, allured by Angelica's assertions that she could make gold, he had allowed himself to assist her in her weird operations.

"It would be quite unnecessary," thus the physician ended his story, "to say anything more to you about the deeper inward relationship of all these strange things. It is clear to my mind that it was you who brought about the catastrophe, a catastrophe which will mean recovery or speedy death for the sick woman. And now I will confess to you that I was not a little alarmed, horrified even, to discover that—when I had set myself in magnetic communication with you by placing my hand on your neck—I could see the picture in the mirror with my own eyes. We both know now that the reflection in the glass was the face of Countess Edwina."

I repeat Dr. K.'s words in saying that, to my mind also, there is no further comment that can be made on all these facts. I consider it equally unnecessary to discuss at any further length with you now the mysterious relationship between Angelica, Edwina, the old valet, and myself—a relationship which seemed the work of a malicious demon who was playing his tricks with us. I will add only that I left the city soon after all these events, driven from the place by an oppression I could not shake off. The uncanny sensation left me suddenly a month or so later, giving way to a feeling of intense relief that flowed through all my veins with the warmth of an electric current. I am convinced that this change within me came about in the moment when the mad woman died.

Thus did Theodore end his narrative. His friends had much to say about his strange adventure, and they agreed with him that the odd and unusual, and the truly marvelous as well, were mingled in a strange and gruesome manner in his story. When they parted for the night, Franz shook Theodore's hand gently, as he said with a smile: "Good night, you Spallanzani[2] bat, you."

---

[2] Lazzaro Spallanzini (1729-1799), Italian born biologist and physiologist who experimented with bats to learn their sense of direction in the dark.

EDGAR ALLAN POE
(1809-1849)

Φ

The Tell-Tale Heart

This is Poe's classic gothic tale of insanity and murder that was first published in the January issue of the *Pioneer* magazine of 1843. It involves the famous Evil Eye that people have been rumored to posses for hundreds of years. It is often confused with those having an extreme lazy eye or even a glass eye. During this time period many viewed the eyes as denoting good or evil within, a window to the soul. Many believed it could drive a person to insanity, as Poe artfully demonstrated.

Poe was orphaned at a young age when his parents, both theatre actors, died. Poe was haunted by thoughts of ghosts and encounters from the undead when a child. Poe's friend, Susan Archer Talley Weiss, recounted in "Home Life of Poe" for 1907: . . . *the most horrible thing he could imagine as a boy was to feel an ice-cold hand laid upon his face in a pitch-dark room when alone at night; or to awaken in semi-darkness and see an evil face gazing close into his own; and that these fancies had so haunted him that he would often keep his head under the bed-covering until nearly suffocated.*

The Tell-Tale Heart

TRUE! –NERVOUS –VERY, VERY dreadfully nervous I had been and am; but why *will* you say that I am mad? The disease had sharpened my senses –not destroyed –not dulled them. Above all was the sense of hearing acute. I heard all things in the heaven and in the earth. I heard many things in hell. How, then, am I mad? Hearken! and observe how healthily –how calmly I can tell you the whole story.

It is impossible to say how first the idea entered my brain; but once conceived, it haunted me day and night. Object there was none. Passion there was none. I loved the old man. He had never wronged me. He had never given me insult. For his gold I had no desire. I think it was his eye! yes, it was this! He had the eye of a vulture –a pale blue eye, with a film over it. Whenever it fell upon me, my blood ran cold; and so by degrees –very gradually –I made up my mind to take the life of the old man, and thus rid myself of the eye forever.

Now this is the point. You fancy me mad. Madmen know nothing. But you should have seen *me*. You should have seen how wisely I proceeded – with what caution – with what foresight – with what dissimulation I went to work! I was never kinder to the old man than during the whole week before I killed him. And every night, about midnight, I turned the latch of his door and opened it – oh so gently! And then, when I had made an opening sufficient for my head, I put in a dark lantern, all closed, closed, that no light shone out, and then I thrust in my head. Oh, you would have laughed to see how cunningly I thrust it in! I moved it slowly – very, very slowly, so that I might not disturb the old man's sleep. It took me an hour to place my whole head within the opening so far that I could see him as he lay upon his bed. Ha! would a madman have been so wise as this, And then, when my head was well in the room, I undid the lantern cautiously- oh, so cautiously – cautiously (for the hinges creaked) – I undid it just so much that a single thin ray fell upon the vulture eye. And this I did for seven long nights – every night just at midnight – but I found the eye always closed; and so it was impossible to do the work; for it was not the old man who vexed me, but his Evil Eye. And every morning, when the day broke, I went boldly into the chamber, and spoke courageously to him, calling him by name in a hearty tone, and inquiring how he has passed the night. So you see he would have been a very profound old man, indeed, to suspect that every night, just at twelve, I looked in upon him while he slept.

Upon the eighth night I was more than usually cautious in opening the door. A watch's minute hand moves more quickly than did mine. Never before that night had I *felt* the extent of my own powers – of my sagacity. I could scarcely contain my feelings of triumph. To think that there I was, opening the door, little by little, and he not even to dream of my secret deeds or thoughts. I fairly chuckled at the idea; and perhaps he heard me; for he moved on the bed suddenly, as if startled. Now you may think that I drew back – but no. His room was as black as pitch with the thick darkness, (for the shutters were close fastened, through fear of robbers,) and so I knew that he could not see the opening of the door, and I kept pushing it on steadily, steadily.

I had my head in, and was about to open the lantern, when my thumb slipped upon the tin fastening, and the old man sprang up in bed, crying out – "Who's there?"

I kept quite still and said nothing. For a whole hour I did not move a muscle, and in the meantime I did not hear him lie down. He was still sitting up in the bed listening; – just as I have done, night after night, hearkening to the death watches in the wall.[1]

Presently I heard a slight groan, and I knew it was the groan of mortal terror. It was not a groan of pain or of grief – oh, no! – it was the low stifled sound that arises from the bottom of the soul when overcharged with awe. I knew the sound well. Many a night, just at midnight, when all the world slept, it has welled up from my own bosom, deepening, with its dreadful echo, the terrors that

---

[1] "Certain small beetles bore into the woodwork of old houses, and there 'make a clicking sound by standing up on their hind legs and knocking their heads against the wood quickly and forcibly several times in succession.' *(Century Dictionary.)* Both the beetles and the noise they make are called 'death watches,' because superstitious people regard the sounds as ominous of death." "Poems and Tales from the Writings of Edgar Allan Poe," William Peterfield Trent, 1898, pg. 81.

distracted me. I say I knew it well. I knew what the old man felt, and pitied him, although I chuckled at heart. I knew that he had been lying awake ever since the first slight noise, when he had turned in the bed. His fears had been ever since growing upon him. He had been trying to fancy them causeless, but could not. He had been saying to himself – "It is nothing but the wind in the chimney – it is only a mouse crossing the floor," or "It is merely a cricket which has made a single chirp."

Yes, he had been trying to comfort himself with these suppositions: but he had found all in vain. *All in vain*; because Death, in approaching him had stalked with his black shadow before him, and enveloped the victim. And it was the mournful influence of the unperceived shadow that caused him to feel – although he neither saw nor heard – to *feel* the presence of my head within the room.

When I had waited a long time, very patiently, without hearing him lie down, I resolved to open a little – a very, very little crevice in the lantern. So I opened it – you cannot imagine how stealthily, stealthily – until, at length a simple dim ray, like the thread of the spider, shot from out the crevice and fell full upon the vulture eye.

It was open – wide, wide open – and I grew furious as I gazed upon it. I saw it with perfect distinctness – all a dull blue, with a hideous veil over it that chilled the very marrow in my bones; but I could see nothing else of the old man's face or person: for I had directed the ray as if by instinct, precisely upon the damned spot.

And have I not told you that what you mistake for madness is but over-acuteness of the sense? – now, I say, there came to my ears a low, dull, quick sound, such as a watch makes when enveloped in cotton. I knew *that* sound well, too. It was the beating of the old man's heart. It increased my fury, as the beating of a drum stimulates the soldier into courage.

But even yet I refrained and kept still. I scarcely breathed. I held the lantern motionless. I tried how steadily I could maintain the ray upon the eve. Meantime the hellish tattoo of the heart increased. It grew quicker and quicker, and louder and louder every instant. The old man's terror *must* have been extreme! It grew louder, I say, louder every moment! – do you mark me well I have told you that I am nervous: so I am. And now at the dead hour of the night, amid the dreadful silence of that old house, so strange a noise as this excited me to uncontrollable terror. Yet, for some minutes longer I refrained and stood still. But the beating grew louder, louder! I thought the heart must burst. And now a new anxiety seized me – the sound would be heard by a neighbour! The old man's hour had come! With a loud yell, I threw open the lantern and leaped into the room. He shrieked once – once only. In an instant I dragged him to the floor, and pulled the heavy bed over him. I then smiled gaily, to find the deed so far done. But, for many minutes, the heart beat on with a muffled sound. This, however, did not vex me; it would not be heard through the wall. At length it ceased. The old man was dead. I removed the bed and examined the corpse. Yes, he was stone, stone dead. I placed my hand upon the heart and held it there many minutes. There was no pulsation. He was stone dead. His eye would trouble me no more.

If still you think me mad, you will think so no longer when I describe the wise precautions I took for the concealment of the body. The night waned, and I worked hastily, but in silence. First of all I dismembered the corpse. I cut off the head and the arms and the legs.

I then took up three planks from the flooring of the chamber, and deposited all between the scantlings.[2] I then replaced the boards so cleverly, so cunningly, that no human eye – not even *his* – could have detected any thing wrong. There was nothing to wash out – no stain of any kind – no blood-spot whatever. I had been too wary for that. A tub had caught all – ha! ha!

When I had made an end of these labors, it was four o'clock – still dark as midnight. As the bell sounded the hour, there came a knocking at the street door. I went down to open it with a light heart, – for what had I *now* to fear? There entered three men, who introduced themselves, with perfect suavity, as officers of the police. A shriek had been heard by a neighbour during the night; suspicion of foul play had been aroused; information had been lodged at the police office, and they (the officers) had been deputed to search the premises.

I smiled, – for *what* had I to fear? I bade the gentlemen welcome. The shriek, I said, was my own in a dream. The old man, I mentioned, was absent in the country. I took my visitors all over the house. I bade them search – search *well.* I led them, at length, to *his* chamber. I showed them

---

[2] Tiny boards used as floor supports

his treasures, secure, undisturbed. In the enthusiasm of my confidence, I brought chairs into the room, and desired them *here* to rest from their fatigues, while I myself, in the wild audacity of my perfect triumph, placed my own seat upon the very spot beneath which reposed the corpse of the victim.

The officers were satisfied. My *manner* had convinced them. I was singularly at ease. They sat, and while I answered cheerily, they chatted of familiar things. But, ere long, I felt myself getting pale and wished them gone. My head ached, and I fancied a ringing in my ears: but still they sat and still chatted. The ringing became more distinct: – It continued and became more distinct: I talked more freely to get rid of the feeling: but it continued and gained definiteness – until, at length, I found that the noise was not within my ears.

No doubt I now grew *very* pale; – but I talked more fluently, and with a heightened voice. Yet the sound increased – and what could I do? It was *a low, dull, quick sound – much such a sound as a watch makes when enveloped in cotton.* I gasped for breath – and yet the officers heard it not. I talked more quickly – more vehemently; but the noise steadily increased. I arose and argued about trifles, in a high key and with violent gesticulations; but the noise steadily increased. Why *would* they not be gone? I paced the floor to and fro with heavy strides, as if excited to fury by the observations of the men – but the noise steadily increased. Oh God! what *could* I do? I foamed – I raved – I swore! I swung the chair upon which I had been sitting, and grated it upon the boards, but the noise arose over all and continually increased. It grew louder –louder – *louder!* And still the men chatted pleasantly, and smiled. Was it possible they heard not? Almighty God! – no, no! They heard! – they suspected! – they *knew!* – they were making a mockery of my horror!-this I thought, and this I think. But anything was better than this agony! Anything was more tolerable than this derision! I could bear those hypocritical smiles no longer! I felt that I must scream or die! and now – again! – hark! louder! louder! louder! *louder!*

"Villains!" I shrieked, "dissemble no more! I admit the deed! – tear up the planks! here, here! – It is the beating of his hideous heart!"

HONORÉ DE BALZAC
(1799-1850)

Φ

El Verdugo
(The Executioner)

"El Verdugo" is cherished for the artistic way in which its acute horror is presented to readers. Honoré de Balzac, who was best known in his time for stories of romance, was adept at bringing the interplay of human experiences and emotions to his stories. When he decided to include elements of horror, this blending of genres resulted in a short story that hinged on relationships and bloodlines. "El Verdugo" is a fine example of this method and it is very effective. It has resulted in Honoré de Balzac having multiple horror stories in this collection. The only other author to accomplish the same is Edgar Allan Poe.

El Verdugo

MIDNIGHT HAD JUST SOUNDED from the belfry tower of the little town of Menda. A young French officer, leaning over the parapet[1] of the long terrace at the further end of the castle gardens, seemed to be unusually absorbed in deep thought for one who led the reckless life of a soldier; but it must be admitted that never was the hour, the scene, and the night more favorable to meditation.

The blue dome of the cloudless sky of Spain was overhead; he was looking out over the coy windings of a lovely valley lit by the uncertain starlight and the soft radiance of the moon. The officer, leaning against an orange-tree in blossom, could also see, a hundred feet below him, the town of Menda, which seemed to nestle for shelter from the north wind at the foot of the crags on which the castle itself was built. He turned his head and caught sight of the sea; the moonlit waves made a broad frame of silver for the landscape.

There were lights in the castle windows. The mirth and movement of a ball, the sounds of the violins, the laughter of the officers and their partners in the dance was borne towards him, and blended with the far-off murmur of the waves. The cool night had a certain bracing effect upon his frame, wearied as he had been by the heat of the day. He seemed to bathe in the air, made fragrant by the strong, sweet scent of flowers and of aromatic trees in the gardens.

The castle of Menda belonged to a Spanish grandee,[2] who was living in it at that time with his family. All through the evening the oldest daughter of the house had watched the officer with such a wistful interest that the Spanish lady's compassionate eyes might well have set the young Frenchman dreaming. Clara was beautiful; and although she had three brothers and a sister, the broad lands of the Marqués de Légañès appeared to be sufficient warrant for Victor Marchand's belief that the young lady

---

[1] Wall
[2] Aristocrat

would have a splendid dowry.[3] But how could he dare to imagine that the most fanatical believer in blue blood,[4] in all Spain would give his daughter to the son of a grocer in Paris? Moreover, the French were hated. It was because the Marquis had been suspected of an attempt to raise the country in favor of Ferdinand VII. that General Q , who governed the province, had stationed Victor Marchand's battalion in the little town of Menda to overawe the neighboring districts which received the Marqués de Légañès's word as law. A recent dispatch from Marshal Ney had given ground for fear that the English might ere long effect a landing on the coast, and had indicated the Marquis as being in correspondence with the Cabinet in London.

In spite, therefore, of the welcome with which the Spaniards had received Victor Marchand and his soldiers, that officer was always on his guard. As he went towards the terrace, where he had just surveyed the town and the districts confided to his charge, he had been asking himself what construction he ought to put upon the friendliness which the Marquis had invariably shown him, and how to reconcile the apparent tranquility of the country with his General's uneasiness. But a moment later these thoughts were driven from his mind by the instinct of caution and very legitimate curiosity. It had just struck him that there was a very fair number of lights in the town below. Although it was the Feast of Saint James,[5] he himself had issued orders that very morning that all lights must be put out in the town at the hour prescribed by military regulations. The castle alone had been excepted in this order. Plainly here and there he saw the gleam of bayonets,[6] where his own men were at their accustomed posts; but in the town there was a solemn silence, and not a sign that the Spaniards had given themselves up to the intoxication of a festival. He tried vainly for awhile to explain this breach of the regulations on the part of the inhabitants; the mystery seemed but so much the more obscure because he had left instructions

---

[3] The wealth, in whatever form, a woman brings to her husband when married
[4] A term for aristocracy
[5] July 25th religious celebration of St. James, the apostle of Jesus Christ
[6] Dagger affixed to the end of a riffle

with some of his officers to do police duty that night, and make the rounds of the town.

With the impetuosity of youth, he was about to spring through a gap in the wall preparatory to a rapid scramble down the rocks, thinking to reach a small guard-house at the nearest entrance into the town more quickly than by the beaten track, when a faint sound stopped him. He fancied that he could hear the light footstep of a woman along the graveled garden walk. He turned his head and saw no one; for one moment his eyes were dazzled by the wonderful brightness of the sea, the next he saw a sight so ominous that he stood stock-still with amazement, thinking that his senses must be deceiving him. The white moonbeams lighted the horizon, so that he could distinguish the sails of ships still a considerable distance out at sea. A shudder ran through him; he tried to persuade himself that this was some optical illusion brought about by chance effects of moonlight on the waves; and even as he made the attempt, a hoarse voice called to him by name. The officer glanced at the gap in the wall; saw a soldier's head slowly emerge from it, and knew the grenadier[7] whom he had ordered to accompany him to the castle.

"Is that you, Commandant?"

"Yes. What is it?" returned the young officer in a low voice. A kind of presentiment warned him to act cautiously.

"Those beggars down there are creeping about like worms; and, by your leave, I came as quickly as I could to report my little reconnoitering[8] expedition."

"Go on," answered Victor Marchand.

"I have just been following a man from the castle who came round this way with a lantern in his hand. A lantern is a suspicious matter with a vengeance! I don't imagine that there was any need for that good Christian to be lighting tapers at this time of night. Says I to myself, 'They mean to gobble us up!' and I set myself to dogging his heels; and that is how I found out that there is a pile of faggots, sir, two or three steps away from here."

Suddenly a dreadful shriek rang through the town below, and cut the man short. A light flashed in the Commandant's face, and the poor grenadier dropped

---

[7] Powerful and specialized fighting solider
[8] Information gathering

down with a bullet through his head. Ten paces away a
bonfire flared up like a conflagration. The sounds of music
and laughter ceased all at once in the ballroom; the
silence of death, broken only by groans, succeeded to the
rhythmical murmur of the festival. Then the roar of
cannon sounded from across the white plain of the sea.

A cold sweat broke out on the young officer's forehead.
He had left his sword behind. He knew that his men had
been murdered, and that the English were about to land.
He knew that if he lived he would be dishonored; he saw
himself summoned before a court-martial. For a moment
his eyes measured the depth of the valley; the next, just
as he was about to spring down, Clara's hand caught his.

"Fly!" she cried. "My brothers are coming after me to
kill you. Down yonder at the foot of the cliff you will find
Juanito's Andalusian. Go!"

She thrust him away. The young man gazed at her in
dull bewilderment; but obeying the instinct of self-
preservation, which never deserts even the bravest, he
rushed across the park in the direction pointed out to
him, springing from rock to rock in places unknown to
any save the goats. He heard Clara calling to her brothers
to pursue him; he heard their balls whistling about his
ears; but he reached the foot of the cliff, found the horse,
mounted, and fled with lightning speed.

A few hours later the young officer reached General
G—'s quarters, and found him at dinner with the staff.

"I put my life in your hands!" cried the haggard and
exhausted Commandant of Menda.

He sank into a seat, and told his horrible story. It was
received with an appalling silence.

"It seems to me that you are more to be pitied than to
blame," the terrible General said at last. "You are not
answerable for the Spaniard's crimes, and unless the
Marshal decides otherwise, I acquit you."

These words brought but cold comfort to the
unfortunate officer.

"When the Emperor comes to hear about it!" he cried.

"Oh, he will be for having you shot," said the General,
"but we shall see. Now we will say no more about this," he
added severely, "except to plan a revenge that shall strike
a salutary terror into this country, where they carry on
war like savages."

An hour later a whole regiment, a detachment of
cavalry, and a convoy of artillery were upon the road. The

General and Victor marched at the head of the column. The soldiers had been told of the fate of their comrades, and their rage knew no bounds. The distance between headquarters and the town of Menda was crossed at a well-nigh miraculous speed. Whole villages by the way were found to be under arms; every one of the wretched hamlets was surrounded, and their inhabitants decimated.

It so chanced that the English vessels still lay out at sea, and were no nearer the shore, a fact inexplicable until it was known afterwards that they were artillery transports which had out-sailed the rest of the fleet. So the townsmen of Menda, left without the assistance on which they had reckoned when the sails of the English appeared, were surrounded by French troops almost before they had had time to strike a blow. This struck such terror into them that they offered to surrender at discretion. An impulse of devotion, no isolated instance in the history of the Peninsula, led the actual slayers of the French to offer to give themselves up; seeking in this way to save the town, for from the General's reputation for cruelty it was feared that he would give Menda over to the flames, and put the whole population to the sword. General G— took their offer, stipulating that every soul in the castle, from the lowest servant to the Marquis, should likewise be given up to him. These terms being accepted, the General promised to spare the lives of the rest of the townsmen, and to prohibit his soldiers from pillaging or setting fire to the town. A heavy contribution was levied, and the wealthiest inhabitants were taken as hostages to guarantee payment within twenty-four hours.

The General took every necessary precaution for the safety of his troops, provided for the defense of the place, and refused to billet his men in the houses of the town. After they had bivouacked,[9] he went up to the castle and entered it as a conqueror. The whole family of the Léganès and their household were gagged, shut up in the great ballroom, and closely watched. From the windows it was easy to see the whole length of the terrace above the town.

The staff was established in an adjoining gallery, where the General forthwith held a council as to the best means of preventing the landing of the English. An *aide-*

---

[9] Camped on the outskirts in tents

de-camp[10] was dispatched to Marshal Ney, orders were issued to plant batteries along the coast, and then the General and his staff turned their attention to their prisoners. The two hundred Spaniards given up by the townsfolk were shot down then and there upon the terrace. And after this military execution, the General gave orders to erect gibbets to the number of the prisoners in the ballroom in the same place, and to send for the hangman out of the town. Victor took advantage of the interval before dinner to pay a visit to the prisoners. He soon came back to the General.

"I am come in haste," he faltered out, "to ask a favor."

"You!" exclaimed the General, with bitter irony in his tones.

"Alas!" answered Victor, "it is a sorry favor. The Marquis has seen them erecting the gallows, and hopes that you will commute the punishment for his family; he entreats you to have the nobles beheaded."

"Granted," said the General.

"He further asks that they may be allowed the consolations of religion, and that they may be unbound; they give you their word that they will not attempt to escape."

"That I permit," said the General, "but you are answerable for them."

"The old noble offers you all that he has if you will pardon his youngest son."

"Really!" cried the Commander. "His property is forfeit already to King Joseph." He paused; a contemptuous thought set wrinkles in his forehead, as he added, "I will do better than they ask. I understand what he means by that last request of his. Very good. Let him hand down his name to posterity; but whenever it is mentioned, all Spain shall remember his treason and its punishment! I will give the fortune and his life to any one of the sons who will do the executioner's office. . . . There, don't talk any more about them to me."

Dinner was ready. The officers sat down to satisfy an appetite whetted by hunger. Only one among them was absent from the table—that one was Victor Marchand. After long hesitation, he went to the ballroom, and heard the last sighs of the proud house of Légañès. He looked sadly at the scene before him. Only last night, in this very

---

[10] A high-ranking officer's assistant in the military

room, he had seen their faces whirled past him in the waltz, and he shuddered to think that those girlish heads with those of the three young brothers must fall in a brief space by the executioner's sword. There sat the father and mother, their three sons and two daughters, perfectly motionless, bound to their gilded chairs. Eight serving men stood with their hands tied behind them. These fifteen prisoners, under sentence of death, exchanged grave glances; it was difficult to read the thoughts that filled them from their eyes, but profound resignation and regret that their enterprise should have failed so completely was written on more than one brow.

The impassive soldiers who guarded them respected the grief of their bitter enemies. A gleam of curiosity lighted up all faces when Victor came in. He gave orders that the condemned prisoners should be unbound, and himself unfastened the cords that held Clara a prisoner. She smiled mournfully at him. The officer could not refrain from lightly touching the young girl's arm; he could not help admiring her dark hair, her slender waist. She was a true daughter of Spain, with a Spanish complexion, a Spaniard's eyes, blacker than the raven's wing beneath their long curving lashes.

"Did you succeed?" she asked, with a mournful smile, in which a certain girlish charm still lingered.

Victor could not repress a groan. He looked from the faces of the three brothers to Clara, and again at the three young Spaniards. The first, the oldest of the family, was a man of thirty. He was short, and somewhat ill-made; he looked haughty and proud, but a certain distinction was not lacking in his bearing, and he was apparently no stranger to the delicacy of feeling for which in olden times the chivalry of Spain was famous. His name was Juanito. The second eon, Felipe, was about twenty years of age; he was like his sister Clara; and the youngest was a child of eight. In the features of the little Manuel a painter would have discerned something of that Roman steadfastness which David has given to the children's faces in his Republican *genre* pictures. The old Marquis, with his white hair, might have come down from some canvas of Murillo's. Victor threw back his head in despair after this survey; how should one of these accept the General's offer! Nevertheless he ventured to entrust it to Clara. A shudder ran through the Spanish girl, but she recovered herself almost instantly, and knelt before her father.

"Father," she said, "bid Juanito swear to obey the commands that you shall give him, and we shall be content."

The Marquesa trembled with hope, but as she leant towards her husband and learned Clara's hideous secret, the mother fainted away. Juanito understood it all and leant up like a caged lion. Victor took it upon himself to dismiss the soldiers, after receiving an assurance of entire submission from the Marquis. The servants were led away and given over to the hangman and their fate. When only Victor remained on guard in the room, the old Marqués de Légañès rose to his feet.

"Juanito," he said. For an answer Juanito bowed his head in a way that meant refusal; he sank down into his chair, and fixed tearless eyes upon his father and mother in an intolerable gaze. Clara went over to him and sat on his knee; she put her arms about him, and pressed kisses on his eyelids, saying gaily:

"Dear Juanito, if you but knew how sweet death at your hands will be to me! I shall not be compelled to submit to the hateful touch of the hangman's fingers. You will snatch me away from the evils to come and . . . Dear, kind Juanito, you could not bear the thought of my belonging to any one—well, then?"

The velvet eyes gave Victor a burning glance; she seemed to try to awaken in Juanito's heart his hatred for the French.

"Take courage," said his brother Felipe, "or our well-nigh royal line will be extinct."

Suddenly Clara sprang to her feet. The group round Juanito fell back, and the son who had rebelled with such good reason was confronted with his aged father.

"Juanito, I command you!" said the Marquis solemnly.

The young Count gave no sign, and his father fell on his knees; Clara, Manuel, and Felipe unconsciously followed his example, stretching out suppliant hands to him who must save their family from oblivion, and seeming to echo their father's words.

"Can it be that you lack the fortitude of a Spaniard and true sensibility, my son? Do you mean to keep me on my knees? What right have you to think of your own life and of your own sufferings?—Is this my son, Madame?" the old Marquis added, turning to his wife.

"He will consent to it," cried the mother in agony of soul.

She had seen a slight contraction of Juanito's brows which she, his mother, alone understood.

Mariquita, the second daughter, knelt, with her slender clinging arms about her mother; the hot tears fell from her eyes, and her little brother Manuel upbraided her for weeping. Just at that moment the castle chaplain came in; the whole family surrounded him and led him up to Juanito. Victor felt that he could endure the sight no longer, and with a sign to Clara he hurried from the room to make one last effort for them. He found the General in boisterous spirits; the officers were still sitting over their dinner and drinking together; the wine had loosened their tongues.

An hour later, a hundred of the principal citizens of Menda were summoned to the terrace by the General's orders to witness the execution of the family of Légañès. A detachment had been told off to keep order among the Spanish townsfolk, who were marshaled beneath the gallows whereon the Marquis' servants hung; the feet of those martyrs of their cause all but touched the citizens' heads. Thirty paces away stood the block; the blade of a scimitar[11] glittered upon it, and the executioner stood by in case Juanito should refuse at the last.

The deepest silence prevailed, but before long it was broken by the sound of many footsteps, the measured tramp of a picket of soldiers, and the jingling of their weapons. Mingled with these came other noises—loud talk and laughter from the dinner-table where the officers were sitting; just as the music and the sound of the dancers' feet had drowned the preparations for last night's treacherous butchery.

All eyes turned to the castle, and beheld the family of nobles coming forth with incredible composure to their death. Every brow was serene and calm. One alone among them, haggard and overcome, leant on the arm of the priest, who poured forth all the consolations of religion for the one man who was condemned to live. Then the executioner, like the spectators, knew that Juanito had consented to perform his office for a day. The old Marquis and his wife, Clara and Mariquita, and their two brothers knelt a few paces from the fatal spot. Juanito reached it, guided by the priest. As he stood at the block the executioner plucked him by the sleeve, and took him

---

[11] Sharp, curved sword

aside, probably to give him certain instructions. The confessor so placed the victims that they could not witness the executions, but one and all stood upright and fearless, like Spaniards, as they were.

Clara sprang to her brother's side before the others. "Juanito," she said to him, "be merciful to my lack of courage. Take me first!"

As she spoke, the footsteps of a man running at full speed echoed from the walls, and Victor appeared upon the scene. Clara was kneeling before the block; her white neck seemed to appeal to the blade to fall. The officer turned faint, but he found strength to rush to her side.

"The General grants you your life if you will consent to marry me," he murmured.

The Spanish girl gave the officer a glance full of proud disdain.

"Now, Juanito!" she said in her deep-toned voice.

Her head fell at Victor's feet. A shudder ran through the Marqués de Légañès, a convulsive tremor that she could not control, but she gave no other sign of her anguish.

"Is this where I ought to be, dear Juanito? Is it all right?" little Manuel asked his brother.

"Oh, Mariquita, you are weeping!" Juanito said when his sister came.

"Yes," said the girl; "I am thinking of you, poor Juanito; how unhappy you will be when we are gone."

Then the Marquis' tall figure approached. He looked at the block where his children's blood had been shed, turned to the mute and motionless crowd, and said in a loud voice as he stretched out his hands to Juanito:

"Spaniards! I give my son a father's blessing.—Now, *Marquis,* strike 'without fear;' thou art 'without reproach.'"

But when his mother came near, leaning on the confessor's arm—"She fed me from her breast!" Juanito cried, in tones that drew a cry of horror from the crowd. The uproarious mirth of the officers over their wine died away before that terrible cry. The Marquesa knew that Juanito's courage was exhausted; at one bound she sprang to the balustrade,[12] leapt forth, and was dashed to pieces on the rocks below. A cry of admiration broke from the spectators. Juanito swooned.

---

[12] Bannister or railing with ornate supports

"General," said an officer, half drunk by this time, "Marchand has just been telling me something about this execution; I will wager that it was not by your orders "

"Are you forgetting, gentlemen, that in a month's time five hundred families in France will be in mourning, and that we are still in Spain?" cried General G—. "Do you want us to leave our bones here?"

But not a man at the table, not even a subaltern,[13] dared to empty his glass after that speech.

In spite of the respect in which all men hold the Marqués de Légañès, in spite of the title of *El Verdugo* (the executioner) conferred upon him as a patent of nobility by the King of Spain, the great noble is consumed by a gnawing grief. He lives a retired life, and seldom appears in public. The burden of his heroic crime weighs heavily upon him, and he seems to wait impatiently till the birth of a second son shall release him, and he may go to join the Shades[14] that never cease to haunt him.

PARIS, *October* 1830.

---

[13] Low-ranking officer
[14] Spirits

NATHANIEL HAWTHORNE
(1804-1864)

Φ

The Minister's Black Veil

No anthology of greatest horror stories from 1800-1849 would be complete without one from Nathaniel Hawthorne. His greatest horror tales are: "The Minister's Black Veil," "Dr. Heidegger's Experiment," "Rappaccini's Daughter," "The Wedding Knell," "Young Goodman Brown," and "The Ambitious Guest," in that order. Edgar Allan Poe, not focusing on any particular genre, recognized the first two when he reviewed Hawthorne's "Twice Told Tales" in *Graham's Magazine* of April 1842: "Among his best, we may briefly mention 'The Hollow of the Three Hills,' 'The Minister's Black Veil;' 'Wakefield;' 'Mr. Higginbotham's Catastrophe;' 'Fancy's Show-Box;' 'Dr. Heidegger's Experiment;' 'David Swan;' 'The Wedding Knell,' and 'The White Old Maid.' It is remarkable that all these, with one exception, are from the first volume." This story is lacking the traditional horror elements of blood, death, or even murder. It is, however, the creepiest story ever written by Nathaniel Hawthorne in the horror genre and cannot be denied from this collection.

The Minister's Black Veil

A PARABLE[1]

THE SEXTON STOOD IN the porch of Milford meeting-house, pulling busily at the bell-rope. The old people of the village came stooping along the street. Children, with bright faces, tripped merrily beside their parents, or mimicked a graver gait, in the conscious dignity of their Sunday clothes. Spruce bachelors looked sidelong at the pretty maidens, and fancied that the Sabbath sunshine made them prettier than on week days. When the throng had mostly streamed into the porch, the sexton began to toll the bell, keeping his eye on the Reverend Mr. Hooper's door. The first glimpse of the clergyman's figure was the signal for the bell to cease its summons.

"But what has good Parson Hooper got upon his face?" cried the sexton in astonishment.

All within hearing immediately turned about, and beheld the semblance of Mr. Hooper, pacing slowly his meditative way towards the meetinghouse. With one accord they started, expressing more wonder than if some strange minister were coming to dust the cushions of Mr. Hooper's pulpit.

"Are you sure it is our parson?" inquired Goodman Gray of the sexton.

"Of a certainty it is good Mr. Hooper," replied the sexton. "He was to have exchanged pulpits with Parson Shute, of Westbury; but Parson Shute sent to excuse himself yesterday, being to preach a funeral sermon."

The cause of so much amazement may appear sufficiently slight. Mr. Hooper, a gentlemanly person, of about thirty, though still a bachelor, was dressed with due clerical neatness, as if a careful wife had starched his

---

[1] Another clergyman in New England, Mr. Joseph Moody, of York, Maine, made himself remarkable by the same eccentricity that is here related of the Reverend Mr. Hooper. In his case, however, the symbol had a different import. In early life he had accidentally killed a beloved friend, and from that day till the hour of his own death, he hid his face from men.

band, and brushed the weekly dust from his Sunday's garb. There was but one thing remarkable in his appearance. Swathed about his forehead, and hanging down over his face, so low as to be shaken by his breath, Mr. Hooper had on a black veil. On a nearer view it seemed to consist of two folds of crape, which entirely concealed his features, except the mouth and chin, but probably did not intercept his sight, further than to give a darkened aspect to all living and inanimate things. With this gloomy shade before him, good Mr. Hooper walked onward, at a slow and quiet pace, stooping somewhat, and looking on the ground, as is customary with abstracted men, yet nodding kindly to those of his parishioners who still waited on the meeting-house steps. But so wonder-struck were they that his greeting hardly met with a return.

"I can't really feel as if good Mr. Hooper's face was behind that piece of crape," said the sexton.

"I don't like it," muttered an old woman, as she hobbled into the meeting-house. "He has changed himself into something awful, only by hiding his face."

"Our parson has gone mad!" cried Goodman Gray, following him across the threshold.

A rumor of some unaccountable phenomenon had preceded Mr. Hooper into the meeting-house, and set all the congregation astir. Few could refrain from twisting their heads towards the door; many stood upright, and turned directly about; while several little boys clambered upon the seats, and came down again with a terrible racket. There was a general bustle, a rustling of the women's gowns and shuffling of the men's feet, greatly at variance with that hushed repose which should attend the entrance of the minister. But Mr. Hooper appeared not to notice the perturbation of his people. He entered with an almost noiseless step, bent his head mildly to the pews on each side, and bowed as he passed his oldest parishioner, a white-haired great grandsire, who occupied an arm-chair in the centre of the aisle. It was strange to observe how slowly this venerable man became conscious of something singular in the appearance of his pastor. He seemed not fully to partake of the prevailing wonder, till Mr. Hooper had ascended the stairs, and showed himself in the pulpit, face to face with his congregation, except for the black veil. That mysterious emblem was never once withdrawn. It shook with his measured breath, as he gave out the psalm; it threw its obscurity between him and the holy page, as he read the Scriptures; and while he prayed, the veil lay heavily on his uplifted countenance. Did he seek to hide it from the dread Being whom he was addressing?

Such was the effect of this simple piece of crape, that more than one woman of delicate nerves was forced to leave the meeting-house. Yet perhaps the pale-faced congregation was almost as fearful a sight to the minister, as his black veil to them.

Mr. Hooper had the reputation of a good preacher, but not an energetic one: he strove to win his people heavenward by mild, persuasive influences, rather than to drive them thither by the thunders of the Word. The sermon which he now delivered was marked by the same characteristics of style and manner as the general series of his pulpit oratory. But there was something, either in the sentiment of the discourse itself, or in the imagination of the auditors, which made it greatly the most powerful effort that they had ever heard from their pastor's lips. It was tinged, rather more darkly than usual, with the gentle gloom of Mr. Hooper's temperament. The subject had reference to secret sin, and those sad mysteries which we hide from our nearest and dearest, and would fain conceal from our own consciousness, even forgetting that the Omniscient can detect them. A subtle power was breathed into his words. Each member of the congregation, the most innocent girl, and the man of hardened breast, felt as if the preacher had crept upon them, behind his awful veil, and discovered their hoarded iniquity of deed or thought. Many spread their clasped hands on their bosoms. There was nothing terrible in what Mr. Hooper said, at least, no violence; and yet, with every tremor of his melancholy voice, the hearers quaked. An unsought pathos came hand in hand with awe. So sensible were the audience of some unwonted attribute in their minister, that they longed for a breath of wind to blow aside the veil, almost believing that a stranger's visage would be discovered, though the form, gesture, and voice were those of Mr. Hooper.

At the close of the services, the people hurried out with indecorous confusion, eager to communicate their pent-up amazement, and conscious of lighter spirits the moment they lost sight of the black veil. Some gathered in little circles, huddled closely together, with their mouths all whispering in the centre; some went homeward alone, wrapt in silent meditation; some talked loudly, and profaned the Sabbath day with ostentatious laughter. A few shook their sagacious heads, intimating that they could penetrate the mystery; while one or two affirmed that there was no mystery at all, but only that Mr. Hooper's eyes were so weakened by the midnight lamp, as to require a shade. After a brief interval, forth came good Mr. Hooper also, in the rear of his flock. Turning his veiled face from one group to another, he paid due reverence to the hoary heads, saluted the middle aged with kind dignity as their friend and spiritual guide, greeted the young with mingled authority and love, and laid his hands on the little children's heads to bless them. Such was always his custom on the Sabbath day. Strange and bewildered looks repaid him for his courtesy. None, as on former occasions, aspired to the honor of walking by their pastor's side. Old Squire Saunders, doubtless by an accidental lapse of memory, neglected to invite Mr. Hooper to his table, where the good clergyman had been wont to bless the food, almost every Sunday since his settlement. He returned, therefore, to the parsonage, and, at the moment of closing the door, was observed to look back upon the people, all of whom had their eyes fixed upon the minister. A sad smile gleamed faintly from beneath the black veil, and flickered about his mouth, glimmering as he disappeared.

"How strange," said a lady, "that a simple black veil, such as any woman might wear on her bonnet, should become such a terrible thing on Mr. Hooper's face!"

"Something must surely be amiss with Mr. Hooper's intellects," observed her husband, the physician of the village. "But the strangest part of the affair is the effect of this vagary, even on a sober-minded man like myself. The black veil, though it covers only our pastor's face, throws its influence over his whole person, and makes him ghostlike from head to foot. Do you not feel it so?"

"Truly do I," replied the lady; "and I would not be alone with him for the world. I wonder he is not afraid to be alone with himself!"

"Men sometimes are so," said her husband.

The afternoon service was attended with similar circumstances. At its conclusion, the bell tolled for the funeral of a young lady. The relatives and friends were assembled in the house, and the more distant acquaintances stood about the door, speaking of the good qualities of the deceased, when their talk was interrupted by the appearance of Mr. Hooper, still covered with his black veil. It was now an appropriate emblem. The clergyman stepped into the room where the corpse was laid, and bent over the coffin, to take a last farewell of his deceased parishioner. As he stooped, the veil hung straight down from his forehead, so that, if her eyelids had not been closed forever, the dead maiden might have seen his face. Could Mr. Hooper be fearful of her glance, that he so hastily caught back the black veil? A person who watched the interview between the dead and living, scrupled not to affirm, that, at the instant when the clergyman's features were disclosed, the corpse had slightly shuddered, rustling the shroud and muslin cap, though the countenance retained the composure of death. A superstitious old woman was the only witness of this prodigy. From the coffin Mr. Hooper passed into the chamber of the mourners, and thence to the head of the staircase, to make the funeral prayer. It was a tender and heart-dissolving prayer, full of sorrow, yet so imbued with celestial hopes, that the music of a heavenly harp, swept by the fingers of the dead, seemed faintly to be heard among the saddest accents of the minister. The people trembled, though they but darkly understood him when he prayed that they, and himself, and all of mortal race, might be ready, as he trusted this young maiden had been, for the dreadful hour that should snatch the veil from their faces. The bearers went heavily forth, and the mourners followed, saddening all the street, with the dead before them, and Mr. Hooper in his black veil behind.

"Why do you look back?" said one in the procession to his partner.

"I had a fancy," replied she, "that the minister and the maiden's spirit were walking hand in hand."

"And so had I, at the same moment," said the other.

That night, the handsomest couple in Milford village were to be joined in wedlock. Though reckoned a melancholy man, Mr. Hooper had a placid cheerfulness for such occasions, which often excited a sympathetic smile where livelier merriment would have been thrown away. There was no quality of his disposition which made him more beloved than this. The company at the wedding awaited his arrival with impatience, trusting that the strange awe, which had gathered over him throughout the day, would now be dispelled. But such was not the result. When Mr. Hooper came, the first thing that their eyes rested on was the same horrible black veil, which had added deeper gloom to the funeral, and could portend nothing but evil to the wedding. Such was its immediate effect on the guests that a cloud seemed to have rolled duskily from beneath the black crape, and dimmed the light of the candles. The bridal pair stood up before the minister.

But the bride's cold fingers quivered in the tremulous hand of the bridegroom, and her deathlike paleness caused a whisper that the maiden who had been buried a few hours before was come from her grave to be married. If ever another wedding were so dismal, it was that famous one where they tolled the wedding knell. After performing the ceremony, Mr. Hooper raised a glass of wine to his lips, wishing happiness to the new-married couple in a strain of mild pleasantry that ought to have brightened the features of the guests, like a cheerful gleam from the hearth. At that instant, catching a glimpse of his figure in the looking-glass, the black veil involved his own spirit in the horror with which it overwhelmed all others. His frame shuddered, his lips grew white, he spilt the untasted wine upon the carpet, and rushed forth into the darkness. For the Earth, too, had on her Black Veil.

The next day, the whole village of Milford talked of little else than Parson Hooper's black veil. That, and the mystery concealed behind it, supplied a topic for discussion between acquaintances meeting in the street, and good women gossiping at their open windows. It was the first item of news that the tavern-keeper told to his guests. The children babbled of it on their way to school. One imitative little imp covered his face with an old black handkerchief, thereby so affrighting his playmates that the panic seized himself, and he well-nigh lost his wits by his own waggery.

It was remarkable that all of the busybodies and impertinent people in the parish, not one ventured to put the plain question to Mr. Hooper, wherefore he did this thing. Hitherto, whenever there appeared the slightest call for such interference, he had never lacked advisers, nor shown himself averse to be guided by their judgment. If he erred at all, it was by so painful a degree of self-distrust, that even the mildest censure would lead him to consider an indifferent action as a crime. Yet, though so well acquainted with this amiable weakness, no individual among his parishioners chose to make the black veil a subject of friendly remonstrance. There was a feeling of dread, neither plainly confessed nor carefully concealed, which caused each to shift the responsibility upon another, till at length it was found expedient to send a deputation of the church, in order to deal with Mr. Hooper about the mystery, before it should grow into a scandal.

Never did an embassy so ill discharge its duties. The minister received then with friendly courtesy, but became silent, after they were seated, leaving to his visitors the whole burden of introducing their important business. The topic, it might be supposed, was obvious enough. There was the black veil swathed round Mr. Hooper's forehead, and concealing every feature above his placid mouth, on which, at times, they could perceive the glimmering of a melancholy smile. But that piece of crape, to their imagination, seemed to hang down before his heart, the symbol of a fearful secret between him and them. Were the veil but cast aside, they might speak freely of it, but not till then. Thus they sat a considerable time, speechless, confused, and shrinking uneasily from Mr. Hooper's eye, which they felt to be fixed upon them with an invisible glance. Finally, the deputies returned abashed to their constituents, pronouncing the matter too weighty to be handled, except by a council of the churches, if, indeed, it might not require a general synod.

But there was one person in the village unappalled by the awe with which the black veil had impressed all beside herself. When the deputies returned without an explanation, or even venturing to demand one, she, with the calm energy of her character, determined to chase away the strange cloud that appeared to be settling round Mr. Hooper, every moment more darkly than before. As his plighted wife, it should be her privilege to know what the black veil concealed. At the minister's first visit, therefore, she entered upon the subject with a direct simplicity, which made the task easier both for him and her. After he had seated himself, she fixed her eyes steadfastly upon the veil, but could discern nothing of the dreadful gloom that had so overawed the multitude: it was but a double fold of crape, hanging down from his forehead to his mouth, and slightly stirring with his breath.

"No," said she aloud, and smiling, "there is nothing terrible in this piece of crape, except that it hides a face which I am always glad to look upon. Come, good sir, let the sun shine from behind the cloud. First lay aside your black veil: then tell me why you put it on."

Mr. Hooper's smile glimmered faintly.

"There is an hour to come," said he, "when all of us shall cast aside our veils. Take it not amiss, beloved friend, if I wear this piece of crape till then."

"Your words are a mystery, too," returned the young lady. "Take away the veil from them, at least."

"Elizabeth, I will," said he, "so far as my vow may suffer me. Know, then, this veil is a type and a symbol, and I am bound to wear it ever, both in light and darkness, in solitude and before the gaze of multitudes, and as with strangers, so with my familiar friends. No mortal eye will see it withdrawn. This dismal shade must separate me from the world: even you, Elizabeth, can never come behind it!"

"What grievous affliction hath befallen you," she earnestly inquired, "that you should thus darken your eyes forever?"

"If it be a sign of mourning," replied Mr. Hooper, "I, perhaps, like most other mortals, have sorrows dark enough to be typified by a black veil."

"But what if the world will not believe that it is the type of an innocent sorrow?" urged Elizabeth. "Beloved and respected as you are, there may be whispers that you hide your face under the consciousness of secret sin. For the sake of your holy office, do away this scandal!"

The color rose into her cheeks as she intimated the nature of the rumors that were already abroad in the village. But Mr. Hooper's mildness did not forsake him. He even smiled again—that same sad smile, which always appeared like a faint glimmering of light, proceeding from the obscurity beneath the veil.

"If I hide my face for sorrow, there is cause enough," he merely replied; "and if I cover it for secret sin, what mortal might not do the same?"

And with this gentle, but unconquerable obstinacy did he resist all her entreaties. At length Elizabeth sat silent. For a few moments she appeared lost in thought, considering, probably, what new methods might be tried to withdraw her lover from so dark a fantasy, which, if it had no other meaning, was perhaps a symptom of mental disease. Though of a firmer character than his own, the tears rolled down her cheeks. But, in an instant, as it were, a new feeling took the place of sorrow: her eyes were fixed insensibly on the black veil, when, like a sudden twilight in the air, its terrors fell around her. She arose, and stood trembling before him.

"And do you feel it then, at last?" said he mournfully.

She made no reply, but covered her eyes with her hand, and turned to leave the room. He rushed forward and caught her arm.

"Have patience with me, Elizabeth!" cried he, passionately. "Do not desert me, though this veil must be between us here on earth. Be mine, and hereafter there shall be no veil over my face, no darkness between our souls! It is but a mortal veil—it is not for eternity! O! you know not how lonely I am, and how frightened, to be alone behind my black veil. Do not leave me in this miserable obscurity forever!"

"Lift the veil but once, and look me in the face," said she.

"Never! It cannot be!" replied Mr. Hooper.

"Then farewell!" said Elizabeth.

She withdrew her arm from his grasp, and slowly departed, pausing at the door, to give one long shuddering gaze, that seemed almost to penetrate the mystery of the black veil. But, even amid his grief, Mr. Hooper smiled to think that only a material emblem had separated him from happiness, though the horrors, which it shadowed forth, must be drawn darkly between the fondest of lovers.

From that time no attempts were made to remove Mr. Hooper's black veil, or, by a direct appeal, to discover the secret which it was supposed to hide. By persons who claimed a superiority to popular prejudice, it was reckoned merely an eccentric whim, such as often mingles with the sober actions of men otherwise rational, and tinges them all with its own semblance of insanity. But with the multitude, good Mr. Hooper was irreparably a bugbear. He could not walk the street with any peace of mind, so conscious was he that the gentle and timid would turn aside to avoid him, and that others would make it a point of hardihood to throw themselves in his way. The impertinence of the latter class compelled him to give up his customary walk at sunset to the burial ground; for when he leaned pensively over the gate, there would always be faces behind the gravestones, peeping at his black veil. A fable went the rounds that the stare of the dead people drove him thence. It grieved him, to the very depth of his kind heart, to observe how the children fled from his approach, breaking up their merriest sports, while his melancholy figure was yet afar off. Their instinctive dread caused him to feel more strongly than aught else, that a preternatural horror was interwoven with the threads of the black crape.

In truth, his own antipathy to the veil was known to be so great, that he never willingly passed before a mirror, nor stooped to drink at a still fountain, lest, in its peaceful bosom, he should be affrighted by himself. This was what gave plausibility to the whispers, that Mr. Hooper's conscience tortured him for some great crime too horrible to be entirely concealed, or otherwise than so obscurely intimated. Thus, from beneath the black veil, there rolled a cloud into the sunshine, an ambiguity of sin or sorrow, which enveloped the poor minister, so that love or sympathy could never reach him. It was said that ghost and fiend consorted with him there. With self-shudderings and outward terrors, he walked continually in its shadow, groping darkly within his own soul, or gazing through a medium that saddened the whole world. Even the lawless wind, it was believed, respected his dreadful secret, and never blew aside the veil. But still good Mr. Hooper sadly smiled at the pale visages of the worldly throng as he passed by.

Among all its bad influences, the black veil had the one desirable effect, of making its wearer a very efficient clergyman. By the aid of his mysterious emblem—for there was no other apparent cause—he became a man of awful power over souls that were in agony for sin. His converts always regarded him with a dread peculiar to themselves, affirming, though but figuratively, that, before he brought them to celestial light, they had been with him behind the black veil. Its gloom, indeed, enabled him to sympathize with all dark affections. Dying sinners cried aloud for Mr. Hooper, and would not yield their breath till he appeared; though ever, as he stooped to whisper consolation, they shuddered at the veiled face so near their own. Such were the terrors of the black veil, even when Death had bared his visage! Strangers came long distances to attend service at his church, with the mere idle purpose of gazing at his figure, because it was forbidden them to behold his face. But many were made to quake ere they departed! Once, during Governor Belcher's administration, Mr. Hooper was appointed to preach the election sermon. Covered with his black veil, he stood before the chief magistrate, the council, and the representatives, and wrought so deep an impression, that the legislative measures of that year were characterized by all the gloom and piety of our earliest ancestral sway.

In this manner Mr. Hooper spent a long life, irreproachable in outward act, yet shrouded in dismal suspicions; kind and loving, though unloved, and dimly feared; a man apart from men, shunned in their health and joy, but ever summoned to their aid in mortal anguish. As years wore on, shedding their snows above his sable veil, he acquired a name throughout the New England churches, and they called him Father Hooper. Nearly all his parishioners, who were of mature age when he was settled, had been borne away by many a funeral: he had one congregation in the church, and a more crowded one in the churchyard; and having wrought so late into the evening, and done his work so well, it was now good Father Hooper's turn to rest.

Several persons were visible by the shaded candlelight, in the death chamber of the old clergyman. Natural connections he had none. But there was the decorously grave, though unmoved physician, seeking only to mitigate the last pangs of the patient whom he could not save. There were the deacons, and other eminently pious members of his church. There, also, was the Reverend Mr. Clark, of Westbury, a young and zealous divine, who had ridden in haste to pray by the bedside of the expiring minister. There was the nurse, no hired handmaiden of death, but one whose calm affection had endured thus long in secrecy, in solitude, amid the chill of age, and would not perish, even at the dying hour. Who, but Elizabeth! And there lay the hoary head of good Father Hooper upon the death pillow, with the black veil still swathed about his brow, and reaching down over his face, so that each more difficult gasp of his faint breath caused it to stir. All through life that piece of crape had hung between him and the world: it had separated him from cheerful brotherhood and woman's love, and kept him in that saddest of all prisons, his own heart; and still it lay upon his face, as if to deepen the gloom of his darksome chamber, and shade him from the sunshine of eternity.

For some time previous, his mind had been confused, wavering doubtfully between the past and the present, and hovering forward, as it were, at intervals, into the indistinctness of the world to come. There had been feverish turns, which tossed him from side to side, and wore away what little strength he had. But in his most convulsive struggles, and in the wildest vagaries of his intellect, when no other thought retained its sober influence, he still showed an awful solicitude lest the black veil should slip aside. Even if his bewildered soul could have forgotten, there was a faithful woman at this pillow, who, with averted eyes, would have covered that aged face, which she had last beheld in the comeliness of manhood. At length the death-stricken old man lay quietly in the torpor of mental and bodily exhaustion, with an imperceptible pulse, and breath that grew fainter and fainter, except when a long, deep, and irregular inspiration seemed to prelude the flight of his spirit.

The minister of Westbury approached the bedside.

"Venerable Father Hooper," said he, "the moment of your release is at hand. Are you ready for the lifting of the veil that shuts in time from eternity?"

Father Hooper at first replied merely by a feeble motion of his head; then, apprehensive, perhaps, that his meaning might be doubted, he exerted himself to speak.

"Yea," said he, in faint accents, "my soul hath a patient weariness until that veil be lifted."

"And is it fitting," resumed the Reverend Mr. Clark, "that a man so given to prayer, of such a blameless example, holy in deed and thought, so far as mortal judgment may pronounce; is it fitting that a father in the church should leave a shadow on his memory, that may seem to blacken a life so pure? I pray you, my venerable brother, let not this thing be! Suffer us to be gladdened by your triumphant aspect as you go to your reward. Before the veil of eternity be lifted, let me cast aside this black veil from your face!"

And thus speaking, the Reverend Mr. Clark bent forward to reveal the mystery of so many years. But, exerting a sudden energy, that made all the beholders stand aghast, Father Hooper snatched both his hands from beneath the bedclothes, and pressed them strongly on the black veil, resolute to struggle, if the minister of Westbury would contend with a dying man.

"Never!" cried the veiled clergyman. "On earth, never!"

"Dark old man!" exclaimed the affrighted minister, "with what horrible crime upon your soul are you now passing to the judgment?"

Father Hooper's breath heaved; it rattled in his throat; but, with a mighty effort, grasping forward with his hands, he caught hold of life, and held it back till he should speak. He even raised himself in bed; and there he sat, shivering with the arms of death around him, while the black veil hung down, awful, at that last moment, in the gathered terrors of a lifetime. And yet the faint, sad smile, so often there, now seemed to glimmer from its obscurity, and linger on Father Hooper's lips.

"Why do you tremble at me alone?" cried he, turning his veiled face round the circle of pale spectators. "Tremble also at each other! Have men avoided me, and women shown no pity, and children screamed and fled, only for my black veil? What, but the mystery which it obscurely typifies, has made this piece of crape so awful? When the friend shows his inmost heart to his friend; the lover to his best beloved; when man does not vainly shrink from the eye of his Creator, loathsomely treasuring up the secret of his sin; then deem me a monster, for the symbol beneath which I have lived, and die! I look around me, and, lo! on every visage a Black Veil!"

While his auditors shrank from one another, in mutual affright, Father Hooper fell back upon his pillow, a veiled corpse, with a faint smile lingering on the lips. Still veiled, they laid him in his coffin, and a veiled corpse they bore him to the grave. The grass of many years has sprung up and withered on that grave, the burial stone is moss-grown, and good Mr. Hooper's face is dust; but awful is still the thought that it mouldered beneath the Black Veil!

EDGAR ALLAN POE
(1809-1849)

Φ

The Pit and the Pendulum

Poe's famous tale "The Pit and the Pendulum," was first published in *The Gift* for 1843. It is his horrific perspective on the Spanish Inquisition that occurred until 1808 when the French invaded Spain. While differing elements of the story appeared in publication before Poe wrote the tale, he combined them with original elements and a perfect gothic style to render it an unforgettable horror tale.

Here Poe incorporates the most horrific use of rats experienced in the literature for this time period. Poe was very effective in using animals in his horror tales and poems. The first was in "The Conqueror Worm" of 1842, followed in 1843 by "The Black Cat," with its obvious use of a feline, and the rats of this story. He outdid them all in early 1845 with his unique use of a bird in "The Raven."

"The Pit and the Pendulum" incorporates the use of verticality in the swinging blade as it moves ever downward. One nearly hears the hiss of the blade as it passes the victim. Poe's fantastic use of the auditory in this tale makes readers feel each pass of the blade. One can also hear it. That is why "The Pit and the Pendulum"

belongs in this collection along with three other stories by
Poe.

The Pit and the Pendulum

Impia tortorum longos hic turba furores
Sanguinis innocui, non satiata, aluit.
Sospite nunc patria, fracto nunc funeris antro,
Mors ubi dira fuit vita salusque patent.[1]

(Quatrain composed for the gates of a market to be erected upon the site of the Jacobin Club House at Paris.)

I WAS SICK — SICK UNTO DEATH with that long agony; and when they at length unbound me, and I was permitted to sit, I felt that my senses were leaving me. The sentence — the dread sentence of death — was the last of distinct accentuation which reached my ears. After that, the sound of the inquisitorial voices seemed merged in one dreamy indeterminate hum. It conveyed to my soul the idea of *revolution* — perhaps from its association in fancy with the burr of a mill wheel. This only for a brief period; for presently I heard no more. Yet, for a while, I saw; but with how terrible an exaggeration!

I saw the lips of the black-robed judges. They appeared to me white — whiter than the sheet upon which I trace these words — and thin even to grotesqueness; thin with the intensity of their expression of firmness — of immoveable resolution — of stern contempt of human torture. I saw that the decrees of what to me was Fate, were still issuing from those lips. I saw them writhe with a deadly locution. I saw them fashion the syllables of my name; and I shuddered because no sound succeeded. I saw, too, for a few moments of delirious horror, the soft and nearly imperceptible waving of the sable[2] draperies which enwrapped the walls of the apartment. And then my

---

[1] Here the wicked mob, unappeased, long cherished a hatred of innocent blood. Now that the fatherland is saved, and the cave of death demolished; where grim death has been, life and health appear; "Tales & Sketches": Thomas Ollive Mabbott, *University of Illinois Press*, 697, 1978, Vol. I

[2] Black

vision fell upon the seven tall candles[3] upon the table. At first they wore the aspect of charity, and seemed white and slender angels who would save me; but then, all at once, there came a most deadly nausea over my spirit, and I felt every fibre in my frame thrill as if I had touched the wire of a galvanic battery,[4] while the angel forms became meaningless spectres, with heads of flame, and I saw that from them there would be no help. And then there stole into my fancy, like a rich musical note, the thought of what sweet rest there must be in the grave. The thought came gently and stealthily, and it seemed long before it attained full appreciation; but just as my spirit came at length properly to feel and entertain it, the figures of the judges vanished, as if magically, from before me; the tall candles sank into nothingness; their flames went out utterly; the blackness of darkness supervened; all sensations appeared swallowed up in a mad rushing descent as of the soul into Hades. Then silence, and stillness, and night were the universe.

I had swooned; but still will not say that all of consciousness was lost. What of it there remained I will not attempt to define, or even to describe; yet all was not lost. In the deepest slumber — no! In delirium — no! In a swoon — no! In death — no! even in the grave all *is not* lost. Else there is no immortality for man. Arousing from the most profound of slumbers, we break the gossamer web of some dream. Yet in a second afterward, (so frail may that web have been) we remember not that we have dreamed. In the return to life from the swoon there are two stages; first, that of the sense of mental or spiritual; secondly, that of the sense of physical, existence. It seems probable that if, upon reaching the second stage, we could recall the impressions of the first, we should find these impressions eloquent in memories of the gulf beyond. And that gulf is — what? How at least shall we distinguish its shadows from those of the tomb? But if the impressions of what I have termed the first stage, are not, at will, recalled, yet, after long interval, do they not come unbidden, while we marvel whence they come? He who has never swooned, is not he who finds strange palaces and wildly familiar faces in coals that glow; is not he who

---

[3] Perhaps symbolic of the seven stages of life, just as Poe presented us with the seven rooms in "Masque of the Red Death"

[4] Rudimentary battery used to shock people back to life

beholds floating in mid-air the sad visions that the many may not view; is not he who ponders over the perfume of some novel flower — is not he whose brain grows bewildered with the meaning of some musical cadence which has never before arrested his attention.

Amid frequent and thoughtful endeavors to remember; amid earnest struggles to regather some token of the state of seeming nothingness into which my soul had lapsed, there have been moments when I have dreamed of success; there have been brief, very brief periods when I have conjured up remembrances which the lucid reason of a later epoch[5] assures me could have had reference only to that condition of seeming unconsciousness. These shadows of memory tell, indistinctly, of tall figures that lifted and bore me in silence down — down — still down — till a hideous dizziness oppressed me at the mere idea of the interminableness of the descent. They tell also of a vague horror at my heart, on account of that heart's unnatural stillness. Then comes a sense of sudden motionlessness throughout all things; as if those who bore me (a ghastly train!) had outrun, in their descent, the limits of the limitless, and paused from the wearisomeness of their toil. After this I call to mind flatness and dampness; and then all is *madness* — the madness of a memory which busies itself among forbidden things.

Very suddenly there came back to my soul motion and sound — the tumultuous motion of the heart, and, in my ears, the sound of its beating. Then a pause in which all is blank. Then again sound, and motion, and touch — a tingling sensation pervading my frame. Then the mere consciousness of existence, without thought — a condition which lasted long. Then, very suddenly, *thought*, and shuddering terror, and earnest endeavor to comprehend my true state. Then a strong desire to lapse into insensibility. Then a rushing revival of soul and a successful effort to move. And now a full memory of the trial, of the judges, of the sable draperies, of the sentence, of the sickness, of the swoon. Then entire forgetfulness of all that followed; of all that a later day and much earnestness of endeavor have enabled me vaguely to recall.

So far, I had not opened my eyes. I felt that I lay upon my back, unbound. I reached out my hand, and it fell

---

[5] Point in time

heavily upon something damp and hard. There I suffered it to remain for many minutes, while I strove to imagine where and *what* I could be. I longed, yet dared not to employ my vision. I dreaded the first glance at objects around me. It was not that I feared to look upon things horrible, but that I grew aghast lest there should be *nothing* to see. At length, with a wild desperation at heart, I quickly unclosed my eyes. My worst thoughts, then, were confirmed. The blackness of eternal night encompassed me. I struggled for breath. The intensity of the darkness seemed to oppress and stifle me. The atmosphere was intolerably close.

I still lay quietly, and made effort to exercise my reason. I brought to mind the inquisitorial proceedings, and attempted from that point to deduce my real condition. The sentence had passed; and it appeared to me that a very long interval of time had since elapsed. Yet not for a moment did I suppose myself actually dead. Such a supposition, notwithstanding what we read in fiction, is altogether inconsistent with real existence; — but where and in what state was I? The condemned to death, I knew, perished usually at the *autos-da-fe,*[6] and one of these had been held on the very night of the day of my trial. Had I been remanded to my dungeon, to await the next sacrifice, which would not take place for many months? This I at once saw could not be. Victims had been in immediate demand. Moreover, my dungeon, as well as all the condemned cells at Toledo,[7] had stone floors, and light was not altogether excluded.

A fearful idea now suddenly drove the blood in torrents upon my heart, and for a brief period, I once more relapsed into insensibility. Upon recovering, I at once started to my feet, trembling convulsively in every fibre. I thrust my arms wildly above and around me in all directions. I felt nothing; yet dreaded to move a step, lest I should be impeded by the walls of a *tomb.* Perspiration burst from every pore, and stood in cold big beads upon my forehead. The agony of suspense grew at length intolerable, and I cautiously moved forward, with my arms extended, and my eyes straining from their sockets, in the hope of catching some faint ray of light. I proceeded for many paces; but still all was blackness and vacancy. I

---

[6] Indictment proceeding
[7] City in Spain near Tagus River

breathed more freely. It seemed evident that mine was not, at least, the most hideous of fates.

And now, as I still continued to step cautiously onward, there came thronging upon my recollection a thousand vague rumors of the horrors of Toledo. Of the dungeons there had been strange things narrated — fables I had always deemed them — but yet strange, and too ghastly to repeat, save in a whisper. Was I left to perish of starvation in this subterranean world of darkness; or what fate, perhaps even more fearful, awaited me? That the result would be death, and a death of more than customary bitterness, I knew too well the character of my judges to doubt. The mode and the hour were all that occupied or distracted me.

My outstretched hands at length encountered some solid obstruction. It was a wall, seemingly of stone masonry — very smooth, slimy, and cold. I followed it up; stepping with all the careful distrust with which certain antique narratives had inspired me. This process, however, afforded me no means of ascertaining the dimensions of my dungeon; as I might make its circuit, and return to the point whence I set out, without being aware of the fact; so perfectly uniform seemed the wall. I therefore sought the knife which had been in my pocket, when led into the inquisitorial chamber; but it was gone; my clothes had been exchanged for a wrapper of coarse serge.[8]

I had thought of forcing the blade in some minute crevice of the masonry, so as to identify my point of departure. The difficulty, nevertheless, was but trivial; although, in the disorder of my fancy, it seemed at first insuperable. I tore apart of the hem from the robe and placed the fragment at full length, and at right angles to the wall. In groping my way around the prison, I could not fail to encounter this rag upon completing the circuit. So, at least I thought: but I had not counted upon the extent of the dungeon, or upon my own weakness. The ground was moist and slippery. I staggered onward for some time, when I stumbled and fell. My excessive fatigue induced me to remain prostrate;[9] and sleep soon overtook me as I lay.

Upon awaking, and stretching forth an arm, I found beside me a loaf and a pitcher with water. I was too much

---

[8] Material of worsted wool
[9] Face down

exhausted to reflect upon this circumstance, but ate and drank with avidity. Shortly afterward, I resumed my tour around the prison, and with much toil came at last upon the fragment of the serge. Up to the period when I fell I had counted fifty-two paces, and upon resuming my walk, I had counted forty-eight more; — when I arrived at the rag. There were in all, then, a hundred paces; and, admitting two paces to the yard, I presumed the dungeon to be fifty yards in circuit. I had met, however, with many angles in the wall, and thus I could form no guess at the shape of the vault; for vault I could not help supposing it to be.

I had little object — certainly no hope — in these researches; but a vague curiosity prompted me to continue them. Quitting the wall, I resolved to cross the area of the enclosure. At first I proceeded with extreme caution, for the floor, although seemingly of solid material, was treacherous with slime. At length, however, I took courage, and did not hesitate to step firmly; endeavoring to cross in as direct a line as possible. I had advanced some ten or twelve paces in this manner, when the remnant of the torn hem of my robe became entangled between my legs. I stepped on it, and fell violently on my face.

In the confusion attending my fall, I did not immediately apprehend a somewhat startling circumstance, which yet, in a few seconds afterward, and while I still lay prostrate, arrested my attention. It was this — my chin rested upon the floor of the prison, but my lips and the upper portion of my head, although seemingly at a less elevation than the chin, touched nothing. At the same time my forehead seemed bathed in a clammy vapor, and the peculiar smell of decayed fungus arose to my nostrils. I put forward my arm, and shuddered to find that I had fallen at the very brink of a circular pit, whose extent, of course, I had no means of ascertaining at the moment. Groping about the masonry just below the margin, I succeeded in dislodging a small fragment, and let it fall into the abyss. For many seconds I hearkened to its reverberations as it dashed against the sides of the chasm in its descent; at length there was a sullen plunge into water, succeeded by loud echoes. At the same moment there came a sound resembling the quick opening, and as rapid closing of a door overhead, while a faint gleam of light flashed suddenly through the gloom, and as suddenly faded away.

I saw clearly the doom which had been prepared for me, and congratulated myself upon the timely accident by which I had escaped. Another step before my fall, and the world had seen me no more. And the death just avoided, was of that very character which I had regarded as fabulous and frivolous in the tales respecting the Inquisition. To the victims of its tyranny, there was the choice of death with its direst physical agonies, or death with its most hideous moral horrors. I had been reserved for the latter. By long suffering my nerves had been unstrung, until I trembled at the sound of my own voice, and had become in every respect a fitting subject for the species of torture which awaited me.

Shaking in every limb, I groped my way back to the wall; resolving there to perish rather than risk the terrors of the wells, of which my imagination now pictured many in various positions about the dungeon. In other conditions of mind I might have had courage to end my misery at once by a plunge into one of these abysses; but now I was the veriest of cowards. Neither could I forget what I had read of these pits — that the *sudden* extinction of life formed no part of their most horrible plan.

Agitation of spirit kept me awake for many long hours; but at length I again slumbered. Upon arousing, I found by my side, as before, a loaf and a pitcher of water. A burning thirst consumed me, and I emptied the vessel at a draught.[10] It must have been drugged; for scarcely had I drunk, before I became irresistibly drowsy. A deep sleep fell upon me — a sleep like that of death. How long it lasted of course, I know not; but when, once again, I unclosed my eyes, the objects around me were visible. By a wild sulphurous lustre, the origin of which I could not at first determine, I was enabled to see the extent and aspect of the prison.

In its size I had been greatly mistaken. The whole circuit of its walls did not exceed twenty-five yards. For some minutes this fact occasioned me a world of vain trouble; vain indeed! for what could be of less importance, under the terrible circumstances which environed me, then the mere dimensions of my dungeon? But my soul took a wild interest in trifles, and I busied myself in

---

[10] Deep gulp

endeavors to account for the error I had committed in my measurement. The truth at length flashed upon me. In my first attempt at exploration I had counted fifty-two paces, up to the period when I fell; I must then have been within a pace or two of the fragment of serge; in fact, I had nearly performed the circuit of the vault. I then slept, and upon awaking, I must have returned upon my steps — thus supposing the circuit nearly double what it actually was. My confusion of mind prevented me from observing that I began my tour with the wall to the left, and ended it with the wall to the right.

I had been deceived, too, in respect to the shape of the enclosure. In feeling my way I had found many angles, and thus deduced an idea of great irregularity; so potent is the effect of total darkness upon one arousing from lethargy or sleep! The angles were simply those of a few slight depressions, or niches, at odd intervals. The general shape of the prison was square. What I had taken for masonry seemed now to be iron, or some other metal, in huge plates, whose sutures or joints occasioned the depression. The entire surface of this metallic enclosure was rudely daubed in all the hideous and repulsive devices to which the charnel superstition of the monks has given rise. The figures of fiends in aspects of menace, with skeleton forms, and other more really fearful images, overspread and disfigured the walls. I observed that the outlines of these monstrosities were sufficiently distinct, but that the colors seemed faded and blurred, as if from the effects of a damp atmosphere. I now noticed the floor, too, which was of stone. In the centre yawned the circular pit from whose jaws I had escaped; but it was the only one in the dungeon.

All this I saw indistinctly and by much effort: for my personal condition had been greatly changed during slumber. I now lay upon my back, and at full length, on a species of low framework of wood. To this I was securely bound by a long strap resembling a surcingle.[11] It passed in many convolutions about my limbs and body, leaving at liberty only my head, and my left arm to such extent that I could, by dint of much exertion, supply myself with food from an earthen dish which lay by my side on the floor. I saw, to my horror, that the pitcher had been removed. I say to my horror; for I was consumed with intolerable

---

[11] Belt used to secure items to a horse

thirst. This thirst it appeared to be the design of my persecutors to stimulate: for the food in the dish was meat pungently seasoned.

Looking upward, I surveyed the ceiling of my prison. It was some thirty or forty feet overhead, and constructed much as the side walls. In one of its panels a very singular figure riveted my whole attention. It was the painted figure of Time as he is commonly represented, save that, in lieu of a scythe,[12] he held what, at a casual glance, I supposed to be the pictured image of a huge pendulum such as we see on antique clocks. There was something, however, in the appearance of this machine which caused me to regard it more attentively. While I gazed directly upward at it (for its position was immediately over my own) I fancied that I saw it in motion. In an instant afterward the fancy was confirmed. Its sweep was brief, and of course slow. I watched it for some minutes, somewhat in fear, but more in wonder. Wearied at length with observing its dull movement, I turned my eyes upon the other objects in the cell.

A slight noise attracted my notice, and, looking to the floor, I saw several enormous rats traversing it. They had issued from the well, which lay just within view to my right. Even then, while I gazed, they came up in troops, hurriedly, with ravenous eyes, allured by the scent of the meat. From this it required much effort and attention to scare them away.

It might have been half an hour, perhaps even an hour, (for in cast my I could take but imperfect note of time) before I again cast my eyes upward. What I then saw confounded and amazed me. The sweep of the pendulum had increased in extent by nearly a yard. As a natural consequence, its velocity was also much greater. But what mainly disturbed me was the idea that had perceptibly *descended.* I now observed — with what horror it is needless to say — that its nether extremity was formed of a crescent of glittering steel, about a foot in length from horn to horn; the horns upward, and the under edge evidently as keen as that of a razor. Like a razor also, it seemed massy and heavy, tapering from the edge into a solid and broad structure above. It was appended to a weighty rod of brass, and the whole *hissed* as it swung through the air.

---

[12] Curved blade, long handle

I could no longer doubt the doom prepared for me by monkish ingenuity in torture. My cognizance of the pit had become known to the inquisitorial agents — *the pit,* whose horrors had been destined for so bold a recusant as myself — *the pit,* typical of hell, and regarded by rumor as the Ultima Thule[13] of all their punishments. The plunge into this pit I had avoided by the merest of accidents, I knew that surprise, or entrapment into torment, formed an important portion of all the grotesquerie of these dungeon deaths. Having failed to fall, it was no part of the demon plan to hurl me into the abyss; and thus (there being no alternative) a different and a milder destruction awaited me. Milder! I half smiled in my agony as I thought of such application of such a term.

What boots it to tell of the long, long hours of horror more than mortal, during which I counted the rushing vibrations of the steel! Inch by inch — line by line — with a descent only appreciable at intervals that seemed ages — down and still down it came! Days passed — it might have been that many days passed — ere it swept so closely over me as to fan me with its acrid breath. The odor of the sharp steel forced itself into my nostrils. I prayed — I wearied heaven with my prayer for its more speedy descent. I grew frantically mad, and struggled to force myself upward against the sweep of the fearful scimitar. And then I fell suddenly calm, and lay smiling at the glittering death, as a child at some rare bauble.

There was another interval of utter insensibility; it was brief; for, upon again lapsing into life there had been no perceptible descent in the pendulum. But it might have been long; for I knew there were demons who took note of my swoon, and who could have arrested the vibration at pleasure. Upon my recovery, too, I felt very — oh, inexpressibly sick and weak, as if through long inanition. Even amid the agonies of that period, the human nature craved food. With painful effort I outstretched my left arm as far as my bonds permitted, and took possession of the small remnant which had been spared me by the rats. As I put a portion of it within my lips, there rushed to my mind a half formed thought of joy — of hope. Yet what business had I with hope? It was, as I say, a half formed thought — man has many such which are never completed. I felt that it was of joy — of hope; but felt also that it had perished in

---

[13] Final destination

its formation. In vain I struggled to perfect — to regain it. Long suffering had nearly annihilated all my ordinary powers of mind. I was an imbecile — an idiot.

The vibration of the pendulum was at right angles to my length. I saw that the crescent was designed to cross the region of the heart. It would fray the serge of my robe — it would return and repeat its operations — again — and again. Notwithstanding terrifically wide sweep (some thirty feet or more) and the hissing vigor of its descent, sufficient to sunder these very walls of iron, still the fraying of my robe would be all that, for several minutes, it would accomplish. And at this thought I paused. I dared not go farther than this reflection. I dwelt upon it with a pertinacity of attention — as if, in so dwelling, I could arrest here the descent of the steel. I forced myself to ponder upon the sound of the crescent as it should pass across the garment — upon the peculiar thrilling sensation which the friction of cloth produces on the nerves. I pondered upon all this frivolity until my teeth were on edge.

Down — steadily down it crept. I took a frenzied pleasure in contrasting its downward with its lateral velocity. To the right — to the left — far and wide — with the shriek of a damned spirit; to my heart with the stealthy pace of the tiger! I alternately laughed and howled as the one or the other idea grew predominant.

Down — certainly, relentlessly down! It vibrated within three inches of my bosom! I struggled violently, furiously, to free my left arm. This was free only from the elbow to the hand. I could reach the latter, from the platter beside me, to my mouth, with great effort, but no farther. Could I have broken the fastenings above the elbow, I would have seized and attempted to arrest the pendulum. I might as well have attempted to arrest an avalanche!

Down — still unceasingly — still inevitably down! I gasped and struggled at each vibration. I shrunk convulsively at its every sweep. My eyes followed its outward or upward whirls with the eagerness of the most unmeaning despair; they closed themselves spasmodically at the descent, although death would have been a relief, oh! how unspeakable! Still I quivered in every nerve to think how slight a sinking of the machinery would precipitate that keen, glistening axe upon my bosom. It was *hope* that prompted the nerve to quiver — the frame to shrink. It was *hope* — the hope that triumphs on the rack — that whispers to the death — condemned even in the dungeons of the Inquisition.

I saw that some ten or twelve vibrations would bring the steel in actual contact with my robe, and with this observation there suddenly came over my spirit all the keen, collected calmness of despair. For the first time during many hours — or perhaps days — I *thought*. It now occurred to me that the bandage, or surcingle, which enveloped me, was *unique*. I was tied by no separate cord. The first stroke of the razor like crescent athwart any portion of the band, would so detach it that it might be unwound from my person by means of my left hand. But how fearful, in that case, the proximity of the steel! The result of the slightest struggle how deadly! Was it likely, moreover, that the minions of the torturer had not foreseen and provided for this possibility! Was it probable that the bandage crossed my bosom in the track of the pendulum? Dreading to find my faint, and, as it seemed, in last hope frustrated, I so far elevated my head as to obtain a distinct view of my breast. The surcingle enveloped my limbs and body close in all directions — *save in the path of the destroying crescent.*

Scarcely had I dropped my head back into its original position, when there flashed upon my mind what I cannot better describe than as the unformed half of that idea of deliverance to which I have previously alluded, and of which a moiety only floated indeterminately through my brain when I raised food to my burning lips. The whole thought was now present — feeble, scarcely sane, scarcely definite, — but still entire. I proceeded at once, with the nervous energy of despair, to attempt its execution.

For many hours the immediate vicinity of the low framework upon which I lay, had been literally swarming with rats. They were wild, bold, ravenous; their red eyes glaring upon me as if they waited but for motionlessness on my part to make me their prey. "To what food," I thought, "have they been accustomed in the well?"

They had devoured, in spite of all my efforts to prevent them, all but a small remnant of the contents of the dish. I had fallen into an habitual see-saw, or wave of the hand about the platter: and, at length, the unconscious uniformity of the movement deprived it of effect. In their voracity the vermin frequently fastened their sharp fangs in my fingers. With the particles of the oily and spicy viand[14] which now remained, I thoroughly rubbed the bandage wherever I could reach it; then, raising my hand from the floor, I lay breathlessly still.

At first the ravenous animals were startled and terrified at the change — at the cessation of movement. They shrank alarmedly back; many sought the well. But this was only for a moment. I had not counted in vain upon their voracity. Observing that I remained without motion, one or two of the boldest leaped upon the framework, and smelt at the surcingle. This seemed the signal for a general rush. Forth from the well they hurried in fresh troops. They clung to the wood — they overran it, and leaped in hundreds upon my person. The measured movement of the pendulum disturbed them not at all. Avoiding its strokes they busied themselves with the anointed bandage.

They pressed — they swarmed upon me in ever accumulating heaps. They writhed upon my throat; their cold lips sought my own; I was half stifled by their thronging pressure; disgust, for which the world has no name, swelled my bosom, and chilled, with a heavy clamminess, my heart. Yet one minute, and I felt that the struggle would be over. Plainly I perceived the loosening of the bandage. I knew that in more than one place it must be already severed. With a more than human resolution I lay *still*.

Nor had I erred in my calculations — nor had I endured in vain. I at length felt that I was *free*. The surcingle hung in ribands from my body. But the stroke of the pendulum already pressed upon my bosom. It had divided the serge of the robe. It had cut through the linen beneath. Twice again it swung, and a sharp sense of pain shot through every nerve. But the moment of escape had arrived. At a wave of my hand my deliverers hurried tumultuously away. With a steady movement — cautious, sidelong, shrinking, and slow — I slid from the embrace of the bandage and beyond the reach of the scimitar. For the moment, at least, *I was free.*

Free! — and in the grasp of the Inquisition! I had scarcely stepped from my wooden bed of horror upon the stone floor of the prison, when the motion of the hellish machine ceased and I beheld it drawn up, by some invisible force, through the ceiling. This was a lesson

---

[14] Item of food

which I took desperately to heart. My every motion was undoubtedly watched.

Free! — I had but escaped death in one form of agony, to be delivered unto worse than death in some other. With that thought I rolled my eyes nervously around on the barriers of iron that hemmed me in. Something unusual — some change which, at first, I could not appreciate distinctly — it was obvious, had taken place in the apartment. For many minutes of a dreamy and trembling abstraction, I busied myself in vain, unconnected conjecture. During this period, I became aware, for the first time, of the origin of the sulphurous light which illumined the cell. It proceeded from a fissure, about half an inch in width, extending entirely around the prison at the base of the walls, which thus appeared, and were, completely separated from the floor. I endeavored, but of course in vain, to look through the aperture.

As I arose from the attempt, the mystery of the alteration in the chamber broke at once upon my understanding. I have observed that, although the outlines of the figures upon the walls were sufficiently distinct, yet the colors seemed blurred and indefinite. These colors had now assumed, and were momentarily assuming, a startling and most intense brilliancy, that gave to the spectral and fiendish portraitures an aspect that might have thrilled even firmer nerves than my own. Demon eyes, of a wild and ghastly vivacity, glared upon me in a thousand directions, where none had been visible before, and gleamed with the lurid lustre of a fire that I could not force my imagination to regard as unreal.

Unreal! — Even while I breathed there came to my nostrils the breath of the vapour of heated iron! A suffocating odour pervaded the prison! A deeper glow settled each moment in the eyes that glared at my agonies! A richer tint of crimson diffused itself over the pictured horrors of blood. I panted! I gasped for breath! There could be no doubt of the design of my tormentors — oh! most unrelenting! oh! most demoniac of men! I shrank from the glowing metal to the centre of the cell. Amid the thought of the fiery destruction that impended, the idea of the coolness of the well came over my soul like balm. I rushed to its deadly brink. I threw my straining vision below. The glare from the enkindled roof illumined its inmost recesses. Yet, for a wild moment, did my spirit refuse to comprehend the meaning of what I saw. At length it forced

— it wrestled its way into my soul — it burned itself in upon my shuddering reason. — Oh! for a voice to speak! — oh! horror! — oh! any horror but this! With a shriek, I rushed from the margin, and buried my face in my hands — weeping bitterly.

The heat rapidly increased, and once again I looked up, shuddering as with a fit of the ague.[15] There had been a second change in the cell — and now the change was obviously in the *form*. As before, it was in vain that I, at first, endeavoured to appreciate or understand what was taking place. But not long was I left in doubt. The Inquisitorial vengeance had been hurried by my two-fold escape, and there was to be no more dallying with the King of Terrors. The room had been square. I saw that two of its iron angles were now acute — two, consequently, obtuse. The fearful difference quickly increased with a low rumbling or moaning sound. In an instant the apartment had shifted its form into that of a lozenge. But the alteration stopped not here — I neither hoped nor desired it to stop. I could have clasped the red walls to my bosom as a garment of eternal peace.

"Death," I said, "any death but that of the pit!" Fool! might I have not known that *into the pit* it was the object of the burning iron to urge me? Could I resist its glow? or, if even that, could I withstand its pressure? And now, flatter and flatter grew the lozenge, with a rapidity that left me no time for contemplation. Its centre, and of course, its greatest width, came just over the yawning gulf. I shrank back — but the closing walls pressed me resistlessly onward. At length for my seared and writhing body there was no longer an inch of foothold on the firm floor of the prison. I struggled no more, but the agony of my soul found vent in one loud, long, and final scream of despair. I felt that I tottered upon the brink — I averted my eyes —

There was a discordant hum of human voices! There was a loud blast as of many trumpets! There was a harsh grating as of a thousand thunders! The fiery walls rushed back! An outstretched arm caught my own as I fell, fainting, into the abyss. It was that of General Lasalle. The French army had entered Toledo. The Inquisition was in the hands of its enemies.

---

[15] Intense shivering

HONORÉ DE BALZAC
(1799-1850)

Φ

The Mysterious Mansion

"*La Grande Breteche*" was first published in 1830 and is part of Honoré de Balzac's "Studies of Women." The horror short story was included in his series titled "Scenes from Private Life." In it he gives us an excellent story of marital infidelity that culminates into a horrific outcome that is sure to induce nightmares. Surely the ending will be remembered the next time any reader steps foot inside a closet.

His building of terror in "The Mysterious Mansion," along with a haunting ending, make this story one of the foremost in this collection. It rises in almost every aspect above Edgar Allan Poe's "The Cask of Amontillado."

One can always rest assured that they are in good hands with Honoré de Balzac who forged new ground in the horror genre. He is the only author, apart from Poe, with more than one horror story in this collection of the best from 1800-1849.

The Mysterious Mansion

ABOUT A HUNDRED YARDS from the town of Vendome, on the borders of the Loire, there is an old gray house, surmounted by very high gables, and so completely isolated that neither tanyard[1] nor shabby hostelry,[2] such as you may find at the entrance to all small towns, exists in its immediate neighborhood.

In front of this building, overlooking the river, is a garden, where the once well-trimmed box borders that used to define the walks now grow wild as they list. Several willows that spring from the Loiré[3] have grown as rapidly as the hedge that encloses it, and half conceal the house. The rich vegetation of those weeds that we call foul adorns the sloping shore. Fruit trees, neglected for the last ten years, no longer yield their harvest, and their shoots form coppices. The wall-fruit grows like hedges against the walls. Paths once graveled are overgrown with moss, but, to tell the truth, there is no trace of a path. From the height of the hill, to which cling the ruins of the old castle of the Dukes of Vendôme, the only spot whence the eye can plunge into this enclosure, it strikes you that, at a time not easy to determine, this plot of land was the delight of a country gentleman, who cultivated roses and tulips and horticulture in general, and who was besides a lover of fine fruit. An arbor is still visible, or rather the debris of an arbor, where there is a table that time has not quite destroyed.

The aspect of this garden of bygone days suggests the negative joys of peaceful, provincial life, as one might reconstruct the life of a worthy tradesman by reading the epitaph on his tombstone. As if to complete the sweetness and sadness of the ideas that possess one's soul, one of the walls displays a sun-dial decorated with the following commonplace Christian inscription: "Ultimam cogita!"[4]

---

[1] Place where animal skins and tanned
[2] Hotel
[3] Longest river in France
[4] "Think about the final hour!" This inscription is on the sundial of old Chateau of Vendôme.

The roof of this house is horribly dilapidated, the shutters are always closed, the balconies are covered with swallows' nests, the doors are perpetually shut, weeds have drawn green lines in the cracks of the flights of steps, the locks and bolts are rusty. Sun, moon, winter, summer, and snow have worn the paneling, warped the boards, gnawed the paint. The lugubrious silence which reigns there is only broken by birds, cats, martins, rats and mice, free to course to and fro, to fight and to eat each other. Everywhere an invisible hand has graven the word *mystery*.

Should your curiosity lead you to glance at this house from the side that points to the road, you would perceive a great door which the children of the place have riddled with holes. I afterward heard that this door had been closed for the last ten years. Through the holes broken by the boys you would have observed the perfect harmony that existed between the façades of both garden and courtyard. In both the same disorder prevails. Tufts of weed encircle the paving-stones. Enormous cracks furrow the walls, round whose blackened crests twine the thousand garlands of the pellitory.[5] The steps are out of joint, the wire of the bell is rusted, the spouts are cracked. What fire from heaven has fallen here? What tribunal has decreed that salt should be strewn on this dwelling? Has God been blasphemed, has France been here betrayed? These are the questions we ask ourselves, but get no answer from the crawling things that haunt the place. The empty and deserted house is a gigantic enigma, of which the key is lost. In bygone times it was a small fief, and bears the name of the Grande Breteche.

I inferred that I was not the only person to whom my good landlady had communicated the secret of which I was to be the sole recipient, and I prepared to listen.

"Sir," she said, "when the Emperor sent the Spanish prisoners of war and others here, the Government quartered on me a young Spaniard who had been sent to Vendome on parole. Parole notwithstanding he went out every day to show himself to the *sous-prefet*.[6] He was a Spanish grandee! Nothing less! His name ended in os and dia, something like Burgos de Feredia. I have his name on my books; you can read it if you like. Oh! but he was a

---

[5] Flowering herb that grows in wall crevices
[6] Deputy to chief of police

handsome young man for a Spaniard; they are all said to be ugly. He was only five feet and a few inches high, but he was well-grown; he had small hands that he took such care of; and you should have seen! He had as many brushes for his hands as a woman for her whole dressing apparatus! He had thick black hair, a fiery eye, his skin was rather bronzed, but I liked the look of it. He wore the finest linen I have ever seen on any one, although I have had princesses staying here, and, among others, General Bertrand, the Duke and Duchess d'Abrantes, Monsieur Decazes, and the King of Spain.

He didn't eat much; but his manners were so polite, so amiable, that one could not owe him a grudge. Oh! I was very fond of him, although he didn't open his lips four times in the day, and it was impossible to keep up a conversation with him. For if you spoke to him, he did not answer. It was a fad, a mania with them all, I heard say. He read his breviary like a priest, he went to Mass and to all the services regularly. Where did he sit? Two steps from the chapel of Madame de Merret. As he took his place there the first time he went to church, nobody suspected him of any intention in so doing.

Besides, he never raised his eyes from his prayer-book, poor young man! After that, sir, in the evening he would walk on the mountains, among the castle ruins. It was the poor man's only amusement, it reminded him of his country. They say that Spain is all mountains! From the commencement of his imprisonment he stayed out late. I was anxious when I found that he did not come home before midnight; but we got accustomed to this fancy of his. He took the key of the door, and we left off sitting up for him. He lodged in a house of ours in the *Rue des Casernes*. After that, one of our stable-men told us that in the evening when he led the horses to the water, he thought he had seen the Spanish grandee swimming far down the river like a live fish. When he returned, I told him to take care of the rushes; he appeared vexed to have been seen in the water. At last, one day, or rather one morning, we did not find him in his room; he had not returned. After searching everywhere, I found some writing in the drawer of a table, where there were fifty gold pieces of Spain that are called doubloons and were worth about five thousand francs; and ten thousand francs' worth of diamonds in a small sealed box. The writing said, that in case he did not return, he left us the money and the diamonds, on condition of paying for Masses to thank God for his escape, and for his salvation. In those days my husband had not been taken from me; he hastened to seek him everywhere.

"And now for the strange part of the story. He brought home the Spaniard's clothes, that he had discovered under a big stone, in a sort of pilework by the river-side near the castle, nearly opposite to the Grande Breteche. My husband had gone there so early that no one had seen him. After reading the letter, he burned the clothes, and according to Count Feredia's desire we declared that he had escaped. The *sous-prefet* sent all the gendarmerie in pursuit of him; but brust! they never caught him. Lepas believed that the Spaniard had drowned himself. I, sir, don't think so; I am more inclined to believe that he had something to do with the affair of Madame de Merret, seeing that Rosalie told me that the crucifix that her mistress thought so much of, that she had it buried with her, was of ebony and silver. Now in the beginning of his stay here, Monsieur de Feredia had one in ebony and silver, that I never saw him with later. Now, sir, don't you consider that I need have no scruples about the Spaniard's fifteen thousand francs, and that I have a right to them?"

"Certainly; but you haven't tried to question Rosalie?" I said.

"Oh, yes, indeed, sir; but to no purpose! the girl's like a wall. She knows something, but it is impossible to get her to talk."

After exchanging a few more words with me, my landlady left me a prey to vague and gloomy thoughts, to a romantic curiosity, and a religious terror not unlike the profound impression produced on us when by night, on entering a dark church, we perceive a faint light under high arches; a vague figure glides by—the rustle of a robe or cassock is heard, and we shudder.

Suddenly the Grande Breteche and its tall weeds, its barred windows, its rusty ironwork, its closed doors, its deserted apartments, appeared like a fantastic apparition before me. I essayed to penetrate the mysterious dwelling, and to find the knot of its dark story—the drama that had killed three persons. In my eyes Rosalie became the most interesting person in Vendome.

As I studied her, I discovered the traces of secret care, despite the radiant health that shone in her plump countenance. There was in her the germ of remorse or hope; her attitude revealed a secret, like the attitude of a bigot who prays to excess, or of the infanticide who ever hears the last cry of her child. Yet her manners were rough and ingenuous—her silly smile was not that of a criminal, and could you but have seen the great kerchief that encompassed her portly bust, framed and laced in by a lilac and blue cotton gown, you would have dubbed her innocent. No, I thought, I will not leave Vendome without learning the history of the Grande Breteche. To gain my ends I will strike up a friendship with Rosalie, if needs be.

"Rosalie," said I, one evening.

"Sir?"

"You are not married?"

She started slightly.

"Oh, I can find plenty of men, when the fancy takes me to be made miserable," she said, laughing.

She soon recovered from the effects of her emotion, for all women, from the great lady to the maid of the inn, possess a composure that is peculiar to them.

"You are too good-looking and well favored to be short of lovers. But tell me, Rosalie, why did you take service in an inn after leaving Madame de Merret? Did she leave you nothing to live on?"

"Oh, yes! But, sir, my place is the best in all Vendome."

The reply was one of those that judges and lawyers would call evasive. Rosalie appeared to me to be situated in this romantic history like the square in the midst of a chessboard. She was at the heart of the truth and chief interest; she seemed to me to be bound in the very knot of it. The conquest of Rosalie was no longer to be an ordinary siege—in this girl was centred the last chapter of a novel; therefore from this moment Rosalie became the object of my preference.

One morning I said to Rosalie: "Tell me all you know about Madame de Merret."

"Oh!" she replied in terror, "do not ask that of me, Monsieur Horace."

Her pretty face fell—her clear, bright color faded—and her eyes lost their innocent brightness.

"Well, then," she said, at last, "if you must have it so, I will tell you about it; but promise to keep my secret!"

"Done! my dear girl, I must keep your secret with the honor of a thief, which is the most loyal in the world."

Were I to transcribe Rosalie's diffuse eloquence faithfully, an entire volume would scarcely contain it; so I shall abridge.

The room occupied by Madame de Merret at the Breteche was on the ground floor. A little closet about four feet deep, built in the thickness of the wall, served as her wardrobe. Three months before the eventful evening of which I am about to speak, Madame de Merret had been so seriously indisposed that her husband had left her to herself in her own apartment, while he occupied another on the first floor.

By one of those chances that it is impossible to foresee, he returned home from the club (where he was accustomed to read the papers and discuss politics with the inhabitants of the place) two hours later than usual. His wife supposed him to be at home, in bed and asleep. But the invasion of France had been the subject of a most animated discussion; the billiard-match had been exciting, he had lost forty francs, an enormous sum for Vendome, where every one hoards, and where manners are restricted within the limits of a praiseworthy modesty, which perhaps is the source of the true happiness that no Parisian covets.

For some time past Monsieur de Merret had been satisfied to ask Rosalie if his wife had gone to bed; and on her reply, which was always in the affirmative, had immediately gained his own room with the good temper engendered by habit and confidence. On entering his house, he took it into his head to go and tell his wife of his misadventure, perhaps by way of consolation. At dinner he found Madame de Merret most coquettishly attired. On his way to the club it had occurred to him that his wife was restored to health, and that her convalescence had added to her beauty. He was, as husbands are wont to be, somewhat slow in making this discovery. Instead of calling Rosalie, who was occupied just then in watching the cook and coachman play a difficult hand at brisque,[7] Monsieur de Merret went to his wife's room by the light of a lantern that he deposited on the first step of the staircase.

His unmistakable step resounded under the vaulted corridor. At the moment that the Count turned the handle of his wife's door, he fancied he could hear the door of the closet I spoke of close; but when he entered Madame de

---

[7] French card game

Merret was alone before the fireplace. The husband thought ingenuously that Rosalie was in the closet, yet a suspicion that jangled in his ear put him on his guard. He looked at his wife and saw in her eyes I know not what wild and hunted expression.

"You are very late," she said. Her habitually pure, sweet voice seemed changed to him.

Monsieur de Merret did not reply, for at that moment Rosalie entered. It was a thunderbolt for him. He strode about the room, passing from one window to the other, with mechanical motion and folded arms.

"Have you heard bad news, or are you unwell?" inquired his wife timidly, while Rosalie undressed her.

He kept silent.

"You can leave me," said Madame de Merret to her maid; "I will put my hair in curl papers myself."

From the expression of her husband's face she foresaw trouble, and wished to be alone with him. When Rosalie had gone, or was supposed to have gone (for she stayed in the corridor for a few minutes), Monsieur de Merret came and stood in front of his wife, and said coldly to her:

"Madame, there is some one in your closet!" She looked calmly at her husband and replied simply:

"No, sir."

This answer was heartrending to Monsieur de Merret; he did not believe in it. Yet his wife had never appeared to him purer or more saintly than at that moment. He rose to open the closet door; Madame de Merret took his hand, looked at him with an expression of melancholy, and said in a voice that betrayed singular emotion:

"If you find no one there, remember this, all will be over between us!" The extraordinary dignity of his wife's manner restored the Count's profound esteem for her, and inspired him with one of those resolutions that only lack a vaster stage to become immortal.

"No," said he, "Josephine, I will not go there. In either case it would separate us forever. Hear me, I know how pure you are at heart, and that your life is a holy one. You would not commit a mortal sin to save your life."

At these words Madame de Merret turned a haggard gaze upon her husband.

"Here, take your crucifix," he added. "Swear to me before God that there is no one in there; I will believe you, I will never open that door."

Madame de Merret took the crucifix and said:

"I swear."

"Louder," said the husband, "and repeat 'I swear before God that there is no one in that closet.'"

She repeated the sentence calmly.

"That will do," said Monsieur de Merret, coldly.

After a moment of silence:

"I never saw this pretty toy before," he said, examining the ebony crucifix inlaid with silver, and most artistically chiseled.

"I found it at Duvivier's, who bought it of a Spanish monk when the prisoners passed through Vendome last year."

"Ah!" said Monsieur de Merret, as he replaced the crucifix on the nail, and he rang. Rosalie did not keep him waiting. Monsieur de Merret went quickly to meet her, led her to the bay window that opened on to the garden and whispered to her:

"Listen! I know that Gorenflot wishes to marry you, poverty is the only drawback, and you told him that you would be his wife if he found the means to establish himself as a master mason. Well! go and fetch him, tell him to come here with his trowel and tools. Manage not to awaken any one in his house but himself; his fortune will be more than your desires. Above all, leave this room without babbling, otherwise—" He frowned. Rosalie went away, he recalled her.

"Here, take my latch-key," he said. "Jean!" then cried Monsieur de Merret, in tones of thunder in the corridor. Jean, who was at the same time his coachman and his confidential servant, left his game of cards and came.

"Go to bed, all of you," said his master, signing to him to approach; and the Count added, under his breath: "When they are all asleep—*asleep,* d'ye hear?—you will come down and tell me." Monsieur de Merret, who had not lost sight of his wife all the time he was giving his orders, returned quietly to her at the fireside and began to tell her of the game of billiards and the talk of the club. When Rosalie returned she found Monsieur and Madame de Merret conversing very amicably.

The Count had lately had all the ceilings of his reception rooms on the ground floor repaired. Plaster of Paris is difficult to obtain in Vendome; the carriage raises its price. The Count had therefore bought a good deal, being well aware that he could find plenty of purchasers for whatever might remain over. This circumstance inspired him with the design he was about to execute.

"Sir, Gorenflot has arrived," said Rosalie in low tones.

"Show him in," replied the Count in loud tones.

Madame de Merret turned rather pale when she saw the mason.

"Gorenflot," said her husband, "go and fetch bricks from the coach-house, and bring sufficient to wall up the door of this closet; you will use the plaster I have over to coat the wall with." Then calling Rosalie and the workman aside:

"Listen, Gorenflot," he said in an undertone, "you will sleep here to-night. But to-morrow you will have a passport to a foreign country, to a town to which I will direct you. I shall give you six thousand francs for your journey. You will stay ten years in that town; if you do not like it, you may establish yourself in another, provided it be in the same country. You will pass through Paris, where you will await me. There I will insure you an additional six thousand francs by contract, which will be paid to you on your return, provided you have fulfilled the conditions of our bargain.

This is the price for your absolute silence as to what you are about to do to-night. As to you, Rosalie, I will give you ten thousand francs on the day of your wedding, on condition of your marrying Gorenflot; but if you wish to marry, you must hold your tongues; or—no dowry."

"Rosalie," said Madame de Merret, "do my hair."

The husband walked calmly up and down, watching the door, the mason, and his wife, but without betraying any insulting doubts. Madame de Merret chose a moment when the workman was unloading bricks and her husband was at the other end of the room to say to Rosalie: "A thousand francs a year for you, my child, if you can tell Gorenflot to leave a chink at the bottom." Then out loud, she added coolly:

"Go and help him!"

Monsieur and Madame de Merret were silent all the time that Gorenflot took to brick up the door. This silence, on the part of the husband, who did not choose to furnish his wife with a pretext for saying things of a double meaning, had its purpose; on the part of Madame de Merret it was either pride or prudence. When the wall was about half-way up, the sly workman took advantage of a moment when the Count's back was turned, to strike a blow with his trowel in one of the glass panes of the closet-door. This act informed Madame de Merret that Rosalie had spoken to Gorenflot.

All three then saw a man's face; it was dark and gloomy with black hair and eyes of flame. Before her husband turned, the poor woman had time to make a sign to the stranger that signified: Hope!

At four o'clock, toward dawn, for it was the month of September, the construction was finished. The mason was handed over to the care of Jean, and Monsieur de Merret went to bed in his wife's room.

On rising the following morning, he said carelessly:

"The deuce! I must go to the Maine for the passport." He put his hat on his head, advanced three steps toward the door, altered his mind and took the crucifix.

His wife trembled for joy. "He is going to Duvivier," she thought. As soon as the Count had left, Madame de Merret rang for Rosalie; then in a terrible voice:

"The trowel, the trowel!" she cried, "and quick to work! I saw how Gorenflot did it; we shall have time to make a hole and to mend it again."

In the twinkling of an eye, Rosalie brought a sort of mattock to her mistress, who with unparalleled ardor set about demolishing the wall. She had already knocked out several bricks and was preparing to strike a more decisive blow when she perceived Monsieur de Merret behind her. She fainted.

"Lay Madame on her bed," said the Count coldly. He bad foreseen what would happen in his absence and had set a trap for his wife; he had simply written to the mayor, and had sent for Duvivier. The jeweler arrived just as the room had been put in order.

"Duvivier," inquired the Count, did you buy crucifixes of the Spaniards who passed through here?"

"No, sir."

"That will do, thank you," he said, looking at his wife like a tiger. "Jean," he added, "you will see that my meals are served in the Countess's room; she is ill, and I shall not leave her until she has recovered."

The cruel gentleman stayed with his wife for twenty days. In the beginning, when there were sounds in the walled closet, and Josephine attempted to implore his pity for the dying stranger, he replied, without permitting her to say a word:

"You have sworn on the cross that there is no one there."

 EDGAR ALLAN POE
(1809-1849)

Φ

The Fall of the House of Usher

This classic gothic tale is perhaps the best Poe ever wrote. To this day it is widely read worldwide.

Washington Irving explained to Poe in a letter dated November 6, 1839 that he thought it was overwritten and could be improved. "You have been too anxious to present your pictures vividly to the eye, or too distrustful of your effect, and have laid on too much colouring. It is erring on the best side–the side of luxuriance. That tale might be improved by relieving the Style from some of the epithets."

It is little known that Roderick Usher and his sister, Madeline Usher, are based on actual people. Noble Luke Usher and Harriet L'Estrange Usher founded the Montreal Theatre in 1808 and were theatre acquaintances of Poe's parents', David and Elizabeth Poe, for a brief period. Their second son, James Usher, and his sister Agnes Usher, were both "held in the bondage of blighted nervous equipment," as Mary E. Phillips stated in "Edgar Allan Poe the Man" of 1926. Phillips believed that Poe met Agnes and James Usher in Philadelphia during 1829-1831 since it is likely he would have sought out information about his parents from their parents, Noble Luke Usher and Harriet L'Estrange Usher.

The Fall of the House of Usher

Son coeur est un luth suspendu;
Sitot qu'on le touche il resonne.[1]
De Beranger.[2]

DURING THE WHOLE OF a dull, dark, and soundless day in the autumn of the year, when the clouds hung oppressively low in the heavens, had been passing alone, on horseback, through a singularly dreary tract of country; and at length found myself, as the shades of the evening drew on, within view of the melancholy House of Usher. I know not how it was –but, with the first glimpse of the building, a sense of insufferable gloom pervaded my spirit.

I say insufferable; for the feeling was unrelieved by any of that half-pleasurable, because poetic, sentiment, with which the mind usually receives even the sternest natural images of the desolate or terrible. I looked upon the scene before me –upon the mere house, and the simple landscape features of the domain –upon the bleak walls – upon the vacant eye-like windows –upon a few rank sedges[3] –and upon a few white trunks of decayed trees – with an utter depression of soul which I can compare to no earthly sensation more properly than to the after-dream of the reveler upon opium[4] –the bitter lapse into everyday life–the hideous dropping off of the reveler upon opium–the bitter lapse into everyday life –the hideous dropping off of the veil.

There was an iciness, a sinking, a sickening of the heart –an unredeemed dreariness of thought which no goading of the imagination could torture into aught of the sublime. What was it –I paused to think –what was it that so unnerved me in the contemplation of the House of Usher? It was a mystery all insoluble; nor could I grapple with the shadowy fancies that crowded upon me as I pondered. I was forced to fall back upon the unsatisfactory

---

[1] His heart is a suspended lute; As soon as it is touched, it resonates
[2] Pierre Jean de Beranger (1780-1857), French poet
[3] Grasslike plants
[4] Drug derived from the poppy

conclusion, that while, beyond doubt, there *are* combinations of very simple natural objects which have the power of thus affecting us, still the analysis of this power lies among considerations beyond our depth. It was possible, I reflected, that a mere different arrangement of the particulars of the scene, of the details of the picture, would be sufficient to modify, or perhaps to annihilate its capacity for sorrowful impression; and, acting upon this idea, I reined my horse to the precipitous brink of a black and lurid tarn[5] that lay in unruffled lustre by the dwelling, and gazed down –but with a shudder even more thrilling than before –upon the remodeled and inverted images of the gray sedge, and the ghastly tree-stems, and the vacant and eye-like windows.

Nevertheless, in this mansion of gloom I now proposed to myself a sojourn of some weeks. Its proprietor, Roderick Usher, had been one of my boon companions in boyhood; but many years had elapsed since our last meeting. A letter, however, had lately reached me in a distant part of the country –a letter from him –which, in its wildly importunate nature, had admitted of no other than a personal reply.

The MS. gave evidence of nervous agitation. The writer spoke of acute bodily illness –of a mental disorder which oppressed him–and of an earnest desire to see me, as his best, and indeed his only personal friend, with a view of attempting, by the cheerfulness of my society, some alleviation of his malady. It was the manner in which all this, and much more, was said –it the apparent *heart* that went with his request –which allowed me no room for hesitation; and I accordingly obeyed forthwith what I still considered a very singular summons.

Although, as boys, we had been even intimate associates, yet really knew little of my friend. His reserve had been always excessive and habitual. I was aware, however, that his very ancient family had been noted, time out of mind, for a peculiar sensibility of temperament, displaying itself, through long ages, in many works of exalted art, and manifested, of late, in repeated deeds of munificent yet unobtrusive charity, as well as in a passionate devotion to the intricacies, perhaps even more than to the orthodox and easily recognizable beauties, of musical science. I had learned, too, the very remarkable

---

[5] Languid pond of dark water

fact, that the stem of the Usher race, all time-honoured as it was, had put forth, at no period, any enduring branch; in other words, that the entire family lay in the direct line of descent, and had always, with very trifling and very temporary variation, so lain.

It was this deficiency, I considered, while running over in thought the perfect keeping of the character of the premises with the accredited character of the people, and while speculating upon the possible influence which the one, in the long lapse of centuries, might have exercised upon the other –it was this deficiency, perhaps, of collateral issue, and the consequent undeviating transmission, from sire to son, of the patrimony with the name, which had, at length, so identified the two as to merge the original title of the estate in the quaint and equivocal appellation of the "House of Usher" –an appellation which seemed to include, in the minds of the peasantry who used it, both the family and the family mansion.

I have said that the sole effect of my somewhat childish experiment –that of looking down within the tarn –had been to deepen the first singular impression. There can be no doubt that the consciousness of the rapid increase of my superstition –for why should I not so term it? –served mainly to accelerate the increase itself. Such, I have long known, is the paradoxical law of all sentiments having terror as a basis. And it might have been for this reason only, that, when I again uplifted my eyes to the house itself, from its image in the pool, there grew in my mind a strange fancy –a fancy so ridiculous, indeed, that I but mention it to show the vivid force of the sensations which oppressed me. I had so worked upon my imagination as really to believe that about the whole mansion and domain there hung an atmosphere peculiar to themselves and their immediate vicinity– an atmosphere which had no affinity with the air of heaven, but which had reeked up from the decayed trees, and the gray wall, and the silent tarn –a pestilent and mystic vapour, dull, sluggish, faintly discernible, and leaden-hued.

Shaking off from my spirit what *must* have been a dream, I scanned more narrowly the real aspect of the building. Its principal feature seemed to be that of an excessive antiquity. The discoloration of ages had been great. Minute fungi overspread the whole exterior, hanging in a fine tangled web-work from the eaves. Yet all this was apart from any extraordinary dilapidation. No portion of the masonry had fallen; and there appeared to be a wild inconsistency between its still perfect adaptation of parts, and the crumbling condition of the individual stones. In this there was much that reminded me of the specious totality of old wood-work which has rotted for long years in some neglected vault, with no disturbance from the breath of the external air.

Beyond this indication of extensive decay, however, the fabric gave little token of instability. Perhaps the eye of a scrutinizing observer might have discovered a barely perceptible fissure, which, extending from the roof of the building in front, made its way down the wall in a zigzag direction, until it became lost in the sullen waters of the tarn.

Noticing these things, I rode over a short causeway to the house. A servant in waiting took my horse, and I entered the Gothic archway of the hall. A valet, of stealthy step, thence conducted me, in silence, through many dark and intricate passages in my progress to the *studio* of his master. Much that I encountered on the way contributed, I know not how, to heighten the vague sentiments of which I have already spoken.

While the objects around me –while the carvings of the ceilings, the sombre tapestries of the walls, the ebon blackness of the floors, and the phantasmagoric[6] armorial[7] trophies which rattled as I strode, were but matters to which, or to such as which, I had been accustomed from my infancy –while I hesitated not to acknowledge how familiar was all this –I still wondered to find how unfamiliar were the fancies which ordinary images were stirring up. On one of the staircases, I met the physician of the family. His countenance, I thought, wore a mingled expression of low cunning and perplexity. He accosted me with trepidation and passed on. The valet now threw open a door and ushered me into the presence of his master.

The room in which I found myself was very large and lofty. The windows were long, narrow, and pointed, and at so vast a distance from the black oaken floor as to be altogether inaccessible from within. Feeble gleams of encrimsoned light made their way through the trellised

---

[6] Fantastic imagery as if in a dream
[7] Coat of arms

panes, and served to render sufficiently distinct the more prominent objects around the eye, however, struggled in vain to reach the remoter angles of the chamber, or the recesses of the vaulted and fretted[8] ceiling. Dark draperies hung upon the walls. The general furniture was profuse, comfortless, antique, and tattered. Many books and musical instruments lay scattered about, but failed to give any vitality to the scene. I felt that I breathed an atmosphere of sorrow. An air of stern, deep, and irredeemable gloom hung over and pervaded all.

Upon my entrance, Usher arose from a sofa on which he had been lying at full length, and greeted me with a vivacious warmth which had much in it, I at first thought, of an overdone cordiality –of the constrained effort of the *ennuyé*[9] man of the world. A glance, however, at his countenance, convinced me of his perfect sincerity. We sat down; and for some moments, while he spoke not, I gazed upon him with a feeling half of pity, half of awe. Surely, man had never before so terribly altered, in so brief a period, as had Roderick Usher!

It was with difficulty that I could bring myself to admit the identity of the wan[12] being before me with the companion of my early boyhood. Yet the character of his face had been at all times remarkable. A cadaverousness of complexion; an eye large, liquid, and luminous beyond comparison; lips somewhat thin and very pallid, but of a surpassingly beautiful curve; a nose of a delicate Hebrew model, but with a breadth of nostril unusual in similar formations; a finely moulded chin, speaking, in its want of prominence, of a want of moral energy; hair of a more than web-like softness and tenuity; these features, with an inordinate expansion above the regions of the temple, made up altogether a countenance not easily to be forgotten.

And now in the mere exaggeration of the prevailing character of these features, and of the expression they were wont to convey, lay so much of change that I doubted to whom I spoke. The now ghastly pallor of the skin, and the now miraculous lustre of the eye, above all things startled and even awed me. The silken hair, too, had been suffered to grow all unheeded, and as, in its wild

---

[8] Repeating ornamental designs
[9] Weary, exhausted
[12] Pallid

gossamer[10] texture, it floated rather than fell about the face, I could not, even with effort, connect its Arabesque expression with any idea of simple humanity.

In the manner of my friend I was at once struck with an incoherence –an inconsistency; and I soon found this to arise from a series of feeble and futile struggles to overcome an habitual trepidancy –an excessive nervous agitation. For something of this nature I had indeed been prepared, no less by his letter, than by reminiscences of certain boyish traits, and by conclusions deduced from his peculiar physical conformation and temperament. His action was alternately vivacious and sullen. His voice varied rapidly from a tremulous indecision (when the animal spirits seemed utterly in abeyance) to that species of energetic concision –that abrupt, weighty, unhurried, and hollow-sounding enunciation –that leaden, self-balanced and perfectly modulated guttural utterance, which may be observed in the lost drunkard, or the irreclaimable eater of opium, during the periods of his most intense excitement.

It was thus that he spoke of the object of my visit, of his earnest desire to see me, and of the solace he expected me to afford him. He entered, at some length, into what he conceived to be the nature of his malady. It was, he said, a constitutional and a family evil, and one for which he despaired to find a remedy –a mere nervous affection, he immediately added, which would undoubtedly soon pass off. It displayed itself in a host of unnatural sensations. Some of these, as he detailed them, interested and bewildered me; although, perhaps, the terms, and the general manner of the narration had their weight. He suffered much from a morbid acuteness of the senses; the most insipid[11] food was alone endurable; he could wear only garments of certain texture; the odours of all flowers were oppressive; his eyes were tortured by even a faint light; and there were but peculiar sounds, and these from stringed instruments, which did not inspire him with horror.

To an anomalous species of terror I found him a bounden slave. "I shall perish," said he, "I *must* perish in this deplorable folly. Thus, thus, and not otherwise, shall I be lost. I dread the events of the future, not in themselves,

[10] Delicate
[11] Bland

but in their results. I shudder at the thought of any, even the most trivial, incident, which may operate upon this intolerable agitation of soul. I have, indeed, no abhorrence of danger, except in its absolute effect –in terror. In this unnerved –in this pitiable condition –I feel that the period will sooner or later arrive when I must abandon life and reason together, in some struggle with the grim phantasm, FEAR."

I learned, moreover, at intervals, and through broken and equivocal hints, another singular feature of his mental condition. He was enchained by certain superstitious impressions in regard to the dwelling which he tenanted, and whence, for many years, he had never ventured forth –in regard to an influence whose supposititious force was conveyed in terms too shadowy here to be re-stated –an influence which some peculiarities in the mere form and substance of his family mansion, had, by dint of long sufferance, he said, obtained over his spirit-an effect which the *physique* of the gray walls and turrets, and of the dim tarn into which they all looked down, had, at length, brought about upon the *morale* of his existence.

He admitted, however, although with hesitation, that much of the peculiar gloom which thus afflicted him could be traced to a more natural and far more palpable[12] origin –to the severe and long-continued illness –indeed to the evidently approaching dissolution-of a tenderly beloved sister –his sole companion for long years –his last and only relative on earth. "Her decease," he said, with a bitterness which I can never forget, "would leave him (him the hopeless and the frail) the last of the ancient race of the Ushers." While he spoke, the lady Madeline (for so was she called) passed slowly through a remote portion of the apartment, and, without having noticed my presence, disappeared.

I regarded her with an utter astonishment not unmingled with dread –and yet I found it impossible to account for such feelings. A sensation of stupor oppressed me, as my eyes followed her retreating steps. When a door, at length, closed upon her, my glance sought instinctively and eagerly the countenance of the brother –but he had buried his face in his hands, and I could only perceive that a far more than ordinary wanness had overspread the

---

[12] Physical characteristics

emaciated fingers through which trickled many passionate tears.

The disease of the lady Madeline had long baffled the skill of her physicians. A settled apathy, a gradual wasting away of the person, and frequent although transient affections of a partially cataleptical[13] character, were the unusual diagnosis. Hitherto she had steadily borne up against the pressure of her malady, and had not betaken herself finally to bed; but, on the closing in of the evening of my arrival at the house, she succumbed (as her brother told me at night within expressible agitation) to the prostrating[14] power of the destroyer; and I learned that the glimpse I had obtained of her person would thus probably be the last I should obtain –that the lady, at least while living, would be seen by me no more.

For several days ensuing, her name was unmentioned by either Usher or myself: and during this period I was busied in earnest endeavours to alleviate the melancholy of my friend. We painted and read together; or I listened, as if in a dream, to the wild improvisations of his speaking guitar. And thus, as a closer and still intimacy admitted me more unreservedly into the recesses of his spirit, the more bitterly did I perceive the futility of all attempt at cheering a mind from which darkness, as if an inherent positive quality, poured forth upon all objects of the moral and physical universe, in one unceasing radiation of gloom.

I shall ever bear about me a memory of the many solemn hours I thus spent alone with the master of the House of Usher. Yet I should fail in any attempt to convey an idea of the exact character of the studies, or of the occupations, in which he involved me, or led me the way. An excited and highly distempered ideality threw a sulphureous[15] lustre over all. His long improvised dirges[15] will ring forever in my ears. Among other things, I hold painfully in mind a certain singular perversion and amplification of the wild air of the last waltz of Von Weber.[16] From the paintings over which his elaborate

---

[13] Unresponsive to external stimulus
[14] Humbling
[15] Yellowy qualities of sulfur
[15] Funeral songs
[16] Waltz of German conductor Karl Gottlieb Reissiger (1798-1859), copied by Baron Karl Maria Friedrich Ernst von Weber (1786-1826)

fancy brooded, and which grew, touch by touch, into vaguenesses at which I shuddered the more thrillingly, because I shuddered knowing not why; –from these paintings (vivid as their images now are before me) I would in vain endeavour to educe more than a small portion which should lie within the compass of merely written words. By the utter simplicity, by the nakedness of his designs, he arrested and overawed attention. If ever mortal painted an idea, that mortal was Roderick Usher. For me at least –in the circumstances then surrounding me –there arose out of the pure abstractions which the hypochondriac[17] contrived to throw upon his canvas, an intensity of intolerable awe, no shadow of which felt I ever yet in the contemplation of the certainly glowing yet too concrete reveries[18] of Fuseli.[19]

One of the phantasmagoric conceptions of my friend, partaking not so rigidly of the spirit of abstraction, may be shadowed forth, although feebly, in words. A small picture presented the interior of an immensely long and rectangular vault or tunnel, with low walls, smooth, white, and without interruption or device. Certain accessory points of the design served well to convey the idea that this excavation lay at an exceeding depth below the surface of the earth. No outlet was observed in any portion of its vast extent, and no torch, or other artificial source of light was discernible; yet a flood of intense rays rolled throughout, and bathed the whole in a ghastly and inappropriate splendour.

I have just spoken of that morbid condition of the auditory nerve which rendered all music intolerable to the sufferer, with the exception of certain effects of stringed instruments. It was, perhaps, the narrow limits to which he thus confined himself upon the guitar, which gave birth, in great measure, to the fantastic character of his performances. But the fervid *facility* of his *impromptus*[20] could not be so accounted for. They must have been, and were, in the notes, as well as in the words of his wild fantasias (for he not unfrequently accompanied himself with rhymed verbal improvisations), the result of that

---

[17] Imagined perpetual sickness
[18] Daydreams
[19] Henry Fuseli (1741-1825), Swiss painter, works include *The Nightmare*
[20] Prompted by the occasion

intense mental collectedness and concentration to which I have previously alluded as observable only in particular moments of the highest artificial excitement. The words of one of these rhapsodies I have easily remembered. I was, perhaps, the more forcibly impressed with it, as he gave it, because, in the under or mystic current of its meaning, I fancied that I perceived, and for the first time, a full consciousness on the part of Usher, of the tottering of his lofty reason upon her throne. The verses, which were entitled "The Haunted Palace," ran very nearly, if not accurately, thus:

I.

In the greenest of our valleys,
By good angels tenanted,
Once fair and stately palace –
Radiant palace –reared its head.
In the monarch Thought's dominion –
It stood there!
Never seraph spread a pinion
Over fabric half so fair.

II.

Banners yellow, glorious, golden,
On its roof did float and flow;
(This –all this –was in the olden Time long ago)
And every gentle air that dallied,
In that sweet day,
Along the ramparts plumed and pallid,
A winged odour went away.

III.

Wanderers in that happy valley
Through two luminous windows saw
Spirits moving musically
To a lute's well-tuned law,
Round about a throne, where sitting
(Porphyrogene!)
In state his glory well befitting,
The ruler of the realm was seen.

IV.

And all with pearl and ruby glowing
Was the fair palace door,
Through which came flowing, flowing, flowing
And sparkling evermore,
A troop of Echoes whose sweet duty
Was but to sing,
In voices of surpassing beauty,
The wit and wisdom of their king.

V.

But evil things, in robes of sorrow,
Assailed the monarch's high estate;
(Ah, let us mourn, for never morrow
Shall dawn upon him, desolate!)
And, round about his home, the glory
That blushed and bloomed
Is but a dim-remembered story
Of the old time entombed.

VI.

And travelers now within that valley,
Through the red-litten windows, see
Vast forms that move fantastically
To a discordant melody;
While, like a rapid ghastly river,
Through the pale door,
A hideous throng rush out forever,
And laugh –but smile no more.

I well remember that suggestions arising from this ballad led us into a train of thought wherein there became manifest an opinion of Usher's which I mention not so much on account of its novelty, (for other men have thought thus,) as on account of the pertinacity with which he maintained it. This opinion, in its general form, was that of the sentience[21] of all vegetable things. But, in his disordered fancy, the idea had assumed a more daring character, and trespassed, under certain conditions, upon the kingdom of inorganization. I lack words to express the full extent, or the earnest *abandon* of his persuasion. The

---

[21] Feeling apart from perception

belief, however, was connected (as I have previously hinted) with the gray stones of the home of his forefathers.

The conditions of the sentience had been here, he imagined, fulfilled in the method of collocation[22] of these stones –in the order of their arrangement, as well as in that of the many *fungi* which overspread them, and of the decayed trees which stood around –above all, in the long undisturbed endurance of this arrangement, and in its reduplication in the still waters of the tarn. Its evidence – the evidence of the sentience –was to be seen, he said, (and I here started as he spoke,) in the gradual yet certain condensation of an atmosphere of their own about the waters and the walls. The result was discoverable, he added, in that silent, yet importunate and terrible influence which for centuries had moulded the destinies of his family, and which made *him* what I now saw him – what he was. Such opinions need no comment, and I will make none.

Our books –the books which, for years, had formed no small portion of the mental existence of the invalid –were, as might be supposed, in strict keeping with this character of phantasm. We pored together over such works as the Ververt et Chartreuse of Gresset;[23] the Belphegor of Machiavelli;[24] the Heaven and Hell of Swedenborg;[25] the Subterranean Voyage of Nicholas Klimm by Holberg;[26] the Chiromancy of Robert Flud,[27] of Jean D'Indaginé, and of De la Chambre;[28] the Journey into the Blue Distance of Tieck;[29] and the City of the Sun

---

[22] Act of placing

[23] Poem "Vert-Vert, the Parrot" by Jean-Baptiste Gresset (1709-1777)

[24] "The Marriage of Belphegor" by Niccolò Machiavelli (1469-1527), tells of demon that returns to Hell instead of staying married to his Christian wife

[25] "Heaven and It's Wonders, and Hell from Things Heard and Seen" by Emanuel Swedenbord (1688-1772)

[26] Ludvig Holberg (1684-1754), Danish author who penned *"Nicolai Klimii iter subterraneum"* in 1741

[27] Robert Flud (1574-1637), theologist and author, who proposed the foretelling of the future through palm reading

[28] Jean D'Indagine (early 16th century) and Maria Cireau de la Chaimbre (1594-1669), both wrote treatises of palm reading

[29] German gothic writer Ludwig Tieck (1773-1853), wrote *"Das Alte Buch, oder Die Reise in das Blaue Hinein,"* about a trip to the netherworld

of Campanella.[30] One favourite volume was a small octavo edition[31] of the Directorium Inquisitorum, by the Dominican Eymeric de Gironne;[32] and there were passages in Pomponius Mela,[33] about the old African Satyrs[34] and AEgipans,[35] over which Usher would sit dreaming for hours. His chief delight, however, was found in the perusal of an exceedingly rare and curious book in quarto Gothic –the manual of a forgotten church –the *Vigilæ Mortuorum secundum Chorum Ecclesiae Maguntinæ.*[36]

I could not help thinking of the wild ritual of this work, and of its probable influence upon the hypochondriac, when, one evening, having informed me abruptly that the lady Madeline was no more, he stated his intention of preserving her corpse for a fortnight, (previously to its final interment,) in one of the numerous vaults within the main walls of the building. The worldly reason, however, assigned for this singular proceeding, was one which I did not feel at liberty to dispute. The brother had been led to his resolution (so he told me) by consideration of the unusual character of the malady of the deceased, of certain obtrusive and eager inquiries on the part of her medical men, and of the remote and exposed situation of the burial-ground of the family. I will not deny that when I called to mind the sinister countenance of the person whom I met upon the stair case, on the day of my arrival at the house, I had no desire to oppose what I regarded as at best but a harmless, and by no means an unnatural, precaution.

At the request of Usher, I personally aided him in the arrangements for the temporary entombment. The body having been encoffined, we two alone bore it to its rest. The vault in which we placed it (and which had been so long unopened that our torches, half smothered in its

---

[30] Tommaso Campanella (1568-1639), wrote *"La città del Sole"* in 1602 that uses astrology to predict the future

[31] Book pages each folded into eight leaves

[32] Nicola Emeric de Gerone, Inquistor Gerneral in Castile, recorded torturing practices

[33] Pomponius Mela, penned wild accounts of people and animals in faraway lands

[34] Satyroi Libyes were African tribes believed to inhabit Atlas Mountains of North Africa by the Greeks

[35] Greek Woodland god Pan, similar to Centaur but with goat body

[36] Vigils of the dead

oppressive atmosphere, gave us little opportunity for investigation) was small, damp, and entirely without means of admission for light; lying, at great depth, immediately beneath that portion of the building in which was my own sleeping apartment. It had been used, apparently, in remote feudal times,[37] for the worst purposes of a donjon-keep,[38] and, in later days, as a place of deposit for powder, or some other highly combustible substance, as a portion of its floor, and the whole interior of a long archway through which we reached it, were carefully sheathed with copper. The door, of massive iron, had been, also, similarly protected. Its immense weight caused an unusually sharp grating sound, as it moved upon its hinges.

Having deposited our mournful burden upon tressels[39] within this region of horror, we partially turned aside the yet unscrewed lid of the coffin, and looked upon the face of the tenant. A striking similitude between the brother and sister now first arrested my attention; and Usher, divining, perhaps, my thoughts, murmured out some few words from which I learned that the deceased and himself had been twins, and that sympathies of a scarcely intelligible nature had always existed between them. Our glances, however, rested not long upon the dead –for we could not regard her unawed. The disease which had thus entombed the lady in the maturity of youth, had left, as usual in all maladies of a strictly cataleptical character, the mockery of a faint blush upon the bosom and the face, and that suspiciously lingering smile upon the lip which is so terrible in death. We replaced and screwed down the lid, and, having secured the door of iron, made our way, with toll, into the scarcely less gloomy apartments of the upper portion of the house.

And now, some days of bitter grief having elapsed, an observable change came over the features of the mental disorder of my friend. His ordinary manner had vanished. His ordinary occupations were neglected or forgotten. He roamed from chamber to chamber with hurried, unequal, and objectless step.

The pallor of his countenance had assumed, if possible, a more ghastly hue –but the luminousness of his eye had

---

[37] Land held in fee by feudal lords
[38] Dungeon keeper
[39] Frame or support

utterly gone out. The once occasional huskiness of his tone was heard no more; and a tremulous quaver, as if of extreme terror, habitually characterized his utterance. There were times, indeed, when I thought his unceasingly agitated mind was labouring with some oppressive secret, to divulge which he struggled for the necessary courage. At times, again, I was obliged to resolve all into the mere inexplicable vagaries of madness, for I beheld him gazing upon vacancy for long hours, in an attitude of the profoundest attention, as if listening to some imaginary sound. It was no wonder that his condition terrified-that it infected me. I felt creeping upon me, by slow yet certain degrees, the wild influences of his own fantastic yet impressive superstitions.

It was, especially, upon retiring to bed late in the night of the seventh or eighth day after the placing of the lady Madeline within the donjon, that I experienced the full power of such feelings. Sleep came not near my couch – while the hours waned and waned away. I struggled to reason off the nervousness which had dominion over me. I endeavoured to believe that much, if not all of what I felt, was due to the bewildering influence of the gloomy furniture of the room –of the dark and tattered draperies, which, tortured into motion by the breath of a rising tempest, swayed fitfully to and fro upon the walls, and rustled uneasily about the decorations of the bed. But my efforts were fruitless. An irrepressible tremour gradually pervaded my frame; and, at length, there sat upon my very heart an incubus[40] of utterly causeless alarm. Shaking this off with a gasp and a struggle, I uplifted myself upon the pillows, and, peering earnestly within the intense darkness of the chamber, hearkened –I know not why, except that an instinctive spirit prompted me –to certain low and indefinite sounds which came, through the pauses of the storm, at long intervals, I knew not whence.

Overpowered by an intense sentiment of horror, unaccountable yet unendurable, I threw on my clothes with haste (for I felt that I should sleep no more during the night), and endeavoured to arouse myself from the pitiable condition into which I had fallen, by pacing rapidly to and fro through the apartment.

I had taken but few turns in this manner, when a light step on an adjoining staircase arrested my attention. I

---

[40] Evil spirit, descends on sleeping women

presently recognised it as that of Usher. In an instant afterward he rapped, with a gentle touch, at my door, and entered, bearing a lamp. His countenance was, as usual, cadaverously wan –but, moreover, there was a species of mad hilarity in his eyes –an evidently restrained *hysteria* in his whole demeanour. His air appalled me –but anything was preferable to the solitude which I had so long endured, and I even welcomed his presence as a relief.

"And you have not seen it?" he said abruptly, after having stared about him for some moments in silence – "you have not then seen it? –but, stay! you shall." Thus speaking, and having carefully shaded his lamp, he hurried to one of the casements,[41] and threw it freely open to the storm.

The impetuous fury of the entering gust nearly lifted us from our feet. It was, indeed, a tempestuous yet sternly beautiful night, and one wildly singular in its terror and its beauty. A whirlwind had apparently collected its force in our vicinity; for there were frequent and violent alterations in the direction of the wind; and the exceeding density of the clouds (which hung so low as to press upon the turrets of the house) did not prevent our perceiving the life-like velocity with which they flew careering from all points against each other, without passing away into the distance. I say that even their exceeding density did not prevent our perceiving this –yet we had no glimpse of the moon or stars –nor was there any flashing forth of the lightning. But the under surfaces of the huge masses of agitated vapour, as well as all terrestrial objects immediately around us, were glowing in the unnatural light of a faintly luminous and distinctly visible gaseous exhalation which hung about and enshrouded the mansion.

"You must not –you shall not behold this!" said I, shudderingly, to Usher, as I led him, with a gentle violence, from the window to a seat. "These appearances, which bewilder you, are merely electrical phenomena not uncommon –or it may be that they have their ghastly origin in the rank miasma[42] of the tarn. Let us close this casement; –the air is chilling and dangerous to your frame. Here is one of your favourite romances. I will read,

---

[41] Window sash, opens outward
[42] Vaporous atmosphere

and you shall listen; –and so we will pass away this terrible night together."

The antique volume which I had taken up was the "Mad Trist" of Sir Launcelot Canning;[43] but I had called it a favourite of Usher's more in sad jest than in earnest; for, in truth, there is little in its uncouth and unimaginative prolixity[44] which could have had interest for the lofty and spiritual ideality of my friend. It was, however, the only book immediately at hand; and I indulged a vague hope that the excitement which now agitated the hypochondriac, might find relief (for the history of mental disorder is full of similar anomalies) even in the extremeness of the folly which I should read. Could I have judged, indeed, by the wild over-strained air of vivacity with which he hearkened, or apparently hearkened, to the words of the tale, I might well have congratulated myself upon the success of my design.

I had arrived at that well-known portion of the story where Ethelred, the hero of the Trist, having sought in vain for peaceable admission into the dwelling of the hermit, proceeds to make good an entrance by force. Here, it will be remembered, the words of the narrative run thus: "And Ethelred, who was by nature of a doughty heart, and who was now mighty withal, on account of the powerfulness of the wine which he had drunken, waited no longer to hold parley with the hermit, who, in sooth, was of an obstinate and maliceful turn, but, feeling the rain upon his shoulders, and fearing the rising of the tempest, uplifted his mace[45] outright, and, with blows, made quickly room in the plankings of the door for his gauntleted hand; and now pulling there-with sturdily, he so cracked, and ripped, and tore all asunder, that the noise of the dry and hollow-sounding wood alarumed and reverberated throughout the forest.

At the termination of this sentence I started, and for a moment, paused; for it appeared to me (although I at once concluded that my excited fancy had deceived me) –it appeared to me that, from some very remote portion of the mansion, there came, indistinctly, to my ears, what might have been, in its exact similarity of character, the echo (but a stifled and dull one certainly) of the very cracking

---

[43] Author and book are Poe fabrications

[44] Prolonged

[45] Medieval club with spiked end

and ripping sound which Sir Launcelot had so particularly described. It was, beyond doubt, the coincidence alone which had arrested my attention; for, amid the rattling of the sashes of the casements, and the ordinary commingled noises of the still increasing storm, the sound, in itself, had nothing, surely, which should have interested or disturbed me. I continued the story:

"But the good champion Ethelred, now entering within the door, was sore enraged and amazed to perceive no signal of the maliceful hermit; but, in the stead thereof, a dragon of a scaly and prodigious demeanour, and of a fiery tongue, which sate in guard before a palace of gold, with a floor of silver; and upon the wall there hung a shield of shining brass with this legend enwritten –

Who entereth herein, a conqueror hath bin;
Who slayeth the dragon, the shield he shall win;

And Ethelred uplifted his mace, and struck upon the head of the dragon, which fell before him, and gave up his pesty breath, with a shriek so horrid and harsh, and withal so piercing, that Ethelred had fain to close his ears with his hands against the dreadful noise of it, the like whereof was never before heard."

Here again I paused abruptly, and now with a feeling of wild amazement –for there could be no doubt whatever that, in this instance, I did actually hear (although from what direction it proceeded I found it impossible to say) a low and apparently distant, but harsh, protracted, and most unusual screaming or grating sound –the exact counterpart of what my fancy had already conjured up for the dragon's unnatural shriek as described by the romancer.

Oppressed, as I certainly was, upon the occurrence of the second and most extraordinary coincidence, by a thousand conflicting sensations, in which wonder and extreme terror were predominant, I still retained sufficient presence of mind to avoid exciting, by any observation, the sensitive nervousness of my companion. I was by no means certain that he had noticed the sounds in question; although, assuredly, a strange alteration had, during the last few minutes, taken place in his demeanour. From a position fronting my own, he had gradually brought round his chair, so as to sit with his face to the door of the chamber; and thus I could but partially perceive his features, although I saw that his lips trembled as if he were murmuring inaudibly. His head had dropped upon his breast –yet I knew that he was not asleep, from the wide and rigid opening of the eye as I caught a glance of it in profile. The motion of his body, too, was at variance with this idea –for he rocked from side to side with a gentle yet constant and uniform sway. Having rapidly taken notice of all this, I resumed the narrative of Sir Launcelot, which thus proceeded:

"And now, the champion, having escaped from the terrible fury of the dragon, bethinking himself of the brazen shield, and of the breaking up of the enchantment which was upon it, removed the carcass from out of the way before him, and approached valorously over the silver pavement of the castle to where the shield was upon the wall; which in sooth tarried not for his full coming, but fell down at his feet upon the silver floor, with a mighty great and terrible ringing sound."

No sooner had these syllables passed my lips, than –as if a shield of brass had indeed, at the moment, fallen heavily upon a floor of silver became aware of a distinct, hollow, metallic, and clangorous, yet apparently muffled reverberation. Completely unnerved, I leaped to my feet; but the measured rocking movement of Usher was undisturbed. I rushed to the chair in which he sat. His eyes were bent fixedly before him, and throughout his whole countenance there reigned a stony rigidity. But, as I placed my hand upon his shoulder, there came a strong shudder over his whole person; a sickly smile quivered about his lips; and I saw that he spoke in a low, hurried, and gibbering murmur, as if unconscious of my presence. Bending closely over him, I at length drank in the hideous import of his words.

"Not hear it? –yes, I hear it, and *have* heard it. Long – long –long –many minutes, many hours, many days, have I heard it –yet I dared not –oh, pity me, miserable wretch that I am! –I dared not –I *dared* not speak! *We have put her living in the tomb!* Said I not that my senses were acute? I *now* tell you that I heard her first feeble movements in the hollow coffin. I heard them –many, many days ago –yet I dared not –*I dared not speak!* And now –tonight –Ethelred –ha! ha! –the breaking of the hermit's door, and the death-cry of the dragon, and the clangour of the shield! –say, rather, the rending of her coffin, and the grating of the iron hinges of her prison, and her struggles within the coppered archway of the vault! Oh whither shall I fly?

Will she not be here anon?[46] Is she not hurrying to upbraid me for my haste? Have I not heard her footstep on the stair? Do I not distinguish that heavy and horrible beating of her heart? Madman!" here he sprang furiously to his feet, and shrieked out his syllables, as if in the effort he were giving up his soul – *"Madman! I tell you that she now stands without the door!"*

As if in the superhuman energy of his utterance there had been found the potency of a spell –the huge antique panels to which the speaker pointed, threw slowly back, upon the instant, ponderous and ebony jaws. It was the work of the rushing gust –but then without those doors there *did* stand the lofty and enshrouded figure of the lady Madeline of Usher. There was blood upon her white robes, and the evidence of some bitter struggle upon every portion of her emaciated frame. For a moment she remained trembling and reeling to and fro upon the threshold, then, with a low moaning cry, fell heavily inward upon the person of her brother, and in her violent and now final death-agonies, bore him to the floor a corpse, and a victim to the terrors he had anticipated.

From that chamber, and from that mansion, I fled aghast. The storm was still abroad in all its wrath as I found myself crossing the old causeway. Suddenly there shot along the path a wild light, and I turned to see whence a gleam so unusual could have issued; for the vast house and its shadows were alone behind me. The radiance was that of the full, setting, and blood-red moon which now shone vividly through that once barely-discernible fissure of which I have before spoken as extending from the roof of the building, in a zigzag direction, to the base.

While I gazed, this fissure rapidly widened –there came a fierce breath of the whirlwind –the entire orb of the satellite burst at once upon my sight –my brain reeled as I saw the mighty walls rushing asunder –there was a long tumultuous shouting sound like the voice of a thousand waters –and the deep and dank tarn at my feet closed sullenly and silently over the fragments of the *"House of Usher."*

---

[46] Soon

CHARLES DICKENS
(1812-1870)

Φ

The Old Man's Tale About the Queer Client

"The Old Man's Tale About the Queer Client" was first published in Dickens's series of short stories entitled, "The Pickwick Papers" in November of 1836. The story takes place in Marshalsea, the now famous debtor's prison that housed Charles Dickens, his parents, and siblings when his father was imprisoned for indebtedness in 1824. The prison was hundreds of years old. It origins date back to at least the 1300s. In the 1800s it was known for its harsh living conditions. Marshalsea would later make a more prominent appearance in Dickens's novel "Little Dorrit."

It may come as a surprise that Charles Dickens wrote a horror story. "The Old Man's Tale About the Queer Client" has been collected in various tales of terror and "weird tales" books over the years. While not the best horror story in this collection, it is the foremost tale of revenge and satisfies all the criteria for a great horror story. It has a pervasive sense of dread throughout and readers are emotionally vested in the characters. Who better than Charles Dickens to entwine the hearts of readers with his characters? He does it in such a way that one almost feels it is their own family who is in the dire situation presented. The dialogue in this story is some of

the best in this collection and is only rivaled by that of
George Soane in "The Lighthouse," which is the next story
in this collection.

Similar to Hawthorne's "The Minister's Black Veil,"
which is also contained in this anthology, this story has
none of the blood or gore many associate with modern
horror stories. The horrific effect of the ending contained
in "The Old Man's Tale About the Queer Client" is no less
dramatic and leaves an indelible impression.

The Old Man's Tale
About the Queer Client

'IT MATTERS LITTLE,' SAID the old man, 'where, or how, I picked up this brief history. If I were to relate it in the order in which it reached me, I should commence in the middle, and when I had arrived at the conclusion, go back for a beginning. It is enough for me to say that some of its circumstances passed before my own eyes; for the remainder I know them to have happened, and there are some persons yet living, who will remember them but too well.

'In the Borough High Street, near St. George's Church, and on the same side of the way, stands, as most people know, the smallest of our debtors' prisons,[1] the Marshalsea. Although in later times it has been a very different place from the sink of filth and dirt it once was, even its improved condition holds out but little temptation to the extravagant, or consolation to the improvident. The condemned felon has as good a yard for air and exercise in Newgate, as the insolvent debtor in the Marshalsea Prison.[2]

'It may be my fancy, or it may be that I cannot separate the place from the old recollections associated with it, but this part of London I cannot bear. The street is broad, the shops are spacious, the noise of passing vehicles, the footsteps of a perpetual stream of people—all the busy sounds of traffic, resound in it from morn to midnight; but the streets around are mean and close; poverty and debauchery lie festering in the crowded alleys; want and misfortune are pent up in the narrow prison; an air of gloom and dreariness seems, in my eyes at least, to hang about the scene, and to impart to it a squalid and sickly hue.

'Many eyes, that have long since been closed in the grave, have looked round upon that scene lightly enough, when entering the gate of the old Marshalsea Prison for

---

[1] Prison where those who cannot pay their debts are placed.

[2] Better. But this is past, in a better age, and the prison exists no longer.

the first time; for despair seldom comes with the first severe shock of misfortune. A man has confidence in untried friends, he remembers the many offers of service so freely made by his boon companions when he wanted them not; he has hope—the hope of happy inexperience— and however he may bend beneath the first shock, it springs up in his bosom, and flourishes there for a brief space, until it droops beneath the blight of disappointment and neglect. How soon have those same eyes, deeply sunken in the head, glared from faces wasted with famine, and sallow from confinement, in days when it was no figure of speech to say that debtors rotted in prison, with no hope of release, and no prospect of liberty! The atrocity in its full extent no longer exists, but there is enough of it left to give rise to occurrences that make the heart bleed.

'Twenty years ago, that pavement was worn with the footsteps of a mother and child, who, day by day, so surely as the morning came, presented themselves at the prison gate; often after a night of restless misery and anxious thoughts, were they there, a full hour too soon, and then the young mother turning meekly away, would lead the child to the old bridge, and raising him in her arms to show him the glistening water, tinted with the light of the morning's sun, and stirring with all the bustling preparations for business and pleasure that the river presented at that early hour, endeavour to interest his thoughts in the objects before him. But she would quickly set him down, and hiding her face in her shawl, give vent to the tears that blinded her; for no expression of interest or amusement lighted up his thin and sickly face. His recollections were few enough, but they were all of one kind—all connected with the poverty and misery of his parents. Hour after hour had he sat on his mother's knee, and with childish sympathy watched the tears that stole down her face, and then crept quietly away into some dark corner, and sobbed himself to sleep. The hard realities of the world, with many of its worst privations—hunger and thirst, and cold and want—had all come home to him, from the first dawnings of reason; and though the form of childhood was there, its light heart, its merry laugh, and sparkling eyes were wanting.

'The father and mother looked on upon this, and upon each other, with thoughts of agony they dared not breathe in words. The healthy, strong-made man, who could have borne almost any fatigue of active exertion, was wasting beneath the close confinement and unhealthy atmosphere of a crowded prison. The slight and delicate woman was sinking beneath the combined effects of bodily and mental illness. The child's young heart was breaking.

'Winter came, and with it weeks of cold and heavy rain. The poor girl had removed to a wretched apartment close to the spot of her husband's imprisonment; and though the change had been rendered necessary by their increasing poverty, she was happier now, for she was nearer him. For two months, she and her little companion watched the opening of the gate as usual. One day she failed to come, for the first time. Another morning arrived, and she came alone. The child was dead.

'They little know, who coldly talk of the poor man's bereavements, as a happy release from pain to the departed, and a merciful relief from expense to the survivor—they little know, I say, what the agony of those bereavements is. A silent look of affection and regard when all other eyes are turned coldly away—the consciousness that we possess the sympathy and affection of one being when all others have deserted us—is a hold, a stay, a comfort, in the deepest affliction, which no wealth could purchase, or power bestow. The child had sat at his parents' feet for hours together, with his little hands patiently folded in each other, and his thin wan face raised towards them. They had seen him pine away, from day to day; and though his brief existence had been a joyless one, and he was now removed to that peace and rest which, child as he was, he had never known in this world, they were his parents, and his loss sank deep into their souls.

'It was plain to those who looked upon the mother's altered face, that death must soon close the scene of her adversity and trial. Her husband's fellow-prisoners shrank from obtruding on his grief and misery, and left to himself alone, the small room he had previously occupied in common with two companions. She shared it with him; and lingering on without pain, but without hope, her life ebbed slowly away.

'She had fainted one evening in her husband's arms, and he had borne her to the open window, to revive her with the air, when the light of the moon falling full upon her face, showed him a change upon her features, which made him stagger beneath her weight, like a helpless infant.

"'Set me down, George," she said faintly. He did so, and seating himself beside her, covered his face with his hands, and burst into tears.

"'It is very hard to leave you, George," she said; "but it is God's will, and you must bear it for my sake. Oh! how I thank Him for having taken our boy! He is happy, and in heaven now. What would he have done here, without his mother!"

"'You shall not die, Mary, you shall not die;" said the husband, starting up. He paced hurriedly to and fro, striking his head with his clenched fists; then reseating himself beside her, and supporting her in his arms, added more calmly, "Rouse yourself, my dear girl. Pray, pray do. You will revive yet."

"'Never again, George; never again," said the dying woman. "Let them lay me by my poor boy now, but promise me, that if ever you leave this dreadful place, and should grow rich, you will have us removed to some quiet country churchyard, a long, long way off—very far from here—where we can rest in peace. Dear George, promise me you will."

"'I do, I do," said the man, throwing himself passionately on his knees before her. "Speak to me, Mary, another word; one look—but one!"

'He ceased to speak: for the arm that clasped his neck grew stiff and heavy. A deep sigh escaped from the wasted form before him; the lips moved, and a smile played upon the face; but the lips were pallid, and the smile faded into a rigid and ghastly stare. He was alone in the world.

'That night, in the silence and desolation of his miserable room, the wretched man knelt down by the dead body of his wife, and called on God to witness a terrible oath, that from that hour, he devoted himself to revenge her death and that of his child; that thenceforth to the last moment of his life, his whole energies should be directed to this one object; that his revenge should be protracted and terrible; that his hatred should be undying and inextinguishable; and should hunt its object through the world.

'The deepest despair, and passion scarcely human, had made such fierce ravages on his face and form, in that one night, that his companions in misfortune shrank affrighted from him as he passed by. His eyes were bloodshot and heavy, his face a deadly white, and his body bent as if with age. He had bitten his under lip nearly through in the violence of his mental suffering, and the blood which had flowed from the wound had trickled down his chin, and stained his shirt and neckerchief. No tear, or sound of complaint escaped him; but the unsettled look, and disordered haste with which he paced up and down the yard, denoted the fever which was burning within.

'It was necessary that his wife's body should be removed from the prison, without delay. He received the communication with perfect calmness, and acquiesced in its propriety. Nearly all the inmates of the prison had assembled to witness its removal; they fell back on either side when the widower appeared; he walked hurriedly forward, and stationed himself, alone, in a little railed area close to the lodge gate, from whence the crowd, with an instinctive feeling of delicacy, had retired. The rude coffin was borne slowly forward on men's shoulders. A dead silence pervaded the throng, broken only by the audible lamentations of the women, and the shuffling steps of the bearers on the stone pavement. They reached the spot where the bereaved husband stood: and stopped. He laid his hand upon the coffin, and mechanically adjusting the pall with which it was covered, motioned them onward. The turnkeys in the prison lobby took off their hats as it passed through, and in another moment the heavy gate closed behind it. He looked vacantly upon the crowd, and fell heavily to the ground.

'Although for many weeks after this, he was watched, night and day, in the wildest ravings of fever, neither the consciousness of his loss, nor the recollection of the vow he had made, ever left him for a moment. Scenes changed before his eyes, place succeeded place, and event followed event, in all the hurry of delirium; but they were all connected in some way with the great object of his mind. He was sailing over a boundless expanse of sea, with a blood-red sky above, and the angry waters, lashed into fury beneath, boiling and eddying up, on every side. There was another vessel before them, toiling and labouring in the howling storm; her canvas[3] fluttering in ribbons from the mast, and her deck thronged with figures who were lashed to the sides, over which huge waves every instant burst, sweeping away some devoted creatures into the foaming sea. Onward they bore, amidst the roaring mass of water, with a speed and force which nothing could

---

[3] Sail

resist; and striking the stem of the foremost vessel, crushed her beneath their keel.[4] From the huge whirlpool which the sinking wreck occasioned, arose a shriek so loud and shrill—the death-cry of a hundred drowning creatures, blended into one fierce yell—that it rung far above the war-cry of the elements, and echoed, and re-echoed till it seemed to pierce air, sky, and ocean. But what was that—that old gray head that rose above the water's surface, and with looks of agony, and screams for aid, buffeted with the waves! One look, and he had sprung from the vessel's side, and with vigorous strokes was swimming towards it. He reached it; he was close upon it. They were HIS features. The old man saw him coming, and vainly strove to elude his grasp. But he clasped him tight, and dragged him beneath the water. Down, down with him, fifty fathoms down; his struggles grew fainter and fainter, until they wholly ceased. He was dead; he had killed him, and had kept his oath.

'He was traversing the scorching sands of a mighty desert, barefoot and alone. The sand choked and blinded him; its fine thin grains entered the very pores of his skin, and irritated him almost to madness. Gigantic masses of the same material, carried forward by the wind, and shone through by the burning sun, stalked in the distance like pillars of living fire. The bones of men, who had perished in the dreary waste, lay scattered at his feet; a fearful light fell on everything around; so far as the eye could reach, nothing but objects of dread and horror presented themselves. Vainly striving to utter a cry of terror, with his tongue cleaving to his mouth, he rushed madly forward. Armed with supernatural strength, he waded through the sand, until, exhausted with fatigue and thirst, he fell senseless on the earth. What fragrant coolness revived him; what gushing sound was that? Water! It was indeed a well; and the clear fresh stream was running at his feet. He drank deeply of it, and throwing his aching limbs upon the bank, sank into a delicious trance. The sound of approaching footsteps roused him. An old gray-headed man tottered forward to slake his burning thirst. It was *he* again! He wound his arms round the old man's body, and held him back. He struggled, and shrieked for water—for but one drop of water to save his life! But he held the old man firmly, and watched his agonies with greedy eyes;

---

[4] Beam stretching lengthwise along the hull, or bottom, of a ship

and when his lifeless head fell forward on his bosom, he rolled the corpse from him with his feet.

'When the fever left him, and consciousness returned, he awoke to find himself rich and free, to hear that the parent who would have let him die in jail—*would!* who *had* let those who were far dearer to him than his own existence die of want, and sickness of heart that medicine cannot cure—had been found dead in his bed of down. He had had all the heart to leave his son a beggar, but proud even of his health and strength, had put off the act till it was too late, and now might gnash his teeth in the other world, at the thought of the wealth his remissness had left him. He awoke to this, and he awoke to more. To recollect the purpose for which he lived, and to remember that his enemy was his wife's own father—the man who had cast him into prison, and who, when his daughter and her child sued at his feet for mercy, had spurned them from his door. Oh, how he cursed the weakness that prevented him from being up, and active, in his scheme of vengeance!

'He caused himself to be carried from the scene of his loss and misery, and conveyed to a quiet residence on the sea-coast; not in the hope of recovering his peace of mind or happiness, for both were fled for ever; but to restore his prostrate energies, and meditate on his darling object. And here, some evil spirit cast in his way the opportunity for his first, most horrible revenge.

'It was summertime; and wrapped in his gloomy thoughts, he would issue from his solitary lodgings early in the evening, and wandering along a narrow path beneath the cliffs, to a wild and lonely spot that had struck his fancy in his ramblings, seat himself on some fallen fragment of the rock, and burying his face in his hands, remain there for hours—sometimes until night had completely closed in, and the long shadows of the frowning cliffs above his head cast a thick, black darkness on every object near him.

'He was seated here, one calm evening, in his old position, now and then raising his head to watch the flight of a sea-gull, or carry his eye along the glorious crimson path, which, commencing in the middle of the ocean, seemed to lead to its very verge where the sun was setting, when the profound stillness of the spot was broken by a loud cry for help; he listened, doubtful of his having heard aright, when the cry was repeated with even greater vehemence than before, and, starting to his feet, he hastened in the direction whence it proceeded.

'The tale told itself at once: some scattered garments lay on the beach; a human head was just visible above the waves at a little distance from the shore; and an old man, wringing his hands in agony, was running to and fro, shrieking for assistance. The invalid, whose strength was now sufficiently restored, threw off his coat, and rushed towards the sea, with the intention of plunging in, and dragging the drowning man ashore.

"Hasten here, Sir, in God's name; help, help, Sir, for the love of Heaven. He is my son, Sir, my only son!" said the old man frantically, as he advanced to meet him. "My only son, Sir, and he is dying before his father's eyes!"

'At the first word the old man uttered, the stranger checked himself in his career, and, folding his arms, stood perfectly motionless.

"Great God!" exclaimed the old man, recoiling, "Heyling!"

'The stranger smiled, and was silent.

"Heyling!" said the old man wildly; "my boy, Heyling, my dear boy, look, look!" Gasping for breath, the miserable father pointed to the spot where the young man was struggling for life.

"Hark!" said the old man. "He cries once more. He is alive yet. Heyling, save him, save him!"

'The stranger smiled again, and remained immovable as a statue. "I have wronged you," shrieked the old man, falling on his knees, and clasping his hands together. "Be revenged; take my all, my life; cast me into the water at your feet, and, if human nature can repress a struggle, I will die, without stirring hand or foot. Do it, Heyling, do it, but save my boy; he is so young, Heyling, so young to die!"

"Listen," said the stranger, grasping the old man fiercely by the wrist; "I will have life for life, and here is ONE. *My* child died, before his father's eyes, a far more agonising and painful death than that young slanderer of his sister's worth is meeting while I speak. You laughed— laughed in your daughter's face, where death had already set his hand—at our sufferings, then. What think you of them now! See there, see there!"

'As the stranger spoke, he pointed to the sea. A faint cry died away upon its surface; the last powerful struggle of the dying man agitated the rippling waves for a few seconds; and the spot where he had gone down into his early grave, was undistinguishable from the surrounding water.

*   *   *   *   *

Three years had elapsed, when a gentleman alighted from a private carriage at the door of a London attorney, then well known as a man of no great nicety in his professional dealings, and requested a private interview on business of importance. Although evidently not past the prime of life, his face was pale, haggard, and dejected; and it did not require the acute perception of the man of business, to discern at a glance, that disease or suffering had done more to work a change in his appearance, than the mere hand of time could have accomplished in twice the period of his whole life.

"'I wish you to undertake some legal business for me," said the stranger.

The attorney bowed obsequiously, and glanced at a large packet which the gentleman carried in his hand. His visitor observed the look, and proceeded.

"'It is no common business," said he; "nor have these papers reached my hands without long trouble and great expense."

The attorney cast a still more anxious look at the packet; and his visitor, untying the string that bound it, disclosed a quantity of promissory notes, with copies of deeds, and other documents.

"'Upon these papers," said the client, "the man whose name they bear, has raised, as you will see, large sums of money, for years past. There was a tacit understanding between him and the men into whose hands they originally went—and from whom I have by degrees purchased the whole, for treble and quadruple their nominal value—that these loans should be from time to time renewed, until a given period had elapsed. Such an understanding is nowhere expressed. He has sustained many losses of late; and these obligations accumulating upon him at once, would crush him to the earth."

"'The whole amount is many thousands of pounds," said the attorney, looking over the papers.

"'It is," said the client.

"'What are we to do?" inquired the man of business.

"'Do!" replied the client, with sudden vehemence. "Put every engine of the law in force, every trick that ingenuity can devise and rascality execute; fair means and foul; the open oppression of the law, aided by all the craft of its most ingenious practitioners. I would have him die a harassing and lingering death. Ruin him, seize and sell his lands and goods, drive him from house and home, and drag him forth a beggar in his old age, to die in a common jail."

"'But the costs, my dear Sir, the costs of all this," reasoned the attorney, when he had recovered from his momentary surprise. "If the defendant be a man of straw, who is to pay the costs, Sir?"

"'Name any sum," said the stranger, his hand trembling so violently with excitement, that he could scarcely hold the pen he seized as he spoke—"any sum, and it is yours. Don't be afraid to name it, man. I shall not think it dear, if you gain my object."

The attorney named a large sum, at hazard, as the advance he should require to secure himself against the possibility of loss; but more with the view of ascertaining how far his client was really disposed to go, than with any idea that he would comply with the demand. The stranger wrote a cheque upon his banker, for the whole amount, and left him.

The draft was duly honoured, and the attorney, finding that his strange client might be safely relied upon, commenced his work in earnest. For more than two years afterwards, Mr. Heyling would sit whole days together, in the office, poring over the papers as they accumulated, and reading again and again, his eyes gleaming with joy, the letters of remonstrance, the prayers for a little delay, the representations of the certain ruin in which the opposite party must be involved, which poured in, as suit after suit, and process after process, was commenced. To all applications for a brief indulgence, there was but one reply—the money must be paid. Land, house, furniture, each in its turn, was taken under some one of the numerous executions which were issued; and the old man himself would have been immured in prison had he not escaped the vigilance of the officers, and fled.

The implacable animosity of Heyling, so far from being satiated by the success of his persecution, increased a hundredfold with the ruin he inflicted. On being informed of the old man's flight, his fury was unbounded. He gnashed his teeth with rage, tore the hair from his head, and assailed with horrid imprecations the men who had been intrusted with the writ. He was only restored to comparative calmness by repeated assurances of the certainty of discovering the fugitive. Agents were sent in quest of him, in all directions; every stratagem that could be invented was resorted to, for the purpose of discovering his place of retreat; but it was all in vain. Half a year had passed over, and he was still undiscovered.

'At length late one night, Heyling, of whom nothing had been seen for many weeks before, appeared at his attorney's private residence, and sent up word that a gentleman wished to see him instantly. Before the attorney, who had recognised his voice from above stairs, could order the servant to admit him, he had rushed up the staircase, and entered the drawing-room pale and breathless. Having closed the door, to prevent being overheard, he sank into a chair, and said, in a low voice—

"'Hush! I have found him at last."

"'No!" said the attorney. "Well done, my dear sir, well done."

"'He lies concealed in a wretched lodging in Camden Town," said Heyling. "Perhaps it is as well we *did* lose sight of him, for he has been living alone there, in the most abject misery, all the time, and he is poor—very poor."

"'Very good," said the attorney. "You will have the caption made tomorrow, of course?"

"'Yes," replied Heyling. "Stay! No! The next day. You are surprised at my wishing to postpone it," he added, with a ghastly smile; "but I had forgotten. The next day is an anniversary in his life: let it be done then."

"'Very good," said the attorney. "Will you write down instructions for the officer?"

"'No; let him meet me here, at eight in the evening, and I will accompany him myself."

They met on the appointed night, and, hiring a hackney-coach,[5] directed the driver to stop at that corner of the old Pancras Road, at which stands the parish workhouse. By the time they alighted there, it was quite dark; and, proceeding by the dead wall[6] in front of the Veterinary Hospital, they entered a small by-street, which is, or was at that time, called Little College Street, and which, whatever it may be now, was in those days a desolate place enough, surrounded by little else than fields and ditches.

---

[5] Horse-drawn coach for hire
[6] Solid wall without doors or windows

'Having drawn the travelling-cap he had on half over his face, and muffled himself in his cloak, Heyling stopped before the meanest-looking house in the street, and knocked gently at the door. It was at once opened by a woman, who dropped a curtsey of recognition, and Heyling, whispering the officer to remain below, crept gently upstairs, and, opening the door of the front room, entered at once.

'The object of his search and his unrelenting animosity, now a decrepit old man, was seated at a bare deal table, on which stood a miserable candle. He started on the entrance of the stranger, and rose feebly to his feet.

'"What now, what now?" said the old man. "What fresh misery is this? What do you want here?"

'"A word with *you*," replied Heyling. As he spoke, he seated himself at the other end of the table, and, throwing off his cloak and cap, disclosed his features.

'The old man seemed instantly deprived of speech. He fell backward in his chair, and, clasping his hands together, gazed on the apparition with a mingled look of abhorrence and fear.

'"This day six years," said Heyling, "I claimed the life you owed me for my child's. Beside the lifeless form of your daughter, old man, I swore to live a life of revenge. I have never swerved from my purpose for a moment's space; but if I had, one thought of her uncomplaining, suffering look, as she drooped away, or of the starving face of our innocent child, would have nerved me to my task. My first act of requital you well remember: this is my last."

'The old man shivered, and his hands dropped powerless by his side.

'"I leave England tomorrow," said Heyling, after a moment's pause. "Tonight I consign you to the living death to which you devoted her—a hopeless prison—"

'He raised his eyes to the old man's countenance, and paused. He lifted the light to his face, set it gently down, and left the apartment.

'"You had better see to the old man," he said to the woman, as he opened the door, and motioned the officer to follow him into the street. "I think he is ill." The woman closed the door, ran hastily upstairs, and found him lifeless.

       *   *   *   *   *

'Beneath a plain gravestone, in one of the most peaceful and secluded churchyards in Kent, where wild flowers mingle with the grass, and the soft landscape around forms the fairest spot in the garden of England, lie the bones of the young mother and her gentle child. But the ashes of the father do not mingle with theirs; nor, from that night forward, did the attorney ever gain the remotest clue to the subsequent history of his queer client.'

GEORGE SOANE
(1812-1870)

Φ

The Lighthouse

This fine tale of madness was first published in the London magazine with the cumbersome name, *The Log Book; or Nautical Miscellany.* The year was 1826. The anonymous author—George Soane. He later printed the short story in his three-volume collection titled, "The Last Ball, and Other Stories," which was published in 1841. The story was listed under the new and benign title of "Lucy Ellis." Despite the varying titles and fifteen years of anonymity, this is the best lighthouse horror story to come out of the first half of the nineteenth century. The only qualification is knowing that Edgar Allan Poe failed to finish his own lighthouse story before his untimely death in 1849.

Soane's creation of realistic dialogue and free-spirited outbursts among the characters is excellent. This mastery of the form stems from his work as a London theatre playwright. The characters upstage this "lighthouse on one of the wildest parts of the English coast" and force the structure to take a small role in the overall story.

Although strangely relegated to obscurity in the annals of English literature, Soane's ghost and horror fiction must not be forgotten. Here is his best horror story, "The Lighthouse." Sadly, in over 180 years since it was first published, it has been uncollected in any anthology; that is, until now.

The Lighthouse

RICHARD CLIFTON WAS ONE of those wild, yet commanding, spirits, that are great in good or evil, according to the more or less favourable circumstances in which they may happen to be placed. His earliest years had been devoted to the navy, and in this service, by his own unassisted merits, he had risen to the rank of a first lieutenant, when a blow given by him to his superior officer thrust him on the world a penniless outcast. The same energies, which had before made him the best of seamen, now rendered him the worst of citizens, for *power* is like the fiend that, once evoked, must have something to employ it, or it falls upon its master.

There was a blight on his fame and on his hopes, yet still there was one chance for him; he had long been attached to Lucy Ellis, who on her side most truly loved her sailor in spite of all his faults, real or supposed—and the one list was equal to the other, for calumny, like the raven, is fond of preying on the weak and wounded. Had the father of the maiden consented to their union, it is most probable that the life of Richard would still have proved honourable to himself, and useful to his country; but old Ellis was one of those heartless, selfish beings, who love their children only as they minister to their own comfort or gratification; he wished to see his daughter married to a rich man, not as the possession of wealth might make her lot the happier, but because a rich son-in-law added to his own importance.

Such a proposal therefore excited his warmest indignation; it was a cutting-up of all his prospects—of the hopes he had been toiling for many years to realize; she would be a beggar, an outcast; the alliance would be infamy. In all this, however, there was much less regard shewn for his child than for himself; or rather for his own peculiar fancies; and Lucy felt there was.

This was the cornerstone of the subsequent evils; the harshness of her father made her more open to the false flatteries of her lover, though, at the same time, she was not altogether ignorant of her own weakness; in the hour of temptation she flung herself on the honour of the man she adored; she owned her inability to resist him, in all the fervour of a real passion, and urged that very passion as a plea for his forbearance. With many this plea had been effectual, but not with men like Richard Clifton, who have no settled rule of conduct, and are either bad or good from the impulse only of the moment. The consequence was the seduction of the too-confiding Lucy; and in a few months afterwards her lover joined a band of smugglers, and was either killed, or drowned, or had fled the country, for each of these reports had its particular abettors.

In the meantime the dishonour of Lucy became too gross for longer concealment. On the discovery of her situation, the heartless merchant at once turned her out of doors, as the destroyer of all his dearest expectations, and bade her starve, or live as she could best settle the matter with the world; nor could any after argument of his friends produce the least relaxation in his purpose; he was deaf to all remonstrance, whether on the score of justice or humanity. But the wrath of heaven, which had first smitten the guilty child, was not slow in punishing the relentless parent, who had arrogated to himself the office of vengeance, and executed it with more of passion than of equity.

In his eagerness to amass a fortune, the merchant overstepped the bounds of prudent speculation. The first great loss stimulated him to a second adventure for its retrieval; and, that miscarrying, in turn brought with it a farther hazard, to fail like those before it, 'till the proud and wealthy Ellis found himself a destitute bankrupt, pursued and crushed by the vindictive spirit of disappointed creditors, who pleaded his cruelty in excuse for theirs.

"You shewed no mercy to your own child, how then can you expect it from me, a stranger?" was the answer of one to whom he was deeply indebted, and who had formerly been a fruitless intercessor for poor Lucy. Some, too, were actuated by less disinterested motives, and were glad to shelter their hatred of the father under the show of compassion for the child. But the result was the same to Ellis; he was a ruined man; his ostentatious charities, which had been so much praised in the days of his prosperity, were now viewed in their true light; they had not procured a single friend to assist him in the hour of distress.

So complete had been the failure, and so rigid his creditors, that a few weeks found the man, whose word had once been good for thousands, possessed of a few pounds only. In this dilemma he quitted his native town, which for the last month he had inhabited from mere pride, and, after a long course of suffering, became the guardian of a lighthouse on one of the wildest parts of the English coast. A very short residence in this sad abode made him a weaker, though not a better, man; he grew, not less selfish, but more timid, more impressed with the actual and near presence of a Creator, and he began to feel that there was not only an after, but a present, vengeance. Nor is this to be wondered at; loneliness brings the mind more immediately in contact with the works of Omnipotence,[1] and, from them, with Omnipotence itself. No man of any imagination was ever an Atheist in solitude, and though, in the case of old Ellis, religion was only the worship of fear, still it was better than no faith at all; it taught him a little more lenity to the faults of others.

Nearly two years had thus passed, when one September's evening a poor maniac in squalid weeds, and with a face gaunt from long misery, came to his door, begging for a morsel of bread and a cup of water—it was his child!—The recognition was quick and mutual, but with very opposite feelings. Sorrow, and pain, and remorse, suddenly threw a dark cloud over the old man's face, while the maniac's eye was lit up with an expression of rage and triumph that was truly fiend-like, as she screamed out, "Ho! ho! ho! have I found you at last? take back your curse, old man; I have borne it long enough, and a sad load and a weary one it has been to me; but take it back; it curdled the milk of my bosom to poison, and my poor babe sucked and died. But take it back, and look that it does not sink you into the depths of hell! Many a time it has lain heavy on me, and I felt myself sinking—sinking—sinking—like one that struggled for life in the flood of waters; but then my sweet babe would come, his cherub-face all bright with glory, just like those clouds where the sun is setting,—and his little hand was stronger than my strength, for it would draw me back again when I was up to my breast in fire. But you have no child to save you; therefore look that your heart be strong;

---

[1] All powerful

you had best no child—no child, old man, for I deny you—
I cast you off; go, leave this earth; it is mine; go! do you
hear? you are the only blot upon the face of this bright
and beautiful world, and I'll none of you. Go!—you'll ask
whither? but that's your concern; there's a large realm
above, and a larger one below, and if they refuse you in
the one it will only be a better recommendation to the
other."

She might still have gone on thus, for old Ellis was too
much shocked to interrupt her, but the wild mood had
exhausted itself; her eye was caught by the sun, resting
with his broad, red disk on the ocean, and her thoughts
reverted to the hunger-pains which incessantly gnawed
her, though they had been unfelt, or, at least, unnoticed,
during the violence of her passion.

On a sudden she exclaimed, "I wish the sun would set
that we might go to supper."

Roused by this appeal, the old man took her by the
hand and would have gently forced her into the
lighthouse, but it was all to no purpose; this singular idea
had got possession of her, though it is not easy to say
from what cause, and she positively refused to move a
step till the sun was below the water.

"He has a long way yet to go," she said; and, taking up
a handful of dust, she scattered it slowly in the air
towards the West, at the same time muttering, or rather
chanting, "Speed! speed! speed!" 'till, by degrees, her
memory pieced out the words of a familiar song, which
she poured forth in the wild manner so peculiar to
insanity:—

"Speed, sun, speed through the ocean wave,
Where the mermaid sings in her coral cave,
Where on sands of gold the pearl is white,
And each glance of thine eye wakes something bright;
Where thy fairest beams upon diamonds play,
That shine with a fairer light than they.

Speed, sun, speed, for from out the wave
A voice invites to the mermaid's cave,
Where the waters are rolling o'er her head,
Like the rainbow's arch o'er the evening spread;
And each drop, which falls from that brilliant bow,
Turns to a gem of the same below."

The sun had sunk below the horizon as the last words died on the maniac's lips, and, Ellis having lit the beacon, they sat down to their humble supper. Both for a time were silent, the daughter from the caprice of insanity, the father because he was stunned and stupefied by her appearance, coupled, as it was, by past recollections. Remorse was busy with him, though it was remorse without repentance; and, if he wished the past recalled, it was more with reference to his own pain than to the sufferings of his daughter. Lucy, however, was in a state that made all these things a matter of indifference to her; and as the evening darkened, her madness took a wilder turn.

"Do you hear, old man? ho! ho! ho! the Spirit of the Wind is abroad. Do you hear what a coil he keeps up yonder, bawling into the ear of old Ocean and calling on him to wake? Do you see the billows too? how lazily they lift up their heads, as if unwilling to leave their slumber! how they toss and tumble, and roar and groan!—but it's all to no purpose; you'll sing a wilder tune yet, my merry boys; and I'll sing with you, and the curlew shall whistle, and the rain shall patter, and the thunder shall rumble, and we'll have a brave music to your dancing, such as the foot of king never danced to."

The face of the old man darkened at this raving; it was making his misery more intolerable, and, if remorse had brought any transient feeling of pity into his heart, it was quite extinguished when he found that his daughter's presence would be a constant source of torment to him. He looked at her with a countenance of wrath, but in the next moment something seemed to stifle the expression of his anger before he had time to give it vent, and he resumed his meal in sullen silence.

The change did not escape Lucy; she fixed her elbows on the table, and, resting her head on her hands, gazed on him for several minutes without moving a muscle, to the sore annoyance of the old man, whose blood was already in a ferment; he swallowed the thin sour beer at long draughts, clutched the handle of his knife more firmly, and tried to force his attention from her. But all to no purpose. Her protracted gaze became, at last, unendurable, and he exclaimed, half rising from his seat, "What in the devil's name do you stare at me for? Can you find nothing else for your eyes but my face?"

"I was counting how long you had to live," said the maniac calmly; "you have only a few hours,—I read it in the lines of your brow— only a few hours, and then I shall be the lady of this castle, and Richard will come home to me and bring our little Lucy with him, and we shall be so happy!—oh, so happy!"

This was too much for the patience of Ellis; he started up from his seat, dashing away his plate with a curse on the poor maniac and the mother who had borne her.

"Woman! — witch! — devil! — you were brought into this world for no purpose but to be my torturer. But I'll not bear it many hours longer; either you or I, and I don't much care which."

He raised his hand to strike, perhaps to kill, her, when a deep flash of lightning blazed between them, and the old tower rocked in the wind as if it were going to tumble about their ears. So tremendous, indeed, was this burst of the storm that a large mass of overhanging cliff, which the water had been for years undermining, was hurled down with a horrible crash, and the spray of its fall came beating against the highest windows of the lighthouse.

"Did you see him?" shouted Lucy.

"See whom?" stammered Ellis, pale and motionless from terror, though without knowing any distinct cause for his apprehension.

"Did you hear him?" echoed the maniac.

"Hear whom?" replied the father in a voice that was scarcely audible.

"So, you neither saw nor heard him?"

"Whom? whom?" exclaimed Ellis, now almost frantic with the impatience of fear.

"The Devil—the arch-fiend—the fisherman of souls. He has you, father; he has marked you with his mark, and signed you with his sign. His broad lightning-wings covered you as he spoke upon your head the baptism of hell;—

One drop of thy blood where the stream is red;
One lock of the hair from thy, purchased head;
One touch of baptizing flame to plough
The mark of your Christ from out your brow;
Ho! ho! how the cold and watery sign
Hisses and dries 'neath this touch of mine!
While I'm Lord of the flame, be the waters thine."

The hair on Ellis' head was actually singed by the lightning; his brow, too, was slightly scathed; and, whether it was the electric shock or the mere force of imagination, a single drop of blood did indeed fall from his dilated nostrils. But it is impossible to calculate the power of fancy on such occasions; it is neither to be estimated, nor controuled by reason. The old man was frantic with terror, and dashed out of the lighthouse, as if impelled by some external agency, while the maniac quietly installed herself in a large oak chair before the window, with all the pride of a queen just restored to her lawful throne by the expulsion of its usurper.

"So, so; the old man is gone," she exclaimed, "and I am his heir,—his rightful heir; this house is mine, and all that is in it; I am lord of the castle now. But what do you here?"—it was a large Newfoundland dog that had caught her eye as he lay basking before the fire—"what do you here, I say?—your name and calling—quick!—why, how now! can't you speak?—and with that monstrous tongue too licking your paws!—Sirrah, sirrah, I shall find a way to make you answer."

The dog, for a moment, looked her in the face, wagging his tail in token of recognition, but he did not choose to leave his warm place before the fire, and quietly resumed his occupation of licking his paws. Highly incensed at this supposed obstinacy, the maniac started from her seat and hurled a wooden trencher at his head, upon which the animal, setting up a long piteous howl, slunk back into the farthest corner of the room. But even this timely retreat would not have saved him from her wrath, had not her attention been suddenly drawn away by the appearance of a small brig, that was visible in the flashes of lightning, as it tossed and pitched, and struggled with the waters, like some strong swimmer in the agony of drowning.

"He comes!" she cried—"he comes! my own dear Richard!—missed and mourned for many a long weary day, and come at last!"—the poor thing knew not how truly she was speaking—"Blow, blow, my gentle wind — blow him to me,—my bridegroom, my husband. Oh, how slowly his bark moves towards the shore! 'tis my cruel father holds it back."

But in truth the vessel was driving too fast upon the land, in spite of all the seamen's efforts to keep her off, for they had yet a reef of rocks to weather, which stretched out from the shore, something less than a quarter of a mile, and on which the surf was beating most tremendously. 'Till these were past, the usual dangers of a lee-shore[2] were doubled on them. At this critical juncture the wind veered a point in their favour; the beacon too from the lighthouse marked out to the experienced sailors the extent of their peril, as was evident by their efforts to keep out to sea, and their safety became almost certain.

But this delay was sorely vexatious to the impatient spirit of poor Lucy—"Slow! slow!" she exclaimed, "but 'tis your fault, father; you were always cruel to your daughter; first you took my Richard from me; then, my child; then my reason, and I have been looking for it over many a weary mile of land, and never yet could find it. Some told me it was buried with my babe—it may be so, for the cold hard stone lay upon her grave, and I had no strength to move it and see what lay beneath. But I'll be revenged. I'll quench the fire on your hearth and the light on your tower."

No sooner had this frantic notion got possession of her brain than she hastened to put it into execution by cutting the rope that governed the windlass.[3] In an instant the lamp came down and was dashed to shivers, leaving the whole coast in utter darkness, and the little brig in imminent peril of shipwreck. At first she was startled at her own act; something like a consciousness of her mischief shot across her brain, but the feeling was only transient, and she resumed her lookout for the vessel, that for a time was invisible to her even in the deepest flashes of the lightning. Still she maintained her watch at the window, her eyes intently fixed on the black waste of waters. They were agitated more furiously than ever, and rolled mountain-like against the cliffs, as if contending with them for the empire of the land. At last she caught a glimpse of the vessel, nailed as it were to a rock, but then again it passed away even before the lightning that had shown it.

Still she watched.

Nearly half an hour had thus elapsed when she was roused from this dreamy state by the sound of voices in the room below. A large crevice in the broken floor allowed

---

[2] Shoreline on which wind is blowing

[3] Winch for moving heavy objects such as a boat from the water or, in this instance, the lighthouse lamp

her to see old Ellis in high altercation with three wild-looking strangers in the dress of seamen; two she could easily distinguish, but the third, who stood opposite to her father, and who was by far the most violent, was so placed that she could only see his back; he was evidently the leader of the party by his vehemence in the dispute about the beacon, to the absence of which, and not without cause, he attributed the loss of his vessel and her cargo.

"So, you old scoundrel!" he exclaimed; "after having brought my ship home, in spite of wind and waters, I am to founder in sight of land because you are too lazy a lubber to do your duty! Why were you not aloft in the lighthouse looking after your beacon?"

"Richard Clifton!" cried the old man, who had by this time recognized his voice.

"And who told you I was Richard Clifton, you villainous old wrecker? What!—eh!—yes, it is old Ellis! — huzza, my boys; we have him at last; there is but another of his breed, and that's the Devil. I tell you what, my old one; you had better have sat on a barrel of gunpowder, with a lighted fuse at your tail, than have crossed my path."

"Why, what will you do?"

"Do!—it was you, who set on my creditors to hound me like a pirate; it was you that denied me Lucy; you that drove me to be a villain; and, now that the wind had set fair, and my uncle, the planter, had left me his money, and I was coming home with a wet sail, it was you, you old wrecker, that dowsed the beacon, and—"

"I did no such thing," interrupted Ellis.

"You lie; you did; you wanted to have the picking of my ship's bones, but if you get more than enough timber to make your coffin, may I sup brimstone with the Devil till they pipe all hands for the day of judgment."

And with this he snatched up an axe and split the old man's skull without allowing him a pause for answer. So effectual was the blow that the victim instantly rolled at his feet, a lifeless corpse; but the passion of vengeance was over with its gratification; Clifton, though a daring, and, in some sense of the word, a hard-hearted man, was not totally devoid of feeling, and he would willingly have struck off a dozen years from his own life for the power of recalling the last few minutes. He gazed on the work of his own hands with a sensation of horror, that had hitherto been a stranger to him, when a loud scream from the room above, by diverting his attention gave relief to the poignancy of his feelings. The shriek was repeated—every hand was instinctively placed on its cutlass—a third time, and the fall of a heavy body was heard over their heads.

To catch up a brand from the fire and rush to side of the unfortunate maniac was but the work of an instant, and a very little more time was requisite to show him his own Lucy in the wretched being, that on her recovery to life lay shivering and moaning in hopeless madness. All his efforts to make himself known to her were without avail; she saw in him only the murderer of her father, and, as her mood changed, she either replied to him with curses, or mocked him with idiot malignity, that was even more dreadful than her execrations.

"I see it now," said Clifton in the agony of his heart; "I seduced your innocence,—drove you to madness—and now that madness is made the instrument of vengeance; it wrecks my wealth, makes me a murderer, and consigns me to the gallows-the gallows?—messmates, this is no place for me; I must be off before any one stumbles on the job below. But whither?—no matter; I must be off, or I shall be trapped, and I have no mind to die upon a gallows, if it were only for the name of Clifton."

But it was too late; five minutes before, and escape was not only possible, but without difficulty; now there was not the slightest chance either for cunning or desperation; a party of king's seamen, who were on the preventive service, had observed the sudden disappearance of the beacon, and, supposing it was by some fault of the keeper, had come to warn him of his imagined negligence.

On entering the lighthouse, the first thing they saw was the body of the murdered Ellis, as he lay on the floor, bathed in blood, and his head cleft asunder. This naturally led to the seizure of Clifton and his party, when the latter, in their anxiety to escape from any share in the probable consequences, did not hesitate to bear witness against their captain. Such evidence was of course fatal; a very few days sufficed to settle the whole affair, for it had happened a short time only before the assizes,[4] so that the trial followed close upon the heels of the murder.

---

[4] Criminal courts that ushered in lengthy trials

Richard Clifton was condemned to death, and ordered for execution on the lighthouse rock.

It was the night previous to the fatal day—one of those calm, autumnal nights when the leaf drops noiseless from the tree as if it were a shadow. A thin, clear, white fog mantled the earth, through which the moon seemed floating like a spirit, so little had it dimmed her brightness, and, as the prisoner lay in his dungeon, he could see the carpenters at work on his scaffold. He even heard the coarse jokes of the workmen, their tauntings of each other, and their calculations as to the probable pain of hanging, mixed now and then with a word of self-congratulation that they were not, as they expressed it, in the shoes of the prisoner. Not a syllable escaped him.

"A few more screws in the upright," said the master carpenter, "or our work may chance to give way, and disappoint the poor fellow."

"If it does, I'll give you leave to hang me," said one of his assistants. "But suppose we try it first on Sim, here; if it bears his fat sides, it will bear any thing."

"You had better try it on yourself," replied the object of this taunt; "your throat was made for a hempen neck-cloth, and as well one day as another."

"With all my heart," said the first speaker, and, dexterously flinging a rope over the top-beam, he sprang up so as to catch a grasp of it as high as possible, and swung himself from the scaffold, with his head turned to one shoulder, and his feet flourishing in air, in imitation of one just executed.

The heart of Richard was sick within him at this brutal jest, but, when the first pain of the shock was over, it left behind a kind and gentle effect; the overwrought mind sank into a slumber, and fortunately for him the indolence, or the drowsiness, of the jailor let him remain undisturbed by the usual hourly visitations. His dreams, too, were happier than the waking reality; to his sleep he was no longer in a dungeon, but stood proudly at the helm of his little brig, with every sail set to the wind, and lying gunnel[5] to amidst the dark, green waves that splashed half way up her mast.

There was reason, however, for this perilous speed; Lucy was traversing the shore on her way to church with

---

[5] Same as the more common "gunwale," which is the upper plank or rail on the side of a boat

a bridegroom forced upon her by old Ellis, who, sleeping or waking, seemed to be ever in the way of Richard. The first of the party had already crossed the churchyard stile, while there was still a space of three miles, at least, lying between it and his vessel. Reckless of the consequences, he shouted to his men, "Out with every reef in her mainsail, my lads; sink or swim, 'tis no matter."

This was no sooner said than done, and the mast began to groan and quiver, while the water rose half over the leeward side[6] of the deck; but the purpose was answered; with this fresh stimulus the vessel flew like a bird along the waters, and, just as the priest was challenging the bye-standers to produce any impediment to the union, he was at the altar, and almost breathlessly exclaimed — "I do; I, the bride's husband—mine, by an oath; mine, by this token!" and he lifted up their infant, that now, by another flight of fancy, lay cradled in his arms.

"Mine! mine!" seemed Lucy to reply.

"Mine! mine!" echoed a thousand voices from below, when the organ began to send forth its deepest sounds, and the stones to be heaved up from the vaults, and all those who had been buried for centuries arose from their long sleep, not as shrouded skeletons, but as things of life, each in the costume of his own time. It was, in fact, the masquerade of ages; the thin, tight-laced beau of modern ages gave his hand to the furbelowed[7] antique, with hoop of monstrous dimensions and a turret of caps on her head; the gauntleted warrior stretched out his arm of brass to the half-clad fair one, who returned his formal courtesy with the slight nod of a modern fashionable; lawyers, priests, soldiers, statesmen, women and children, in grotesque assemblage ranged along each side of the chancel.[8] And now the waltz began—at first slow—then quicker—quicker—and the organ, too, increasing its speed—till at last it seemed the jubilee of madness.

But the vision soon melted away into another shape, more pleasing and less fantastic than this dance of the living dead. The grey aisles of the church were succeeded by the humble mansion of his father, even to the minutest article that lived in his waking memory, and twenty years

---

[6] Side protected from the wind

[7] Ruffled

[8] Space around an alter

were struck off from the account of time; he was a boy again, in holiday freedom from school, playing at the feet of his mother, and, by one of the strange incongruities so familiar to dreams, she wore the face and form of Lucy. If a state of sleep can be deemed life, this was with him the happiest moment of life; he hung on her lips, like a young bee on the rose, and the very air, she breathed, seemed a perfume. It was a full and perfect consciousness of bliss, that belongs only to the imagination, and can therefore be tasted by none but the sleeper or the maniac; a glimpse of reason would destroy it; like the figures of the phantasmagoria, it is visible only in the total absence of light.

Such a condition of mind and body, however, could not, and did not, last long, and with every minute his slumber lost something of its soundness. He began to be half conscious that he was only in a dream, and in this middle state, between sleeping and waking, struggled hard to retain the illusion by giving himself up to it as much as possible. He had even partially succeeded, when a rude voice, in breaking up this slumber, awoke him to a full sense of his misery.

It was the jailor with the blacksmith, who came to knock off his fetters previous to his appearance on the scaffold. The transition was anguish unutterable. The mind, too, by this short respite from pain had acquired fresh capabilities of sufferance, and by the time he was led out from prison he was in a state of mental agony more severe than the worst inflictions of the hangman. He had seen many suffer the same form of death, but now that he was called upon to endure it in his own person it seemed as a thing beyond all possible calculation—as an event that had never happened till then.

He gazed on the crowd that were collected to witness his death, as he had often witnessed the death of others, and could hardly believe that he himself was the victim of the present hour; or if his eye by accident glanced on a face of more than usual hardness, he turned away instinctively in horror. It was even a relief to his sufferings to dwell on any countenance that expressed sympathy with his condition; there was a vague idea of safety connected with it, an indefinite feeling of support and friendship; and yet the same man, who yielded to this weakness, would have faced a cannon without shrinking.

He was now within a few yards of the scaffold, when a young woman made her way to him in spite of all opposition, and flung herself, sobbing, on his neck. It was Lucy Ellis. The sheriff's people would fain have forced her from him, but at the earnest prayer of Richard the clergyman interposed, notwithstanding the irregularity of the proceeding, and obtained for her a momentary respite, which she was not slow to employ.

"Why is this?" she exclaimed; "I will not have it so. The old man was my father, and, if I forgive the deed, you surely may. What was he to any of you? by God's light, you make much more ado about the dead man than you ever did about the living one."

"We can delay no longer," said the sheriff, who little expected such an appeal.

"You can't!" exclaimed Lucy, "and who are you?" Then addressing herself to the clergyman, she added in a tone of peculiar bitterness, "Turn over your book, my bonny[9] man, and let them know that they shall do no murder; and what do they call hanging a man on yonder cross-stick till he's black in the face?—isn't that murder, think ye?"

For the first time since his boyhood a tear stood in Richard's eye, but he did not utter a syllable. Lucy stretched out her hand towards him, like a mother questioning her child.

"Answer me, Richard, do you believe there is another world?"

"Most fervently," ejaculated the prisoner, and it was evident the reply was an involuntary one.

"Then give us both your blessing, reverend sir," said Lucy, casting herself on her knees before the clergyman.

The pale cheek of the venerable old man was suffused with a slight glow, and his hand trembled, as be laid it on the suppliant's head, saying, in a voice scarcely audible from emotion, "May God of his infinite mercy forgive the young man the wrong he has done to thee and thine, and take ye both unto himself in a world where there is neither sin nor suffering."

"Amen!" responded Lucy; and the Amen was solemnly echoed back by the whole assemblage.

She now rose from her knees, kissed her lover tenderly between the eyes, and, exclaiming "Farewell!" dashed him

---

[9] Fine

suddenly from the cliff. So unexpected was the action that no hand was quick enough to prevent it, and, before the waters had well closed over his body, she flung herself headlong after him. One cry of the falling suicide—one plash of the broken waters—and all was over!

List of Short Stories Considered

Anonymous
 (1800-1820) The Lunatic and His Turkey
 (1817-1832) The Last Man
 1821 Hallowe'en in Germany, or Walpurgis Night
 1825 The Monster of Scotland
 1826 The Old Wrecker
 1826 The Maniac
 1826 Jan Schalken's Three Wishes
 1826 The Nikkur Holl
 1827 The Possessed One
 1827 The Maid of the Inn
 1827 The Borderer's Leap
 1827 The Bandit Murderers
 1827 The Secret Bandit
 1827 The Fall From the Rock
 1827 Death in the Pot
 1827 The Bohemian
 1827 The Shipwreck
 1827 The Storm
 1827 The Pilgrimage to St. Ganglof
 1827 The Ruin of the Rock
 1827 The Bronze Statue
 1828 The Gored Huntsman
 1828 Maternal Revenge
 1829 A Scene Off Bermuda
 1829 The First and Last Sacrifice
 1829 James Morley, the Murderer!
 1829 The Murder Hole
 1830 The Headsman
 1831 Graveyard Doings
 1831 The Maniac
 1831 The Demon Ship
 1831 The Lonely Man of the Ocean
 1832 Gabriel Lindsay (by author of "The Unrevealed")
 1832 The Enchanted Fusil
 1832 The Monster Made by Man
 1833 Life in Death
 1833 The Tiger's Cave
 1834 The Legend of Buck Island
 1834 The Adventurous Boy
 1834 A Tale of Blood

1835 A Night with a Madman
1835 The Nightmare
1835 The Fiery Vault
1837 The Doctor
1837 The Houri
1837 Mary the Murderess
1839 The Lunatic
1839 The Fairy Shoe
1839 Running the Gauntlet
1844 The Victim
1846 The Haunted Forest
1848 A Legend From Antwerp
1848 The Story of Judar
1848 The Mysterious Bell

William Harrison Ainsworth (1805-1882)
1823 The Mutiny

Hans Andersen (1805-1875)
1847 The Shadow
1848 The Mother and the Dead Child

Honoré de Balzac (1799-1850)
1827 Adieu
1829 The Executioner
1830 The Elixir of Life
1830 An Episode Under the Terror
1830 The Thing at Ghent
1831 Christ in Flanders
1832 La Grande Breteche
1834 Seraphita
1835 Melmoth Reconciled
1835 The Unknown Masterpiece

Milford Bard
1835 The Mysterious Lovers

Richard Barham (1788-1845)
1843 Jerry Jarvis's Wig
1848 Singular Passage in the Life of the Late Henry
Harris, Doctor in Divinity

William Beckford (1760-1844)
1816 "The Episodes of Valthck":

The Story of Prince Alasi and the Princess
Firouzkah
The Story of the Princess Zulka's and the Prince
Kalilah

Peter Borel
    1833 Andreas Vesalius the Anatomist

Charles Brockden Brown (1771-1810)
    1800 Thessalonica

William Carleton (1794-1869)
    1830 Confessions of a Reformed Ribbonman

Rev. Hobart Caunter
    1834 The Drop Scene

Adalbert von Chamisso (1781-1838)
    1813 Peter Schlemihls

Owen Chase (1798-1869)
    1821 The Ship That Was Wrecked by a Whale

W. M. Clarke
    1843 The Robbery of the Astrologer

Thomas Crofton Croker (1798-1854)
    1825 The Legend of Knocksheogowna
    1825 The Legend of Knockfierna
    1826 The Legend of Knockgrafton
    1826 The Priest
    1826 The Young Piper
    1826 The Brewery of Egg-Shells
    1826 The Changeling
    1826 The Two Gossips
    1826 The Legend of Bottle Hill
    1826 Fairies Or No Fairies
    1826 Seeing is Believing
    1826 Master and Man
    1826 The Field of Boliauns
    1826 The Little Shoe
    1826 The Bunworth Banshee
    1826 The M'Carthy Banshee
    1826 The Spirit Horse
    1826 Daniel O Rourke

1826 The Crookened Back
1826 Fior Usga
1826 The Legend of Lough Gur
1826 The Enchanted Lake
1826 The Legend of O'Donoghue
1826 The Lady of Gollerus
1826 Flory Cantillon's Funeral
1826 The Lord of Dunkerron
1826 The Wonderful Tune
1826 Hanlon's Mill
1826 Diarmid Bawn, The Piper
1826 Teigue of the Lee
1826 Ned Sheehy's Excuse
1826 The Lucky Guest
1826 Dreaming Tim Jarvis
1826 Rent-Day
1826 Linn-Na-Payshtha
1826 The Legend of Cairn Thierna
1826 The Rock of the Candle
1826 Clough na Cuddy
1826 The Giant's Stairs
1834 The Legends of the Banshee

Isaac Crookenden (1777-?)
    1802 The Vindictive Monk, or the Fatal Ring

Paul Louis Courier (1773-1825)
    1820 A Tale of Terror

Allan Cunningham (1784-1842)
    Elphin Irving, The Fairies' Cupbearer

T. D.
    1829 The Murderer's Last Night

Charles Dickens (1812-1870)
    1836 The Old Man's Tale About the Queer Client

Dr. Nathan Drake (1766-1836)
    1801 Captive of the Banditti
    1802 Wolkmar and His Dog
    1804 The Abbey of Clunedale

Alexander Dumas (1802-1870)
    1835 A Bal Masque

Joseph von Eichendorff (1788-1857)
    1808-1809 Autumn Sorcery

Baron Friedrich De la Motte Fouquâe (1777-1843)
    1823 The Field of Terror

Théophile Gautier (1811-1872)
    1838 One of Cleopatra's Nights
    1840 The Mummy's Foot

Nikolai Gogol (1809-1852)
    1832 A Terrible Vengeance
    1832 A Bewitched Place
    1836 The Nose

Catherine Gore (1799-1861)
    1839 The Red Man

J. Frederick Hardman
    1843 The Thirteenth. A Tale of Doom.

Wilhelm Hauff (1802-1827)
    1828 The Severed Hand
    1828 The Fortunes of Said

Nathaniel Hawthorne (1804-1864)
    1832 My Kinsman Major Molineux
    1835 The Ambitious Guest
    1836 The Minister's Black Veil
    1836 The Wedding Knell
    1837 Dr. Heidegger's Experiment
    1837 Fancy's Show-Box
    1838 Howe's Masquerade
    1838 Edward Randolph's Portrait
    1843 The Birthmark
    1843 The Christmas Banquet
    1843 Egotism; or, the Bosom Serpent
    1844 Rappaccini's Daughter
    1844 Earth's Holocaust

John Hill Hewitt (1801-1890)
    1847 The Death-Bride

E. P. Hingston
    1847 Confessions of a Deformed Lunatic

James Hogg (1770-1835)
    1823 A Scots Mummy
    1829 A Tale of the Martyrs
    1837 The Fords of Callum
    1837 Cousin Mattie

Charles Fenno Hoffman (1806-1884)
    1847 The Man in the Boiler
    1848 The Man in the Reservoir

Earnest Theodore Hoffmann (1776-1822)
    1817 A New Year's Eve Adventure
    1817 The Deserted House
    1817 The Cremona Violin

Thomas Hood (1799-1845)
    1831 The Shadow of a Shade
    1834 A Tale of the Great Plague

Thomas Henry Huxley (1825-1895)
    1849 Mrs. Thompson Among the Cannibals

G. E. K. I.
    1827 An Italian Legend

John H. Ingraham
    1844 The League Of 'The Thirty'

Washington Irving (1783-1859)
    1824 The Adventure of the Mysterious Picture

Charles Isley
    1837 The Cottage on the Cape

R. J.
    1827 The Tooth Ache: A Dream

Charles Lamb (1775-1834)
    1809 Arabella Hardy; or, the Sea Voyage

Letitia E. Landon (1802-1838)
    1836 The Bride of Lindorf

Charles Lever (1806-1872)
    1836 Post-Mortem Recollections of a Medical
    Lecturer

Matthew Gregory 'Monk' Lewis (1775-1818)
    1808 The Anaconda
    1808 Mistrust

George Lippard (1822-1854)
    1844 A Night in Monk-Hall

Edward Lloyd
    1843 The Dead Alive

Samuel Lover (1797-1868)
    1837 The Burial of the Tithe

Edward Bulwer-Lytton (1803-1873)
    1826 Glenallan

William Maginn (1794-1842)
    1821 The Man in the Bell

Frederick Marryat (1792-1848)
    1836 The Legend of the Bell Rock
    1838 The Story of the Greek Slave

Charles Maturin (1780-1824)
    1825 Leixlip Castle

Prosper Mérimée (1802-1870)
    1829 Federigo
    1829 The Taking of the Redoubt
    1829 The Vision of Charles X
    1829 Mateo Falcone
    1837 *La Vénus d'Ille*

Gérard de Nerval (1808-1855)
    The Enchanted Hand

Edgar Allan Poe (1809-1849)
    1832 A Tale of Jerusalem
    1832 Metzengerstein
    1833 Ms. Found in a Bottle

1835 Berenice
1835 King Pest
1837 Mystification
1839 The Fall of the House of Usher
1841 A Descent into the Maelström
1842 The Masque of the Red Death
1842 The Pit and the Pendulum
1843 The Tell-Tale Heart
1843 The Black Cat
1844 A Premature Burial
1844 Mesmeric Revelation
1844 The Oblong Box
1845 The Facts in the Case of M. Valdemar
1846 The Cask of Amontillado
1849 Hop-Frog

Thomas Peckett Prest (1810-1859)
1833 The Demon of the Hartz
1841 Angelina, or The Mystery of S. Mark's Abbey
1844 The Death Grasp; or, the Father's Curse
1849 The Blighted Heart; or, The Old Priory Ruins

Thomas De Quincey (1785-1859)
1821 Levana and Our Ladies of Sorrow
1821 The Floating Beacon
1832 Klosterheim, or The Masque

W. R.
The Devil's Dyke

George William Macarthur Reynolds (1814-1879)
1845 The Body-Snatchers
The Tribunal of the Inquisition

Edwin F. Roberts (1802-1854)
1848 The Rosicrician

J. B. Rogerson
1843 The Leg
1843 My Nose

James Malcolm Rymer (1804-1882)
1842 Ada the Betrayed; or, The Murder at the Old

Sandwich
    1832 The Shipwrecked Coaster

Daniel Keyte Sanford
    1817-1832 A Night in the Catacombs

D. Scans
    1800-1820 Five Hundred Years Hence

Alois Wilhelm Schreiber
    1822 The Devil's Ladder, or the Gnomes of the Redrich

Michael Scott
    1830 Heat and Thirst,—A Scene in Jamaica

Sir Walter Scott (1771-1832)
    The Bridal of Janet Dalrymple
    1818 Narrative of a Fatal Event
    1828 The Tale of the Mysterious Mirror

Mary Shelley (1797-1851)
    1826-1836 The Evil Eye
    1826-1836 The Invisible Girl
    1826-1836 The Mortal Immortal: A Tale
    1826-1836 The Mourner
    1826-1836 The Heir of Mondolfo
    1826-1836 Crazy Robin
    1826-1836 The Pole
    1826-1836 Roger Dodsworth: The Reanimated
    Englishman
    1826-1836 The Sisters of Albano
    1826-1836 A Tale of the Passions
    1826-1836 Transformation
    1826-1836 Valerius: The Reanimated Roman

Captain Andrew Smith
    1828 The Fever Ship

Horatio Smith (1779-1849)
    1837 Festus and Fadilla

Smithy
    1843 Blanche, or the mystery of the Doomed House

George Soane (1789-1860)
    1823 Harry Woodriff
    1826 The Light-House
    1829 Friar Bacon's Key
    1834 The Singular Trial of Francis Ormiston
    1837 Recollections of a Night of Fever
    1837 Twelve Hours in the Life of a Nervous Man
    1837 The Chamber of the Pale Lady
    1841 The Legend of Narwarth Castle
    1841 Self Sacrifice; with a Supplement on Poisoners

Eugène Sue "Marie-Joseph Sue" (1804-1857)
    (before 1839) The Raft of Death

J. L. Tieck (1773-1853)
    Elphin-Land

Theseus
    1847 A Night with the Dead

Henry Thomson
    1821 Le Revenant

Patrick Fraser-Tytler
    1817 Sketch of a Tradition Related by a Monk in
    Switzerland

G. H. W.
    1846 My Grandmother's Tale

Samuel Warren (1807-1877)
    1832 The Thunder-Struck and the Boxer

Nathaniel P. Willis (1806-1867)
    1834 My Hobby,—Rather

John Wilson "Christopher North" (1785-1854)
    1818 Extracts from Gosschen's Diary
    1842 Highland Snowstorm

John MacKay Wilson (1804-1835)
    1834 The Doom of Soulis
    1835 The Unknown

INDEX OF REAL NAMES

U
Usher, Agnes – 211
Usher, Harriet – 211
Usher, James – 211
Usher, Noble – 211

W
Warren, Samuel – 45
Weber, Baron Karl Maria – 221
Weiss, Susan Archer – 111

OTHER BOTTLETREE TITLES OF INTEREST

The Best Werewolf Short Stories 1800-1849
A Classic Werewolf Anthology
For the first time in one anthology, Andrew Barger has compiled the best werewolf stories from the period when werewolf short stories were first written. The stories are "Hugues the Wer-Wolf: A Kentish Legend of the Middle Ages," "The Man-Wolf," "A Story of a Weir-Wolf," "The Wehr-Wolf: A Legend of the Limousin," and "The White Wolf of the Hartz Mountains." It is believed that two of these stories have never been republished in over one hundred and fifty years since their original printing. Read "The Best Werewolf Short Stories 1800-1849" tonight, just make sure it is not by the light of a full moon!"

Edgar Allan Poe Annotated and Illustrated
Entire Stories and Poems
For the first time in one compilation are background information for Poe's stories and poems, annotations, foreign word translations, illustrations, photographs of individuals Poe wrote about, and poetry to Poe from his many romantic interests. The classic illustrations are by Gustave Dore and Harry Clarke, with a great introduction by Andrew Barger.

Coffee with Poe
A Novel of the Life of Edgar Allan Poe
Like one of his Gothic stories, Poe has been brought to life in the pages of *Coffee with Poe* as he never has before. Orphaned at the age of two, Poe is raised by John Allan—his abusive foster father—who refuses to adopt him until he becomes straight-laced and businesslike. Poe, however, fancies poetry and young women. The contentious relationship culminates in a violent altercation, which causes Poe to leave his wealthy foster father's home to make it as a writer. Poe tries desperately to get established as a writer but is ridiculed by the "Literati of New York." The Raven subsequently gains Poe renown in America yet he slips deeper into poverty, only making $15 off the poem's entire publication history. Desperate for a

motherly figure in his life, Poe marries his first cousin who is only thirteen. Poe lives his last years in abject poverty while suffering through the deaths of his foster mother, grandmother, and young wife. In a cemetery he becomes engaged to Helen Whitman, a dark poet who is addicted to ether, wears a small coffin about her neck, and conducts séances in her home. The engagement is soon broken off because of Poe's drinking. In his final months his health is in a downward spiral. Poe disappears on a trip and is later found delirious and wearing another person's clothes. He dies a few days later, whispering his final words: "God help my poor soul."

Leo Tolstoy's 20 Greatest Short Stories Annotated

"Anna Karenina" and "War and Peace" revealed Leo Tolstoy as one of the greatest writers in modern history. Few, however, have read his wonderful short stories. Now, in one collection, are the greatest short stories of Tolstoy, which give a snapshot of Russia and its people in the late 19th century. Annotations are included of difficult Russian terms. Read these short classics today!

Facebook Fanatic

Make your face royalty on Facebook. Get insanely popular. Buzz a band or book. Zoom a political career or film. Secure privacy in every area. With over 100 million users Facebook is one of the world's largest social networking sites and it has been making major changes. Are you wondering about all those new Facebook applications? Feel lost and overwhelmed? Concerned about privacy? Don't be! "Facebook Fanatic" is a guide on all areas of Facebook. Dominate it instead of being just part of it.

Bottletree®

BottletreeBooks.com

CPSIA information can be obtained
at www.ICGtesting.com
Printed in the USA
BVHW03s1628121018
530011BV00002B/305/P